THE RUNAWAY TROLL

Also available by Matt Haig:

SHADOW FOREST

Blue Peter Book of the Year 2009

Nestlé Children's Book Prize Gold Award Winner 2007

THE RUNAWAY TROLL

MATT HAIG

Illustrated by Julek Heller

CORGI BOOKS

THE RUNAWAY TROLL
A CORGI BOOK 978 0 552 55578 4

First published in Great Britain by the Bodley Head,
an imprint of Random House Children's Books
A Random House Group Company

Bodley Head edition published 2009
Corgi edition published 2010

1 3 5 7 9 10 8 6 4 2

Set in Baskerville Classico

Corgi Books are published by Random House Children's Books,
61–63 Uxbridge Road, London W5 5SA

www.**kidsatrandomhouse**.co.uk
www.**rbooks**.co.uk

Addresses for companies within The Random House Group Limited
can be found at: www.randomhouse.co.uk/offices.htm

THE RANDOM HOUSE GROUP Limited Reg. No. 954009

A CIP catalogue record for this book is available from the British Library.

Printed and bound in Great Britain by CPI Bookmarque, Croydon, CR0 4TD

For Andrea and Lucas

The humans and other creatures you will meet in this book

THE HUMANS

Samuel Blink: A twelve-year-old boy who once had a very normal life, with normal friends, doing normal things. That was before his parents got crushed to death by a falling log. And before he moved to Norway, and before he met a family of trolls, and before he found out that his Uncle Henrik had spent many years as a dog. But now, the day before starting a new school, life is back to being boring again. Until he hears a strange noise coming from under his bed.

Martha Blink: Samuel's ten-year-old sister. The winner of the World's Worst Keeper of Secrets Award, if such a prize existed. She loves: making friends, inventing songs, talking about her time in the forest, eating pickles. She hates: thinking about the day her parents died.

Aunt Eda: Sister of Martha and Samuel's mother, Liv Blink. She's a bit old-fashioned, and can be a little bit strict. A tall lady who always wears her hair in a bun, she tends to worry a lot. But if your husband had turned into a dog, then so might you.

Uncle Henrik: Uncle to Samuel and Martha; husband to Eda. Former ski jumper, goat farmer, cheese-maker and dog. A Norwegian elkhound, to be precise. Now spends most of his time as a kind human uncle, except when he's having one of his 'funny turns'.

Mrs Sturdsen: A teacher in the village school. She is a short, solid-looking woman with cheeks like red apples. She is quite a kind teacher generally, but gets rather annoyed with a certain clever-clogs called Cornelia Myklebust who corrects her in almost every lesson.

Cornelia Myklebust: Spoiled brat. Fluent in numerous languages. Mathematical genius. Owns more ponies than you've got fingers. Oh, and if she tries to make friends with you, run away. Fast.

Mr Myklebust: Cornelia's father. Messy eater. Richest man in Flåm. And the fattest. Has hated Uncle Henrik ever since he– No, I won't tell you that. Not just yet.

Mrs Myklebust: Cornelia's mother. Former beauty queen. Finds her husband repulsive, but will never leave him. He's got too much money.

Mr Tomas Thomassen: A policeman with a face so sour you would think he was sucking a lemon. Loves enforcing ancient laws about trolls. Hates people who waste police time.

THE TROLLS

Troll-Son: A young troll who lives with his family in the village of Trollhelm. He has to share the family's one eyeball with his parents and sister, which he doesn't mind. What he does mind is his mother telling him off for *everything*. Especially when she decides he has to be sent to the Betterer. Secretly, he wishes he was a human, with a proper name, rather like Samuel Blink.

Troll-Mother: Troll-Son's mother is a particularly ugly woman, with wild and matted black hair, a bulbous red nose, hairy nostrils, and five wonky grey teeth. She has been very crotchety since the Troll family lost their eyeball. She spends far too much time clouting Troll-Son around the head and worrying about what the neighbours think to realize that, underneath it all, she is actually quite nice.

Troll-Father: One of the friendliest and most humble trolls there is, although if he has a weakness it is that he rarely dares stand up to Troll-Mother. Mind you, if you'd ever had one of her clouts around the head, then neither would you.

Troll-Daughter: Troll-Son's younger sister. Fast becoming Troll-Mother's favourite child. Has an annoying habit of repeating her favourite words over and over again. Ignore her. She's just seeking attention.

The Betterer: The nastiest creature in the whole of troll history. Well, except for Troll-the-Cannibal, who died 7,552 years ago from a very bad stomach ache. The Betterer hates trolls and hates being one, which probably explains why he gains great pleasure from 'bettering' troll children. This involves sessions in the Dunking Cage and seven-hour maths lessons and numerous other forms of torture. All of which take place in his home, the Bettering Tower.

Troll-the-Left and Troll-the-Right: Two heads of the same troll, who hate each other's guts (which, technically speaking, they share). They were recently separated after a rather nasty incident involving a prison guard's sword, which cut off Troll-the-Right.

Troll-the-Wisest: Leader of the Troll Council. Judged to be the wisest troll in Shadow Forest on account of having the longest beard. In truth, he is one of the most stupid there is. And as most trolls believe the moon is a hole cut out of the sky, this is quite some achievement.

OTHER FOREST CREATURES THAT AREN'T IN THIS BOOK AS MUCH AS THE TROLLS BUT WHICH YOU MIGHT WANT TO KNOW ABOUT

The tomtegubb: A jovial, barrel-shaped creature with a strange taste in colourful clothes. Has the annoying habit of making everything rhyme. All the time. It should be a crime.

The huldre-folk: The huldres once lived underground but now inhabit a village near the southern edge of Shadow Forest. They have long tails, skinny bodies and wide-apart eyes, and spend all their days singing hymns to the sun and making wooden sculptures. Their singing can be heard on a few pages, if you make sure you read this book in a very quiet room.

Skullpeckers: These birds once used to peck skulls and eat brains for supper. Now they are vegetarian and fly around tweeting about how pretty the forest looks.

This book might also contain traces of **caloosh**, **trunklefish** and **truth pixie**.

UNCLE HENRIK'S FUNNY TURN

Samuel Blink was lying on the ground pulling clumps of grass out with his fingers, as if it were the green hair of some rather evil and large-headed monster.

He was bored, you see. Totally, utterly, brain-numbingly bored. Not that he really minded being bored. No. On the scale of Worst Things to Be, being bored was nowhere near the top. It was certainly not as bad as many of the other things he had been this summer. Like being frightened out of his skin, or feeling so sad he could hardly breathe.

But still, if only his stuff had arrived from England. Or if Aunt Eda and Uncle Henrik had a TV. Or a computer. Or a book that wasn't written in Norwegian. If only there were somewhere exciting he could go.

True, it looked *nice* around here. Just by tilting his head left, away from the white wooden house, he could see the still waters of the fjord and, further in the distance, the vast rugged triangle that was Mount Myrdal. But nice as it was, you can't play with a view. You can only look at it. And as it was, according to Uncle Henrik, still three months until the start of the skiing season, it was going to be quite a while before it offered some genuine fun.

Of course, there was one place he could see that offered something exciting. It was the pine forest right in front of him, at the top of the grassy slope where Aunt Eda and Uncle Henrik's land ended. But he wasn't allowed in there.

'We still haff to be careful,' Aunt Eda had told him and his sister, Martha. 'If we don't effer cause trouble with the forest, the forest won't effer cause trouble with us.'

'But the forest's safe now,' he'd said.

'Well, we don't know,' she said. 'Not for sure.'

This was true. There were still a lot of unknown things about the forest, like whether all the trolls who lived there were good or just some of them. And how many had one eye or two heads or some other unusual thing which gave you a shock when you looked at them. And this type of question could do something to lessen the boredom of an afternoon, but not quite as much as seeing a troll face to face.

Samuel was just about to pull up a particularly large clump of grass when he heard the faint sound of the telephone in the house. A few minutes later his aunt was calling out to him from the door.

'Samuel!' she said. 'I haff to tell you something. And what are you doing on the grass? You are far too close to the forest.'

Samuel sighed, and got up to walk over to his aunt. She was quite a stern woman in some ways, and certainly looked it with her pulled-back hair and her buttoned-up cardigan and her tight mouth and prickly chin. But she was a good and kind woman too, who was only really guilty of worrying a bit too much.

'That was Fru Sturdsen on the phone,' she said as Samuel took off his shoes. He saw that Martha was in the kitchen, talking to Uncle Henrik at seven hundred miles an hour while he prepared roast elk and cowberry jam for supper.

It was funny. After their parents died Martha hadn't said a word for weeks, but now you couldn't shut her up. It was as though all those unspoken words had been saved up like money in a bank and she was spending them at every opportunity. And all she would talk about was one thing – the time she had spent in Shadow Forest.

'. . . and so,' she was saying, 'when I was in the underground prison with the Snow Witch, I met this two-headed tro–'

'*Martha*,' said Aunt Eda sharply as she and Samuel went into the kitchen. 'I think we haff heard enough of this conversation. Perhaps we shall talk about something else. Like how you are feeling about your new school. And remember, when you start school you must not mention Shadow Forest. I know it is ferry exciting to liff next to a forest full of such strange creatures, but we must not effer tell anyone about it. This is ferry important, because as I say, Fru Sturdsen has been on the phone and–'

'What kind of a name is Fru?' said Samuel, frowning at the name as if it had an unpleasant smell.

'It's not a name, it's a term of address. *Fru* means Mrs in Norwegian. *Herr* means Mister and *Fru* means Mrs. So I am talking about *Mrs* Sturdsen. Your new teacher.'

Samuel's heart sank. How was he ever going to fit in at a new school if he didn't know the language?

'What did she want?' he asked.

'Well, she telephoned to say how ferry excited she is to haff two new children starting her school tomorrow. And she also said it would be a good idea if you wrote about what you did in your holidays. They do it after effery summer, she says.'

Samuel rolled his eyes. 'Homework before we even start?'

He had already thought schools in Norway sounded strange, with ten-year-olds like his sister being in the same class as twelve-year-olds such as him. But having to do homework *before* term began – that was even worse.

'Apparently, yes,' said Aunt Eda. 'Homework before you start.'

Uncle Henrik stopped crushing cowberries for a moment. 'I remember when I was at school,' he said, his gentle face broadening into a smile. 'Every summer I used to make sure I did something interesting just so I had something to write about.'

'Yes,' said Aunt Eda briskly. 'Well, I haff to say that is not the same problem we face here, is it, Henrik? Quite the contrary in fact. I am worried that there is rather too much for them to say.'

'What's the big deal?' Samuel said. 'Everyone

thinks there are weird creatures in the forest. That's why they're too scared to visit it.'

'They're scared because they don't know for sure,' she said. 'And if they know that Henrik is back after all those years he was meant to be missing in the forest, then efferyone will want answers. So we must pretend we know nothing, and you must not write anything about the creatures of the forest. And tomorrow, when you are both at school and people find out where you liff, you must not try and impress them with stories about the forest.'

'Hey,' said Martha, blushing. 'Why's everyone looking at me?'

'Because you've got an unstoppable mouth,' said Samuel.

'No I–'

'Listen,' said Aunt Eda, raising her hand to stop an argument. 'It's going to be difficult for all of us. But you must pretend you haffn't effer seen Uncle Henrik. Well, not until we decide what we are going to do. And they must not know about trolls and pixies and so forth. What do you think Magnus Myklebust would do if he found out we had seen such things?'

'Who's Magnus Myklebust?' asked Martha, stealing

a pickled onion from a jar she had opened in the kitchen.

Aunt Eda and Uncle Henrik shared a glance, and Samuel noticed there was something strange about this glance, but he couldn't work out what it was.

'Mr Myklebust is a man I used to know before I went into the forest,' said Uncle Henrik in a slow voice, as if each word were precious and breakable and needed to be let out as carefully as porcelain teacups from a chest. 'I met him after I retired from ski jumping and moved to Flåm with Eda.'

'What's so special about him?' said Samuel, staring at the empty dog basket.

Aunt Eda laughed. 'Beleef me, there is nothing ferry special about him. But he is not ferry nice. Not ferry nice at all. And he has neffer liked your uncle ferry much.'

'Why not?' said Martha, taking another pickled onion.

'It is a long story. And you haff your homework to do. But anyway, the point is that if he found out about the forest, he would want to chop it down and make money out of it. If he wasn't so scared of what might be in the forest, then he would do it right now. He already owns half of Flåm. Ski lodges, holiday homes. He is the richest man in the willage. And he has always been wanting to know about the forest. So if he found out we would be in trouble. There are local laws about this kind of thing. Laws that go back hundreds of years, to the time of King Håkon the Good, the first Christian King of Norway. Laws about knowledge of efil creatures. Laws that no one has bothered to update. We must be ferry careful.'

Aunt Eda's attention switched as she noticed Martha pinching another pickled onion. 'Now, Martha, that's enough nibbling. You won't be able to eat your elk. Honestly, what is it with you and pickles?'

Martha shrugged. 'They're tasty,' she said. Indeed, for Martha, this was the very best thing about Norway. There were pickles everywhere. Pickled berries, pickled nuts, pickled onions, pickled cucumbers, pickled gherkins. And she was eating them at every opportunity.

'Right, well, when you do your homework you must not say anything about the creatures that liff in the forest. And when you go to school you must not say that your uncle has come back. That is ferry important.'

Samuel leaned back as far as he could on his chair, supporting himself on tiptoes. 'So . . . you want us to lie?'

Aunt Eda closed her eyes tight, as if someone had just flicked water on her face. 'Well, it is not really *lying*, it is just not telling the whole truth.'

Samuel nodded. 'Yep. Thought so. Lying.'

Aunt Eda was getting flustered. 'No, it's– Could you just *sit still.*'

As soon as she said the word 'sit' in such a sharp way, a rather remarkable thing happened. Uncle Henrik dropped his chopping knife and squatted down on his heels, with his hands on the floor. His tongue was hanging out of the side of his mouth, and he was panting, as if doing an impression of a dog. But if it was an impression, it was a very good one, and Uncle Henrik's eyes showed no sign of a joke. Indeed, Uncle Henrik's eyes showed no sign of Uncle Henrik. It was as though he were in some kind of a trance and had momentarily forgotten he was a human being.

But Aunt Eda didn't look too bothered. She just rolled her eyes as if it were a perfectly normal occurrence.

'What's happening to Uncle Henrik?' asked Martha, so confused that she stopped crunching on her pickle.

'Is he all right?' added Samuel.

'Yes, yes,' said Aunt Eda, through a sigh. 'He had a couple of these turns yesterday.'

'Turns?' said Samuel. He remembered how his mum had used to say his granddad had 'funny turns'. But Samuel was pretty sure Granddad's variety of funny turn never involved sitting on all fours on the kitchen floor, panting like a dog.

'Before you woke up I found Henrik lying in the dog basket,' said Aunt Eda.

And as she said the word 'basket', Uncle Henrik cocked his head to one side and gave her a look of canine bemusement, before charging through the house on all fours. Martha squealed as he nearly ran her over and Samuel jumped out of his chair to get out of his way. But Uncle Henrik flew past the rocking chair and ended up in the dog basket, where he lay down. Obviously he was rather too big for the basket, and seemed most awkward in there, with his head leaning over the side and his legs sticking out. Yet, despite his clear discomfort, he still found time to lick the backs of his hands like paws needing a wash.

'Henrik!' shouted Aunt Eda. 'Henrik! Snap out of it! You are not a dog! Henrik Krohg, get out of that basket immediately. Henrik? Henrik? Can you hear me?'

And Samuel and Martha watched as Uncle Henrik's eyes fluttered, as if he were waking from a bad dream.

'Oh,' he said wearily, pushing himself into an upright, more human position. He blushed when he realized Samuel and Martha were watching the whole thing. 'It's happened again, hasn't it? I thought I was still a–'

'Yes,' said Aunt Eda, stroking his arm. 'But don't worry. You're back with us now. Everything's going to be fine. I'm sure. Yes, everything's going to be fine.'

ROAST ELK AND COWBERRY JAM

Samuel stared at his plate of roast elk and cowberry jam and wondered if he would ever get used to Uncle Henrik's food. Seriously, who would think of putting meat and jam on the same plate? If his mum and dad hadn't died, he and Martha would still be in England, eating normal food. And then, after eating the normal food, he would have gone upstairs and done something equally normal, like play on his computer or read a book or ride his bike to Joseph's house. Joseph was his best friend. Or had been. How could he expect someone to stay best friends with him if he was in a different country?

'Come on,' said Aunt Eda, noticing that Samuel hadn't lifted up his fork. 'It will get cold.'

So Samuel began to eat his meal, which didn't taste

nearly as bad as he had imagined. And neither he nor his sister brought up the subject of Uncle Henrik's funny turn. They didn't want to make him any more embarrassed than he already was, because they liked him very much. He had a more gentle manner than Aunt Eda. You wouldn't think they would go well together but – rather like roast elk and cowberry jam – they somehow made a good combination.

'So,' said Samuel, 'if we're not meant to talk about the forest, why don't we talk about ski jumping? Why don't you put your medal downstairs, where everyone can see it?'

You see, Uncle Henrik had been a ski jumper in his youth, and rather a good one, coming second in the Olympics.

Uncle Henrik laughed quietly and shook his head. 'No, I don't think so. It can stay in the attic, I think . . . And anyway, who would see it?'

This was a good point. After all, no one except the postman ever came round, and for the last two days even he hadn't come by and so Aunt Eda had been collecting letters from the post office in Flåm.

'*We* could see it,' said Samuel. 'And it would be cool to have it on the wall.' *Better than all those rubbish paintings of mountains*, he thought, but didn't say this out loud.

Martha swallowed a large mouthful of elk and decided it had been a while since she'd said anything. 'What did it feel like, when you used to jump? Were you scared? I was *so* scared when I was in the huldres' cage, travelling through Shadow Forest.'

'Yes,' said Uncle Henrik. 'I was sometimes very scared indeed. But sometimes a bit of fear isn't a bad thing. It is how we find out who we are, and what we are made of. You stand at the top of a ski jump tower, like the one that is on Mount Myrdal, and you are on your own and there is no one you can rely on but yourself. I tell you, it is the best feeling in the world.'

'Oh, children, you should haff seen him,' said Aunt Eda, 'flying through the air! It—'

She was interrupted by the telephone, and went to answer it. Everyone stopped to watch as Aunt Eda's face began to look cross and frightened all at once. Even though she was speaking in Norwegian, it was clear to Samuel and Martha that it wasn't a welcome call.

'Yes . . . Magnus, is that you? . . . You heard what? . . . Oh, what nonsense! . . . Don't be ridiculous . . . I can assure you that no such thing happened . . .

No . . . Absolutely not . . . Now, I suggest that a busy man like yourself could do better than listen to silly gossip . . . Now, I must go . . . *Morna*, Magnus. *Morna*.'

Her hand trembled as she put down the receiver.

'Who was that?' asked Martha.

'Mr Myklebust,' said Aunt Eda. 'The man I told you about. The man who wants to destroy the forest. And possibly us too.'

Uncle Henrik's normally calm face creased with worry. 'What on earth did he want?'

'Well, he's heard a story from Johannes. The postman. About what happened three days ago.'

Samuel was confused. 'What *did* happen three days ago?'

Aunt Eda and Uncle Henrik looked at each other, and Henrik's cheeks became the same colour as the cowberry jam on his plate. 'It's all right, Eda,' he said. 'I'll tell them.'

Then he took a deep breath, as if he were standing once again on top of that ski jump tower, and told Samuel and Martha what had happened.

'I had another "funny turn", as your aunt put it. I heard the letters go into the letter box and I lost myself completely. I ran to the door on all fours and

I . . . I . . . I bit Johannes. I bit his hand, and then he pulled it out and I kept . . . I kept barking . . . like a . . . well, like a dog . . . I wasn't aware of it at the time – it was like I went to sleep and became something else for a few seconds, and then when I woke up, I was staring out of the window at the postman's face. And of course, once I saw him I ran upstairs again to hide, but I suppose it must have been too late.'

Samuel and Martha sat there and nodded as if this were a perfectly normal piece of information. They knew that as well as being a goat farmer and a ski jumper, Uncle Henrik had also spent many years as a dog. Yes, a real-life lamppost-wetting, flea-scratching, postman-biting dog.

'No,' said Aunt Eda. 'It is not too late. Not at all. Mr Myklebust knows nothing. Nothing at all. Not for certain. We haff to be careful, that is all. Henrik, you must not go out of the house. And when you are downstairs we must draw the curtains. And children, we do not do anything that puts ourselves in efen more of a situation. You must not think about going back to the forest. We must forget it efen exists. And if you effer see anything leef the forest, then you must tell me or your uncle straight away. This is ferry important. You remember what I always say, don't you?'

Martha and Samuel looked at each other, and recited Aunt Eda's favourite saying word for word: '*If we don't effer cause trouble with the forest, the forest won't effer cause trouble with us.*'

Aunt Eda frowned. 'Why do you say "effer"? I don't speak like that. I say "effer", not "effer", thank you ferry much.'

And Martha nudged Samuel, and Samuel laughed, and the laughter was contagious because pretty soon it had spread to Martha and then to Uncle Henrik, and eventually even Aunt Eda was laughing as well. And, for a considerable few moments, their laughter seemed to make all their worries about new schools and nosy phone calls disappear out of the house and float away on the clean mountain air.

A RUDE INTERRUPTION FROM THE AUTHOR

Hello.

It's the author here.

I'm terribly sorry to interrupt you so early in the book, but I really thought I should explain a few things before we go any further.

I am worried I might have thrown you a little bit there, with that 'Uncle Henrik was once a dog' stuff.

Well, what can I say? Apart from that it's absolutely true. He was a Norwegian elkhound, if you want to know the breed. And if you don't believe *that*, then you probably won't believe that Samuel was once turned into a rabbit, or that Martha spent a short while as a bird. Mind you, if you *are* that type of person, you probably won't believe that trolls really live in Shadow Forest, along with pixies and tomtegubbs and huldre-folk. In which case there is absolutely no point carrying on reading the book.

Seriously, I would put it down and go on your computer or something. What can I do to convince you, other than to tell you that these things are *true*?

Yes, I know, it's hard to believe. But trust me, there are plenty of trolls out there who find *you* just as hard to believe. 'Humans? Pah! Load of rubbish,' they say at Troll Council meetings. 'Never believed in 'em myself. Till I be seeing one with my own eyes I say they be a complete fib.'

Well, not all trolls think like that. There's one troll who believes in humans rather too much. Indeed, he believes all his problems will be solved if only he could run away and see the human boy he met in the summer.

And we'll come to him next, if you are prepared to believe in such things . . .

THE PEOPLE WHO ARE NOT PEOPLE

If you were a bird and you flew directly five miles north of Samuel and Martha's bedroom, you would reach a village in the heart of Shadow Forest. In many ways, this village is rather normal. It has an ale house, where people like to get drunk. It has a meeting hall, where people like to hold meetings. Oh, and it has small stone cottages, where people like to live.

The only difference is that these people aren't *human* people. They are *troll* people. And trolls are different to humans in a number of very important ways. Ten, to be precise:

1. Trolls live a lot longer than humans. The average troll lives to be 807.
2. Trolls never brush their teeth, and grown-up

trolls never wash themselves. Troll children, on the other hand, *are* expected to have baths, but only once a year, on their Annual Washday.

3. Most trolls can't read. There are some trolls who would come out in a violent rash just by touching this page.

4. Trolls are way uglier than even the ugliest humans. They are more lumpy-faced, boil-nosed, wonky-toothed and matted-haired than any of us. Some trolls have only one eye. Others have three eyes. And there's even a few with two heads. About half of the troll population has two eyes and one head, just like humans, but even they are very strange to look at with their hairy nostrils and lumpy skin.

5. Trolls, generally, are much more stupid than humans. Although the humans are really catching up.

6. Trolls don't have supermarkets. They hunt for their supper. And what they hunt is rabbits.

7. Trolls don't have names. Not proper names like Samuel and Martha. They are called things like Troll-Father and Troll-Son and Troll-the-Wisest. Proper names are seen as a bit too fancy, but this creates problems. For instance, there

are now – as I write this – forty-seven children in the village of Trollhelm with the name Troll-Daughter.

8. Trolls don't rot. When they die their bodies turn into stone, which is usually used to build a new cottage.

9. Trolls don't go to school. But naughty troll children still get into trouble, and often get tied to the whipping post for their mother to beat them. And if they are in REALLY BIG trouble, they are sent to a troll called the Betterer. The Betterer is much cleaner and stricter and more cruel than the average troll, and the children who return from the Bettering Tower can hardly speak with fear. However, ever since two troll twins spread tales of what goes on there, no troll parent has sent their child away to learn 'the art of human refinement and dignity', as the Betterer calls it.

10. Trolls don't come out in daylight. They have always been scared of daylight for various reasons. Trolls used to believe they would turn to stone if they were out when it was light, but more recently they believed their shadows would be stolen and that they'd be made evil.

Actually, this *did* happen to a lot of creatures in Shadow Forest. But trolls are too stupid to realize it couldn't happen to them. Their shadows are far too heavy to be stolen by any kind of magic. Humans, on the other hand, have much lighter shadows *and* go out in daylight. Which a troll would think was crazy.

Now, the particular trolls that concern us here are a family who have lived all their lives in the same stone cottage in Trollhelm. Their rather unfancy names are, like those of so many others, Troll-Father, Troll-Mother, Troll-Son and Troll-Daughter.

And right now, as Samuel lies awake in his bed five miles to the south, Troll-Son is being screamed at by his mother. Listen:

'STOP SCRATCHING YOUR EYE-HOLE, YOU GRUBBY LITTLE FLENCH!'

(Oh yes, I nearly forgot. These are one-eyed trolls, who have only one eye-socket each and only one eyeball between the whole family. Which they lost weeks ago and still haven't found.)

'I be not scratching,' said Troll-Son, who was lying.

'Flench! Flench! Flench!' said his younger sister, who was rather annoying.

'I might be having no eyeball but I be hearing some scratching in that there socket of yours.' As usual, Troll-Mother was cross with Troll-Son. She woke up each morning and thought, *Today I be going to be a little less cross with Troll-Son*, but she couldn't help it. He was always doing something that made her angry, and if she wasn't going to tell him how to behave, then who was? A troll with no manners was the lowest kind of creature there was, and Troll-Mother expected better.

'Leave him be, Troll-Mother,' said Troll-Father. 'I don't be hearing hi–'

As always, Troll-Father was unable to finish his sentence owing to the fact that he was being clouted by his wife. And as it was nearly supper time, it wasn't just a hand she was clouting him with. It was a rabbit pan. Although they weren't cooking rabbits – they hadn't caught one since they lost the family eyeball. Now that they had run out of rabbits, they were left to eat a stewish concoction made of grass and earthworms.

Troll-Son *hated* this meal, but as neither he nor Troll-Father had managed to catch a rabbit all night, it looked like they had no choice.

'I be thinking,' said Troll-Father as he felt his way to the table. 'Why don't we be telling one of the neighbours about our rabbit problem. I be sure they be a-helping out.'

This made Troll-Mother even more furious. 'You flenking great lump! You want us to go scrounging to the village? What do you think we be? Pixies?! You be wanting every troll to be knowing our business?'

'No, I–'

'And anyhow, if that there lazy son of yours be finding the eyeball, you'd be catching rabbits every night.'

'Lay-zee! Lay-zee! Lay-zee!' added Troll-Daughter. (I told you she was annoying.)

Now it was Troll-Son who felt cross. Why was he the only one who was forced to hunt all round the garden for the eyeball? It wasn't *his* fault that a blue-feathered bird had flown off with it and dropped it somewhere while his parents were wrestling with a stubborn rabbit on the chopping bench outside. No. But every hour of the night, if he wasn't rabbit-hunting with his father, he was expected to be eye-hunting in the garden.

'I be not lazy,' he said.

And then Troll-Mother, who was now throwing the earthworms and grass into the pan, screamed at Troll-Father, 'Be you letting him speak to his mother like that? BE YOU? BE YOU? WELL?'

'No,' said Troll-Father meekly. 'No . . . Troll-Son, you must not be speaking to your mother like that. Be saying sorry.'

'I be only saying I be not lazy.'

Troll-Mother took a really deep breath to show her horror at this insolence. 'Huh! That horrendous boy. He be needing a strong father. That's what he be needing.'

Taking his cue, Troll-Father spoke again. 'Be saying sorry, Troll-Son. Don't be upsetting your mother.'

And so, with the prospect of no more reward than a plate of cooked earthworms, Troll-Son said, 'Sorry.'

It was the same old story. This was Troll-Son's life. Every night he would work hard trying to find rabbits and eyeballs before having to apologize for his own existence. And every day he would lie on his hard stone bed, imagining the world beyond the forest. That was the one good thing about having no eyeball – it made it easier to *imagine.* He would stay awake and imagine the world where the humans lived, and he knew it was the most wonderful place. And he was thinking of this place right now, as he forced the cooked grass and earthworms into his mouth. In particular he was thinking about the human boy who had once stayed with Troll-Son and his family, while looking for his human sister. This had been a few days before the troll family had lost the eyeball, and so Troll-Son had been able to see him.

He had been so clean and smooth-skinned and well-mannered. The human boy had smiled at Troll-Son as if he were a friend. Imagine that! A human being friendly to a troll.

But the best thing of all about the human boy was his name. He had a *real name*. And every time Troll-Son felt sad, he whispered the name to himself, over and over, like a kind of prayer. If you lean into the page and listen closely, you can hear him whispering it now, between mouthfuls –

'Samuel Blink, Samuel Blink, Samuel–'

'Flenking heck! Will you be quiet, Troll-Son?' asked his mother. 'Honestly! I be trying to eat my worms and all I be hearing is Samuel Blink this and Samuel Blink that. Do you be thinking that a human boy would be speaking the way you speak to your mother? A human boy would not be having time for trolls with no manners. Oh! How will you be coping when you get older? How? How? Oh, Troll-Son . . . be you not understanding? I be only wanting you to be making us proud . . . But it be a hard world for a troll out there,

and if you be carrying on like this I be having to send you to the Betterer. For your own good it be.'

Troll-Mother took a deep breath. She hated the idea of sending her son away, but she had to threaten him with something if he was going to behave himself.

'Bett! Bett! Bett!' chanted Troll-Daughter, knocking her spoon against the table without being told off. (I never knew she was *this* annoying.)

Troll-Son didn't say another word. He knew Troll-Mother wasn't *really* going to send him to the Betterer. After all, no troll parent had sent their child to be bettered for three months – ever since they had heard the tales of the jittery troll twins. But still, Troll-Son knew not to argue with his mother. So he stopped saying the human name, finished his worm supper, and was forced outside to hunt for the eyeball in the garden until the sun came up.

But as always, he had no luck. No eyeball was found. And his mother gave him one clout around the head for being hopeless before morning, and Troll-Son lay down on his stone bed and dreamed of how different his life could be. Beyond the forest. Away from his mother. Among the humans.

'Samuel Blink' – he whispered the name until he fell asleep – 'Samuel Blink, Samuel Blink, Samuel . . .

What happened during the holidays,
by Samuel Blink

My mum and dad were killed by a falling log that crushed their car. If Dad had listened to me and stopped the car when I told him, they would still be alive, so it's his stupid fault that me and Martha had to move to Norway and live with Aunt Eda.

Aunt Eda is OK, apart from being strict and looking like she's from 1838 and having her hair in a bun and her cardigans always buttoned right up to the top.

One day Martha disappeared into the forest near Aunt Eda's house. Aunt Eda had told us never to enter the forest but I had to go into it and rescue her, because Aunt Eda was too scared. Well, that is what I thought. I wasn't on my own though. Ibsen, Aunt Eda's dog (an elkhound, in case you're interested) followed me into the forest. You see, her husband Henrik had disappeared in there years ago too and never came back and she'd spent years with nothing but her dog Ibsen for company.

Anyway, the forest was full of lots of evil creatures who'd had their shadows stolen and been made slaves to an overlord called the Changemaker, who had once been a human being called Professor Horatio Tanglewood. He had gained his power by saving the life of a Shadow Witch and hated his fellow humans so much that he wanted to kill any that entered the forest.

So when Martha went into the forest, she was locked in an underground prison by creatures called huldres – who'd once been good creatures but had been turned very evil by the Changemaker.

I nearly got caught by the huldres too, but luckily I managed to hide with a family of trolls in the village of Trollhelm. You see, trolls are mainly kind creatures who were never made evil because their shadows were too heavy to steal. Oh – and this troll family only had one eyeball between them, which was pretty disgusting because it made a weird kind of sucking sound when they pulled it out of their eye-sockets to pass it around.

And these trolls were very nice to me because they liked humans, especially the boy in the family, who was called Troll-Son.

Samuel scanned his eyes across what he had written, and as he did so, he noted certain words and phrases. *Evil creatures . . . Shadow Witch . . . troll family . . . one eyeball . . . Uncle Henrik . . . into an elkhound.* He imagined the teacher having a heart attack when she read it.

'Hmm,' Samuel thought to himself as he screwed up the sheet of paper. 'Don't think so.'

He wished he'd bothered to do his homework last night, like Martha had – then he wouldn't have to do it in such a rush. He began writing again, on a fresh sheet. Only this time it was a lot shorter:

What happened during the holidays,
by Samuel Blink

Went to live in Norway with my Aunt Eda ~~and Uncle Henrik~~. It is a nice country. I like eating sweet brown cheese and reindeer soup. The scenery is pretty. Everyone is friendly.

Samuel read it back. It was funny how lies could sometimes be so much more believable than the truth. And then he looked at the photograph of his mum and dad that he and Martha kept on their desk. It was taken in front of The Catapult, the world's scariest roller-coaster, which he had pestered his dad to go on. His dad had run to the toilets straight afterwards and been sick. His father hadn't been that brave, but he'd gone on that ride just for him. Which made him the greatest kind of dad in Samuel's eyes.

And then Martha came into the room and said: 'You know that Hek bracelet Aunt Eda had – the one that protects you from *anything* – well, she's just told me where it's hidden. It's in a wooden box with roses on it in her bedroom. Just in case we need it.'

Samuel swallowed, and didn't turn to face his sister so she wouldn't see the tears in his eyes. 'It's a bit too late, isn't it?'

'Too late?'

'I mean, the one thing we needed it to protect us from has already happened. And now we're here – look at us: we live in a house no one even dares visit, next to a forest we can't enter, we go to a school where we don't know the language, and the only family we've got is an aunt who wants us to lie in our homework and an uncle who thinks he's a dog. We need more than a stupid bracelet to protect us from all that.'

'Samuel, what's the matter? I thought you liked Aunt Eda and Unc–'

'It's not about them. They're all right. It's just . . . I don't know – sometimes I get bored and wish we could escape into the forest and live with the trolls, and not have to bother with starting new school and being with human beings any more.'

Martha laughed. '*I'm* a human being. And so were you last time I checked! And anyway, running into the forest is a totally stupid idea.'

'Says you.'

'Yes, well, I've learned my lesson. And it wouldn't make you feel better. However great the forest is now.'

It was true. Wherever Samuel ran away to, he would still have to take himself with him. There was no escape from memories that weren't just contained in a photograph, but were for ever in his mind, preserved like pickles in a jar. And so there was nothing for Samuel to do but carry that mind with him into the bathroom, brush his teeth, get ready for school, and spend a silent breakfast wondering what miserable things lay in store for him.

THE EVER-SO-SUPERIOR CORNELIA

It was Tuesday morning. The first day back from the holidays. Samuel and Martha entered the classroom and looked around. All the girls, of various ages, were seated on one side of the room, and all the boys were seated on the other.

Samuel gulped. He hated the feeling of being watched by so many new faces. Especially faces that examined him as if he were something strange, like a frog to dissect in a biology class. He recognized one of the boys – a boy with glasses who he had seen once before at the grocer's – but the boy made no attempt to look at him or smile. And anyway, he was sitting with another boy. In fact, all the boys were sitting with other boys, and as each desk only had room for two people, he was forced to sit at the empty one at the back of the room.

Martha went to join him, but Mrs Sturdsen (a short, solid-looking woman with rosy cheeks) told her to sit on the girls' side of the room. So she did – in the empty seat next to a girl with blonde, perfectly plaited hair, who was sitting so upright you would think she was riding a horse. The girl's name was Cornelia Myklebust.

Samuel, meanwhile, was at his lonely desk at the back of the classroom while Mrs Sturdsen addressed the class. She was speaking in Norwegian, so he couldn't understand a word of it, except when his and Martha's names were mentioned. Then she spoke in English, with a strong accent.

'Yes, today we have new pupils at our school all the way from England. I am sure they will be made to feel very welcome . . . I will be explaining a lot of the lessons in English – which will help the rest of you learn new words.'

The whole class groaned, and Samuel felt about as popular as a school text book. He sank back in his chair as Mrs Sturdsen collected the homework, wishing he were anywhere but right there.

Cornelia Myklebust was eleven years old, and knew pretty much everything. She spoke eleven languages, and was fluent in English. She was equally excellent at maths, art and science. She could tell you that the sun was four and a half billion years old. Or that Malabo was the capital of Equatorial Guinea. Or that *The Old Curiosity Shop* was a book written by Charles Dickens.

She was so clever that she would often correct Mrs Sturdsen, who didn't very much like to be corrected.

'No,' Cornelia had said recently during a lesson on cloud types, 'I think you will find *that's* a cumulonimbus, not a cirrocumulus formation.'

But although she was the definition of a clever-clogs (look it up in the dictionary and you'll see her picture), she did not enjoy knowledge. Or rather, she enjoyed it only in so far as it helped to make her feel cleverer than other people. She already knew she was the prettiest girl in the school, and she certainly had the richest parents, but she was determined to be the cleverest as well. Then she could make just about everyone feel jealous, and making people feel jealous was the most delicious kind of fun.

Which was why, when the new girl from England chose to sit next to her, she was thrilled. After all, what was a new person but a new victim to whom she could demonstrate her natural superiority.

'Hello, I'm Cornelia,' she said, in the most precise English, as she held out her hand. 'I'm very pleased to meet you.'

Martha shook her hand. 'I'm Martha.'

'Oh, Martha. That's M-A-R-T-H-A, isn't it? In Norway there is a similar name. Marte. It's of Arabic origin, I think, isn't it?'

'I don't know,' said Martha, because she didn't.

'Oh, really! Don't you know *that*? I thought everyone knew where their name comes from and what it means. My name means yellow, so it goes with my hair.'

'I like it,' said Martha. 'Your name – and your hair.'

'Oh, thank you. I get it from my mother. She was a model and is still very beautiful. Now she doesn't need to work. My father's very rich, you see . . . What does your mother do?'

Martha felt sad, suddenly. She remembered the time when her mother had let her put a hundred slides in her hair. 'She's . . . not here.'

Cornelia laughed. 'I know she's *not here*. I think our mothers are a bit too old for school.'

'No,' said Martha. 'She's . . . She . . .' And she realized that this was the first time she had ever had to say it out loud. 'She died. My mum . . . and my dad. Both of them. They died in a car accident . . . That's why we came to live here in Norway. Me and Samuel, my brother. To live with our . . .' She said all this as quickly as she could, but still found the words became stuck. She was too sad to let them out.

'Oh, I'm sorry,' Cornelia said, looking as un-sorry as it is possible to look. 'It must be terrible being an orphan. I'd *hate* it if my parents died and I was left all on my own.'

Martha didn't like Cornelia. There seemed to be something very cold about her. Each of her sentences had the same effect as a sharp pencil, jabbing her where it hurt in order to get a reaction.

'I'm not on my own. I've got my brother. Samuel.'

Cornelia turned to where Martha was pointing and saw a dark-haired, grumpy-looking boy slumped back in his chair and staring right at her.

'Oh, *him*,' she said, with a look of mild disgust. '*That's* your brother. Poor you.'

Secretly, of course, she was rather jealous. You see, Cornelia didn't have a brother or sister, and had often wondered what it would be like to have one.

'No, he's all right really,' Martha said. *Better than you, anyway*, she thought.

'Oh well, I suppose if you're an orphan you must be grateful for anyone.'

'We are lucky because we live with our Uncle Henrik and Aunt Eda and they are the nicest people ever, even if Aunt Eda is a bit strict some–'

And it was at this point in their conversation that Mrs Sturdsen interrupted them, first in Norwegian and then in English, to tell them to be quiet for the start of the lesson. The lesson was mathematics, during which Martha had her sums laughed at by Cornelia. Every other lesson passed in precisely the same way, with Cornelia correcting Martha at every opportunity.

'That girl is *so* annoying,' Martha told Samuel at break.

'Well at least she's talking to you,' said Samuel. 'I tried talking to one boy – that Fredrik boy who's always playing with his calculator – you know, the one we saw at the greengrocer's . . . but he totally blanked me. Like I was invisible.'

'It's because we don't speak Norwegian.'

Samuel nodded. 'I hate this school.'

'It will get better,' Martha said.

And as Samuel looked at his sister's smile, he felt guilty. He was the older brother. Shouldn't he be the one trying to make Martha feel better, not the other way round? He was only two years older than her, but he had to be the parent now. The responsible one.

'I know,' he said, and tried to mirror Martha's smile. 'It will get better . . . Hey, you didn't tell that girl about the forest, did you?'

Martha shook her head. 'No. Course not.'

'Or about Uncle Henrik?'

And Martha shook her head again, and gave another 'No', but Samuel couldn't help noticing it took longer coming than the first 'No'. Nor did he fail to notice his sister's blushing cheeks, but he said nothing more, and trusted she was telling the truth.

THE TWO RABBITS

Troll-Son had once liked nothing better than going out hunting with his father – out on their own, passing the family eyeball back and forth between them as they trekked through the pine trees on the lookout for any rabbits they could put in their sack.

It had been so lovely to talk about the things only a father and son could talk about. Even though the forest had been dangerous in those days, Troll-Son had loved the excitement of travelling through it at night and, when he was allowed the eye, of searching amid the ferns and moonlit undergrowth for any sign of a rabbit, and of catching sight of all the odd creatures in the forest, like the tall, galloping caloosh birds that often raced by.

Now, though, it was different. Every time they

went hunting, Troll-Son knew, like his father, that if they didn't return with a rabbit Troll-Mother would be furious. Night after night after night they had gone out with the sack and the best of intentions, but night after night after night they had returned empty-handed. And now that all the rabbits in the pen had been turned into stew and eaten, things were very desperate indeed.

'We must be finding a rabbit tonight, Troll-Son,' his father was saying. 'If we be not finding one tonight, your mother be in such a temper we won't be knowing what be hitting us, we be not.' He paused a while thoughtfully, then spoke again. 'It be not her fault really. She be just worried, that be all. She be loving us, really. You be knowing that, don't you be?'

Troll-Son said nothing. He supposed, deep down, that his father was telling the truth. But if his mother's love was so well hidden under shouts and clouts around the head, what was the point of it?

He kept following the sound of his father's footsteps and tried not to bang into any of the trees. He knew that tonight would be the same as all the other nights. He knew that without the eyeball they would never be able to catch a rabbit.

'Sssh,' said Troll-Father.

And Troll-Son shushed, even though he hadn't been saying anything in the first place.

'I be hearing rabbits.' His father's voice was now sharp and low. 'To our left. I be hearing rabbits to our left. I be hearing them.'

Troll-Son stood still and listened carefully. At first he heard nothing but the low whisper of the wind through the trees, the same cool wind that brushed against his face and tickled the tender skin inside his eye-socket. Gradually he began to hear other sounds. A rustle of leaves. The crack of a twig. A soft, slow thumping that he recognized as the hop of a rabbit.

'There be two of 'em.' His father's whisper joined that of the wind. 'And if you be listening, son, they be coming this way. If we be staying still enough, they won't be thinking we be trolls or nothing. So let's be still as stones.'

Troll-Son did as his father said, and froze so that he was as still as the trees around him.

'Now, be getting the sack ready – and staying quiet. Wait until I be saying the word, then we be pouncing on them fast as a falling roof.'

'Yes,' whispered Troll-Son, before being silent once again. He held the sack and waited. He knew what to do: when the rabbits got closer, his father would lunge forward and grab them while he covered them with the sack. He knew that if they stayed still enough, the rabbits would keep hopping until they were up close and they would have them. Troll-Son was so excited he could hardly breathe. They were going to catch their first rabbit in days. They weren't going to have to eat a measly bowl of worms and grass, and he wouldn't get told off again by his mother.

But then, just as the rabbits were getting closer – just as they were so close it was almost time to pounce – there was a sound: Troll-Son's stomach rumbled so loudly that the two rabbits were warned off and began hopping in the other direction.

'Keep your hunger quiet,' said Troll-Father. 'It be frightening 'em off.'

'I can't help it!'

'Sssh. Listen – they be hopping fast away now! Grab the sack . . . let's chase 'em.'

And so Troll-Son followed his father, running blindly through the undergrowth in pursuit of the two rabbits.

'Faster, son, faster. We be nearly getting 'em! Faster! Faster!'

Troll-Son ran as fast as he could, because he knew they couldn't afford to return home with an empty rabbit sack, but with such an empty stomach he hardly had any energy.

'Run, Troll-Son, run!'

'I be running,' he said as he sped through the forest. 'I be–'

Doof.

The trouble with chasing after rabbits in a forest when you've got no eyeball is that it is very hard to know exactly where the trees are. Trees, generally speaking, don't warn you that you are about to bump into them. And so Troll-Son slammed into a pine tree and fell back into the undergrowth to hear – he was sure – the quiet laughter of a thousand rabbits throbbing inside his head.

'Ow . . . ow . . . ow,' he moaned.

He tried to sit up – his father was still running after the rabbits – but his head hurt so much he lay back down. Lying there, he thought how angry his mother would be with him. He heard his father's fast and fading footsteps and was about to call after him when there was something else. Another sound. A sound that wasn't made by his father, or by escaping rabbits.

THE SCREAMING HEAD

'Help! . . . Help! . . . Someone! . . . I hear you . . . I hear you . . . Help!'

Troll-Son recognized the voice, but didn't know how. He didn't know what to do. Should he call back? Should he try and ignore his headache and go and see what was the matter? Maybe if he could help whoever it was, he would get a reward. Maybe he would get something to eat.

He inched himself up onto his elbows, then slowly stood up as footsteps raced towards him.

'Troll-Son?' It was his father's voice now, out of breath. 'Troll-Son? Where you be? Where you be? I had the little hoppers – they were right beside my feet and I be saying, "The sack, the sack, put 'em in the sack," and where you be? Where you–?'

But then he heard it too. The shouting.

'Help! . . . Help! . . . I can't move! . . . I can't flenking move!'

Troll-Father fell silent for a moment, and considered. 'I be knowing that voice. I be knowing it as well as my own itching scalp. It be our old neighbour Troll-the-Right, be it not? The head they be chopping off the two-headed troll.'

'Yes,' said Troll-Son, already walking in the direction of the screams. 'It be Troll-the-Right.'

The distant yells continued. 'Argh! . . . Help me . . . Please . . . '

'Troll-Son, come back,' whispered Troll-Father. 'There might be trouble out there. And what use are we being when we can't even catch a rabbit? Troll-Son? Troll-Son?'

Troll-Son headed towards Troll-the-Right, his arms out in front of him so as not to bump into any more trees. He looked – if anyone could have seen him – rather like a sleepwalker who had strayed too far from his bed. Only instead of a bed-sheet hanging down from his fingers he held an empty sack.

'Troll-Son, come back here! What will your mother be saying if we be getting ourselves caught in any mischief? Troll-Son? Troll-Son? If Troll-the-Right is meant to be found, then surely Troll-the-Left is meant to be doing the finding. Troll-Son . . . ?'

But Troll-Son kept walking. After all, Troll-the-Right had been their neighbour, and wasn't it one of the troll commandments to always help a neighbour in need? And wouldn't Troll-the-Left be happy if Troll-the-Right was returned to him? Wouldn't he feel like Troll-Son would feel if he found the eyeball? After all, a two-headed troll who had lost one of his heads would surely be feeling very lonely.

OK, so it was true that Troll-the-Left hadn't stopped whistling happy tunes since he had returned to the village with a set of shoulders all to himself. It was also true that Troll-the-Left hadn't actually searched very hard for the missing head. Troll-the-Left had gone into great detail about how he and Troll-the-Right had been caught trespassing by shadowless huldre-folk, and how they had been sent in a wagon to the evil Changemaker with other prisoners, including a human girl and a witch, and how this witch had helped them escape by conjuring a blizzard out of thin air.

Troll-Son himself had been gripped when his father – who had heard Troll-the-Left tell the story in the ale house – talked of how their two-headed neighbour got into a fight with the huldre prison guards.

Troll-Son had gasped in horror as he heard how Troll-the-Right's head had been sliced off before Troll-the-Left fought back and killed the huldre who had been responsible.

'So why didn't he be picking up Troll-the-Right and taking him home?' Troll-Son had asked.

'He be not saying, now I be thinking on it. Perhaps he be losing it. I mean, we be losing an eyeball. Maybe he be losing a head. 'Tis most possible.'

Troll-Son had wondered exactly *how* it was possible someone could accidentally lose a head – which was another reason why he was determined to reach Troll-the-Right.

'Troll-Son . . . Troll-Son . . . Come back here . . . Please, Troll-Son, let's not be interfering in other people's business. We got to be finding rabbits, not mischief.'

But Troll-Father knew his words never had the strength to control his son's behaviour, and so he too found himself heading through the trees with his arms out in front of him, to feel for rough tree trunks in his way. And all the time, the screams got louder:

'Who's that? Help! Help! Someone – help! I be seeing you. I be seeing you. A troll boy. A troll boy in amongst the trees. Down here! I be down here. I be down here on the path! Be that . . . be that . . . be that Troll-Son? My old neighbour Troll-Son? And be that your father behind you?'

'It be us,' said Troll-Father as he caught up with his son and took his hand to walk down the slope towards the path.

'You be walking all over the place. What be the matter?'

'Oh yes . . . you'll have to be forgiving us. Troll-Son and I can't be seeing you, Troll-the-Right. We be losing our eyeball a while ago, you see, and we–'

'Well, I be down here. On the path. Mind that tree. Yes. There you be. Left a bit. Keep going. Left, left, right. No! Straight on. Left. No! *Left!* Yes, keep walking. Nearly there.'

'Where be you, neighbour?' Troll-Father asked as he felt the ground.

'Here!' Troll-Son said, crouching down and feeling the top of the head that lay on the path.

'Now, you be picking me up and taking me back to the village.'

Troll-Son held the ears and tried to lift the head off the path, but it was too heavy.

'Aaargh!' screamed Troll-the-Right. 'My earaarghs!'

'No, I'll do it, son. Leave it to me.' Troll-Father

crouched down and heaved the head off the ground, drops of blood dripping from Troll-the-Right's severed neck. 'Oof, you are heavy.'

But eventually the head was held safely in his arms, and as Troll-the-Right could see the way ahead, he guided the other two trolls back to the village much faster than they would have made it on their own.

'Why aren't you dead?' Troll-Son asked. 'Why haven't you turned into a rock?'

'*Be*,' Troll-Father said, trying to correct his son. 'Why *be* you not turned into a rock?'

The answer was straightforward. 'So long as Troll-the-Left be staying alive and feeding our stomach, I be staying living myself. Even if I be miles away. That's the way it be going with us two-headed types. And believe me, Troll-the-Left be doing a lot of feeding.' As if to prove the point, Troll-the-Right released a long and deep belch, before smacking his lips together. 'Rabbit stew,' he said, identifying the flavour. 'Washed down with some hurgleberry wine.'

THE BETTERER

The trolls of Trollhelm lived very close together, in stone cottages that were rarely more than a couple of steps from their neighbours'. All these cottages were very similar looking, with low roofs and square doors and windows, and rabbit pens in the garden.

There are only two buildings in Trollhelm that look any different. One of these is the large meeting hall on the village square, where the Troll Council meets every Moon Day night. The other building that looks rather different is the Bettering Tower, which stands on the edge of the village, further into the trees than all the other houses.

The Bettering Tower is different in many ways. Instead of being short and square, like the house where Troll-Son lived, the Bettering Tower was tall and round, like a lighthouse. Only a very wide lighthouse. And one that was covered in deep, dark tree shadows.

The troll who lived in the Bettering Tower was as different from the other inhabitants of Trollhelm as the tower itself was from the other houses. He was just as ugly but he had tried to disguise his ugliness in a number of ways. His beard was a lot better groomed, for one thing. And his clothes, including his long overcoat, were much tidier, and he smelled considerably cleaner owing to the seven baths he had every single day. Of course, he was still a troll. His nose was still lumpy and his teeth were terrible, but he had two eyes and only one head, which in troll terms meant he was quite handsome.

He also spoke a lot more precisely, and tended to use words in a more correct way than the other residents of Trollhelm.

Another difference was his name.

This troll was known to all the others in the village not as Betterer-Troll, or Troll-the-Betterer. No. Just 'the Betterer'. You see, even though the Betterer *was* a troll, he thought he was, well, *better*. And so did many of the other trolls. Which is why, when their children were of a certain age, and misbehaved, they had always sent them to the Betterer to be bettered.

Trolls don't go to school. They don't read, write or work out complicated sums. They don't spend every Sunday praying for Monday never to arrive. No, the only thing a troll child truly has to fear is a week's stay with the Betterer. And one week with him was more terrifying than all your school years put together.

And the Betterer had enjoyed his work: he loved to correct a troll child's bad habits and make them more human-like. The only trouble was, some troll parents had recently gone off the idea of sending their children to be bettered, no matter how naughty they were, because of the bad stories they had heard. In fact, the Betterer hadn't had a troll child to stay for three months, when some unruly troll twins had been sent to him by their exasperated parents. They had been the naughtiest trolls the Betterer had ever seen and needed severe punishments every time they picked their noses or answered back or played with the fleas they found in their hair. The trouble was, his methods worked rather too well, and the twins' parents were appalled to find their children turned into trembling wrecks, stammering about the strict measures the Betterer had been forced to inflict. The stories of the twins' suffering spread fast, and many parents vowed never to send their children off to the Bettering Tower, no matter how naughty they were. No parent wanted to be rid of the Betterer altogether – after all, it was useful to be able to say, 'If you don't be finishing your supper I be sending you to you-know-where!' But very few parents actually *meant* it.

Which is why the Betterer had now decided to go out and actively try and persuade mothers of the values of betterment.

'Hello, my dear. Do you want a clean troll child, a polite troll child, a well-spoken troll child, a troll child who can tidy your house without being asked? If so, I suggest they are sent for a week's stay at the Bettering Tower.'

'Oh, I don't know . . . I mean, there be no such things as Bettering Towers when I be young and I be perfectly all right. And maybe it be better to be proud to be a troll than to better him into something he be never meant to be.'

Yes, the Betterer was suddenly out of fashion. He was having to face the truth that some parents actually preferred their offspring to be noisy, smelly and rude than clean, quiet and – *OK* – a little jittery. But he wasn't going to give up. All he needed was the right kind of mother – one who was at the end of her tether – and he knew he would be able to win her over.

Now, I wonder who that mother might be . . .

TROLL-MOTHER'S VISITOR

Samuel couldn't sleep. His first day at the new school had been a disaster. He knew that he had no reason to expect his second day there to go any better, especially if he got no sleep.

But his mind was racing. He couldn't help but wonder what was going on in the forest. If he didn't have Martha, he thought, he would probably be better off living among the trolls.

At least troll children don't have to go to school, he thought to himself. *And even if they did, it wouldn't be with the likes of Cornelia Myklebust.*

He peeled back the bed covers and went over to the window, poking his head between the curtains. It was a dark night but he could still see the outline of the trees, their top edge jagged against the sky like a torn piece of paper.

He suddenly understood why, earlier in the summer, his sister had decided to head into the forest. It was so easy to imagine that a life you couldn't see or hear – the life beyond the trees – might offer more than the life he knew.

But if he could have seen Troll-Son and Troll-Father struggling to hunt rabbits or feel the hunger in their stomachs, he probably wouldn't have wanted to swap places.

It was impossible for him to see or feel these things, just as it was impossible for him to know that right at that moment – at ten to three in the morning, by Samuel's watch – a certain troll in a long overcoat was leaving the tower on the edge of Trollhelm to pay Troll-Mother a visit.

No, it was as impossible for Samuel to see the Betterer in that dark forest as it is for you to see that same figure in the black ink of these words. But that didn't make the knock on Troll-Mother's door any less real.

'Oh, who be that, I wonder,' she said. 'We not be expecting no visitors, be we, Troll-Daughter? Not unless it be them two lumps come home already with no rabbits!'

She felt her way to the door. 'I be coming . . . I be

coming . . .'

Of course, once she had opened the door she couldn't see who was standing there as she had no eyeball. But whoever it was smelled very nice, and had what she considered to be a very proper and polite type of silence before he spoke.

'Hello, Troll-Mother,' he said eventually, in a voice so crisp and clean it almost sounded human.

'Be this . . . the Betterer?' asked Troll-Mother.

'Indeed it is. I was wondering if I could come in for a conversation.'

This got Troll-Mother into something of a panic. She wasn't used to people speaking all the right words in all the right places, especially words like 'conversation'.

'Oh, Mr Betterer, sir . . . I be awful sorry but Troll-Father be out hunting rabbits and the house be an awful mess being as we have no eyeball.'

The Betterer was looking at Troll-Mother the way you might look at a bowl full of rotting apples with maggots in, but Troll-Mother couldn't see his face. She could only hear his voice, and the perfectly pronounced words it spoke.

'I assure you it won't take long. It is just that I have some information, which I would be delighted to give you, about the services I have to offer.'

The perfectly pronounced words were impossible to argue with. They seemed to fly past Troll-Mother's head like pretty little birds, before making themselves at home in her living room.

'You better be coming in then,' she said.

The Betterer did so, and was appalled at how dirty the house was. He had already been to visit eight other troll parents this week, to encourage them to send their children to the Bettering Tower, but none of their hideous houses were quite so scruffy as this. He saw a young troll girl with a dirty face and greasy hair sitting on the floor and thought he was going to be sick at the sight of her, but he closed his eyes and came to his business as quickly as he could.

'I understand that according to Troll Council records you have a son of bettering age.'

'Aye, that be true,' said Troll-Mother.

'Well, you might not know this, my dear, but recently some parents have been thinking they have no need to send their grubb– their *darling offspring* to be bettered.'

Troll-Mother nodded. 'I be hearing.'

'But already I can see you are very wise, Troll-Mother – quite different from the other parents around here.' The Betterer stared down at the plates left on the dining table. Without Troll-Mother realizing, he picked up a half-eaten earthworm and looked out of the small square window. Even in the gloom he could see that their rabbit pen was empty. 'Yes, my dear, you are a wise and beautiful troll who I am sure wants the best for her son.'

Beautiful. The word made Troll-Mother feel strange and happy, as though she had just tasted a gorgeous drink she never knew existed. 'Of course,' she said as she ran a hand through her hair – unfortunately the hair was so matted that the hand got stuck there for the rest of the conversation. 'We be wanting the best for Troll-Son. It be just that his father be thinking it be best if we be keeping him here.'

The Betterer grimaced at this. What was with parents nowadays? Why had they become so soft, so accepting of their children's grubby, ill-mannered ways? Just because those wimpy troll twins had come out of the tower jibbering wrecks! Surely it was better to be a clean, well-spoken, mathematically competent jibbering wreck than to be left stinking and unbettered.

'I think that's very brave of you,' lied the Betterer. 'In that case I have no reason to tell you about the free stay I was going to offer.'

'*Free stay?*'

'A week at the Bettering Tower free of charge, starting from thirteen o'clock tomorrow night. But obviously that wouldn't matter to you . . . I'm sure you've got enough rabbits to pay for my normal treatment. A troll as beautiful as yourself must surely have a fine rabbit-catching husband. I bet he brings you hundreds every night!'

The Betterer smiled: he could see Troll-Mother was starting to change her mind.

'Oh yes,' said Troll-Mother, laughing desperately. 'We be having so many rabbits they be coming out of our ears!'

'And so there's absolutely no point in my telling you about the new rabbit-hunting lesson I'm starting as part of the Bettering week?'

'Rabbit-hunting lesson?' she said, hoping the Betterer wouldn't notice the rumbling of her stomach.

'Yes, I have devised a new method of rabbit-hunting that is so effective you only have to stand still and wait for rabbits to come to you. Your boy wouldn't even need an eyeball to be able to bring you home a sackful of rabbits a night. But of course, you won't need that . . . And anyway, I'm sure your son isn't the type to have any bad habits that need bettering so I'll be on my way.'

'No, wait,' Troll-Mother said.

The Betterer breathed in triumphantly, as if Troll-Mother's stupidity had its own delicious smell.

'It can be doing no harm to be giving your methodicals a go,' she said.

'No, exactly,' said the Betterer, already relishing the prospect of having a new grubby troll child to stay in the tower. He pulled a rolled-up sheet of paper from one of his many inside pockets. 'Now,' he said, unrolling the paper. 'If you could just put your thumbprint anywhere on here, we'll be in business.'

Troll-Mother was slightly taken aback by the force of the Betterer's grip around her wrist as he pulled her hand out of her hair and guided her filthy thumb to press a small brown smudge on the paper.

'Perfect,' he said, wiping his now dirty hand on his trousers. 'I assure you, Troll-Mother, it's for the best.'

Troll-Mother smiled, and found it impossible to disagree with words that were so well spoken. 'Yes, I be sure you be right, Mr Betterer. It be the best thing to be doing for Troll-Son in the long run and . . .'

She carried on talking for quite some time about

the merits of her decision without realizing that the Betterer had already left. He was halfway back to the Bettering Tower, unable to stand another minute of being polite to what he was sure must be the ugliest troll woman he had ever seen in his life.

TROLL-SON SAYS SOMETHING THAT SHOULDN'T BE SAID

Troll-the-Left wasn't particularly pleased to see Troll-the-Right. You see, the trouble with two-headed trolls is they normally come with two very different personalities. In fact, up until Troll-the-Right's head was chopped off by huldres, their whole life had been one long argument.

As child trolls they had fought over their milk, over their food, over their toys.

They argued about whether the left arm – Troll-the-Left's – was stronger than the right – Troll-the-Right's – and they'd stage arm-wrestling contests that neither of them could win.

Later on, when Troll-the-Left got a girlfriend, Troll-the-Right would spend the whole first date making large belching noises.

When Troll-the-Right began to snore, Troll-the-Left used to squeeze his nose so hard he'd get a nosebleed.

When Troll-the-Left landed them in prison after they were caught trespassing, Troll-the-Right vowed to blame him for ever.

Of course, for ever wasn't going to be a very long time as they were going to be sentenced to death. But then, when the prison wagon broke down on their way to the execution, they ended up in a battle which cost Troll-the-Right his head.

Although Troll-the-Left did the honourable thing and vowed to carry the head back to Trollhelm, he got so fed up with Troll-the-Right telling him 'I told you so' that he plonked him down on a forest path and never looked back.

Which brings us to here.

To Troll-the-Left forcing a smile as Troll-Father handed him Troll-the-Right's head.

'Oh, thank you so much – where be you finding him?'

'*Precisely where you be leaving me,*' snarled Troll-the-Right as blood dripped from his neck onto the wooden floor.

'Well, me and Troll-Son better be going,' said Troll-Father, sensing something of a bad atmosphere.

'All right, bye,' said Troll-the-Left. 'And I be grateful . . . I be so lost without him.'

'Lost!' laughed Troll-the-Right scornfully as he looked over at the rabbit casserole bubbling away on the stove and the new bottle of hurgleberry wine on the table. And then, seeing Troll-Father and Troll-Son were halfway out of the door, he said: 'Wait! Who's going to help stitch me back on? We need the boy. He might be blind but he be having the right-sized fingers. Would you help us, Troll-Son?'

'Can I be helping, Father?' asked Troll-Son, who thought it might make a change from searching for the eyeball. And besides, he had always liked both heads of the two-headed troll, even if they had never liked each other.

'Yes, I don't be seeing why not,' said Troll-Father, a little worried that he was approving something without asking Troll-Mother first. 'But be back for supper.'

'Yes,' said Troll-Son. And the door closed and he was left alone with the two-headed troll, who really *was* two-headed again now Troll-the-Left had put Troll-the-Right back onto the right neck.

'Now,' said Troll-the-Left wearily, 'I suppose we better be stitching him on.'

Troll-Son was directed to the sewing basket. (It might seem strange that a massive two-headed troll should *own* a sewing basket, but in fact the only thing the two heads ever agreed on was their love of needlecraft, and especially making pretty tapestries of lovely woodland scenes. They always found it very relaxing.) And as Troll-Son helped sew on Troll-the-Right's head, he could smell the rabbit casserole that was still bubbling away on the stove.

The smell tantalized his nostrils. He was so hungry after day upon day of earthworm-and-grass stew that he nearly fainted.

His stomach rumbled again. No. It was more of a grumble.

'You be sounding hungry,' said Troll-the-Left.

'Hungry?' huffed Troll-the-Right. 'Surprised you be knowing the word, the amount you been stuffing our stomach since I be gone.'

Troll-the-Left looked at the little eyeless troll boy and his skinny arms as he reached up to sew on the neck. 'You not be eating today?'

'Yes. I be eating worms and grass.'

'Worms and grass! That be no good for a growing troll. Why be you having no rabbits?'

And that was it. That was the moment that changed

everything. For that was when Troll-Son made a mistake, and told Troll-the-Left and Troll-the-Right the one thing his mother wanted to keep private.

The trouble was, Troll-Son was just too hungry to think about what might happen. And so he did it. He told the truth.

'We be not having any rabbits.'

'No rabbits?!' gasped Troll-the-Left.

'No rabbits?!' choked Troll-the-Right.

'Why not?' asked Troll-the-Left.

'We be not catching any. Not since we be losing our eye.'

Troll-the-Left shook his head. 'But I be seeing your parents every day and they be never mentioning it. This be not right. Not right at all!'

So when the right head was stitched back in place, the two-headed troll shared the rabbit casserole with Troll-Son. And Troll-Son was so hungry that he ate it all up and licked the plate clean in less than a minute. Rabbit casserole had never tasted so delicious in all his life.

But when he had eaten it, he began to worry. How would he be able to eat his worm-and-grass supper now?

As it turned out, he had an even bigger problem

to contend with. A problem that began an hour later, when he was back at home, searching for the eyeball in the garden.

'TROLL-SON!'

His mother's scream made him jump out of his skin.

'TROLL-SON! BE GETTING HERE! NOW! YOU BE IN THE TROUBLE OF YOUR LIFE, SO YOU BE!'

TROLL-SON'S BAD NEWS

Samuel was back under his covers and on the verge of falling asleep when Martha suddenly sat up in bed. 'No!' she screamed. 'No! No!'

Samuel jumped out of his bed and shook her by the shoulders. 'Martha, it's all right,' he said. 'Martha, wake up . . . It's all right . . . You're just having a nightmare.'

'Oh,' she said, breathless, as though the bad dream had tried to suffocate her. 'Yes . . . yes . . . Mum and Dad are still here, aren't they? They're still here?'

Samuel swallowed. 'No,' he said, knowing precisely what she was dreaming about. 'They're gone. You were remembering that day in the car, weren't you? Under the bridge.'

Even in the dark Samuel could tell his sister was nodding, and then Aunt Eda arrived and switched on the light and Samuel could see his sister's tear-streaked face.

'What happened?' asked Aunt Eda.

'Nothing . . . I was just having a nightmare,' said Martha, wiping her tears away. Aunt Eda came to sit on the bed and put an arm around Martha's shoulders and spoke comforting words, even though she knew there were no words or hugs that could totally make things all right.

Yet Samuel *was* comforted by his aunt's voice as she spoke to Martha, and he lay back in his bed and looked towards the forest, and wondered what might be happening amidst the trees.

Troll-Mother felt for her son's head and then yanked his ear.

'Ow . . . Mother . . . I be hurt–'

'RABBITS!' she shouted. 'RABBITS! One in each hand! Now where did they be getting the idea we be needing rabbits?'

At first Troll-Son didn't have a clue what she was talking about, but gradually his mistake became clear. You see, a few moments before Troll-Son had been bellowed at by his mother, the two-headed troll had arrived with a rabbit in each hand.

'We be hearing you be out of rabbits,' Troll-the-Left had said.

'A token of thanks,' said the newly-stitched Troll-the-Right. 'For finding me.'

'Mmm,' said Troll-the-Left, less convincingly. 'A token of thanks.'

'Oh, tha–'

But before the incredibly hungry Troll-Father had been able to take either rabbit, Troll-Mother was quick to interrupt.

'Rabbits? Oh, we not be needing any rabbits.'

'But we be hearing you be out of food, and living on grass and worms,' said Troll-the-Left.

At which Troll-Mother had burst out laughing as if she had never heard anything quite so ridiculous in all her life. 'Grass and worms?! Oh, that be funny. Grass and worms? Have you ever be hearing the like? No, I be assuring both you heads I be never cooking my family grass and worms. And who be telling you such stories?'

'Why, Troll-Son . . . After he be stitching me up again and eating rabbit casserole with us, he be telling us you be unable to hunt because of your missing eye.'

Troll-Mother was absolutely furious. Not only had Troll-Son eaten their neighbour's food, but he'd embarrassed the whole family. But of course, *being furious* was one of the many things she could never show the neighbours.

'Oh' – she chuckled – 'that boy. He be a funny one. Always making up stories, so he be. They don't want to be listening to him, do they, Troll-Father?'

Troll-Father, who had been trying to keep out of the conversation, knew what a clouting he would get if he didn't agree. 'Yes,' he said reluctantly as he imagined how nice it would be to have rabbit casserole. 'He be always telling stories.'

'I be telling you it be unlikely,' said Troll-the-Right.

'No, you be not,' said Troll-the-Left.

'I be.'

'You be not. You be saying—'

And they argued their way back out of the door, taking the rabbits with them.

Which brings us back to—

'RABBITS! RABBITS! One in each hand! Now where did they be getting the idea we be needing rabbits?'

'I . . . I . . . I be not knowing,' Troll-Son said eventually.

'You be lying! He be lying!'

Troll-Son didn't know what to do. He was being told off for telling their two-headed neighbour the truth, and now he was being scolded for lying. He couldn't win.

'I be sorry.'

'I be giving you sorry, you flenking useless grubber!'

'Grub! Grub! Grub!' chanted Troll-Daughter, clapping happily.

'It will be round the whole village by now. We be the trolls eating worms for supper! We be the trolls too hopeless to catch a rabbit! The shame! The shame! Oh, Troll-Father, he be your son. Be saying something.'

Troll-Father released a nervous sigh. 'I . . . um . . . well . . . you should not be telling stories, Troll-Son.'

'But it be true,' said Troll-Son.

'True?' said his mother, yanking his ear again. 'Oh, you be liking the truth, be you? You be liking the truth that your mother be never able to go out of her own door? You be liking that, do you? You be liking that the whole village will be saying, "Oh, there be the worm woman. Oh, there be she who be feeding her children grass instead of rabbits."'

'No,' said Troll-Son. 'I be sorry.'

'Come on, Troll-Mother,' said Troll-Father. 'They be not telling anyone . . . And even if the–'

'Well, perhaps you be right. It be a good thing this be happening,' said Troll-Mother.

Troll-Father and Troll-Son were confused, but didn't dare say anything.

'You see, I be having another visitor when you be out. And he be called the Betterer.'

Troll-Son gagged, but Troll-Mother went on, 'I be warning you. I be telling you this be happening and this time I be meaning it – I swear by my dead mother's old stones it be true . . . that we be sending you for a bettering.'

'He don't be needing the Betterer,' said Troll-Father. 'Come on, Troll-Mother, he be not so bad.'

'Not bad! He be making fools of himself and all of us, so he be. We cannot be having him be growing up into the world like that. He be needing an edufication, he be. He be needing to know grammaticals and mathematicals and all them fancy human things. Something me and you be not giving him. It be for his own good, Troll-Father – his own good.' She closed her eye-socket and her nose began to run as she started to cry eyeless tears. Then she pulled herself together and started shouting again. 'Now, boy, be getting outside and finding that eyeball!'

'No Betterer,' said Troll-Son in a frightened voice. 'No. No Betterer. No, Mother, not the–'

'I be sorry, Troll-Son, but you be not learning mannerings from me and your father. We be never having no hoppertunity when we be young to be bettering ourselves – and look where it be leading us! We be here now rabbitless and starving . . . Now, it be one thing if you be like them other trolls with two eyes who be having the best start in life, but it be hard for us who have to be not seeing most of the time. And you be needing all the help you be getting.'

Troll-Father joined in with his wife at about this point. 'Yes, Troll-Son, what your mother be saying be most true. It be not easy being like us. If I could be going back now and be bettered, I would, but it be too late for old trolls like us. There be no bettering that can be done.'

But Troll-Son remembered the terrible stories he'd heard about the Betterer and wasn't having any of it. 'But the Betterer be cruel. That be what they–'

This was too much for Troll-Mother, who realized

her son would never know what was good for him. 'Stop it, Troll-Son. It be hard enough as it is to be doing the right thing without you making it harder . . . Now be getting outside and don't be coming back till you be finding that eyeball!'

THE EYE IN THE HOLE

Troll-Son's hands kept feeling the flat, grassy ground without any luck. It was no good. He would never be able to find the eyeball, and so he would always be punished for it being lost, even though it had been nothing to do with him. It hadn't been his fault that a bird had flown down from the sky and grabbed it right out of his mother's hands as she stood by the chopping table. No.

And now he was to have the greatest punishment of all: a week's stay at the Bettering Tower.

'Cold,' he mumbled as he felt the ground. 'I be cold.'

His hands kept patting and sliding across the grass, while his teeth chattered away. Then, suddenly, under one of his hands, the grass stopped being grass and became nothing. He pressed down into the empty air of a rabbit hole. It was so deep that by the time his hand touched earth again, his entire arm was inside the hole.

Troll-Son's fingers felt around the earth until they touched something round and cold, with a surface that seemed wet and dry all at the same time.

Even before he pulled it out, he knew what it was.

'Eye,' he whispered.

His hand enveloped the eyeball and he drew it out of the hole. There was a change in the breeze, and Troll-Son shivered with cold and excitement. He was about to turn and call to the house. He wanted to tell his parents straight away that he had found the thing they had been seeking for all these days, but he decided to wait a moment. After all, what if this wasn't the eye? What if it was something that felt exactly the same as the eye but was in fact something completely different? Like a caloosh egg. OK, so it was too small and too round to be a caloosh egg, but although Troll-Son had often encountered the tall, three-headed birds running past him while out hunting, he had never seen or felt a caloosh egg so he wasn't to know.

'Troll-Son?' It was his father's voice calling him. 'Troll-Son, it be nearly time for your bath.'

Oh no! His bath. He had forgotten it was his Annual Washday. You see, although troll parents never, *ever* have a bath, they expect their offspring to have one on the second full moon of the year. And if you want to imagine how disgusting the idea of soaking in a bath of water is for a troll, it is roughly the same as you would feel if you had to lower yourself into a tub full of live eels. It's *that* disgusting.

But Troll-Son had heard something even worse. The very jittery troll twins had told him that when you were sent to the Betterer, you were placed in a Dunking Cage and dunked into water filled with soap so strong that it made you itch. The itchiness was made even more excruciating when you were hung on the washing line by your sleeves in such a way that you couldn't scratch yourself. He wondered if the news about finding the eyeball would change his mother's decision. Maybe he wouldn't have to go to the Betterer.

Troll-Father was still calling. 'Troll-Son? Troll-Son? Your bath be ready. Troll-Daughter be out now.'

Troll-Son stayed still a moment longer as he held onto the eye.

He noticed his heart was racing rather fast, but he didn't know why. It felt like it did when he used to chase rabbits, yet he was standing completely still.

'I . . . I . . . I be coming, Father.'

He heard the front door close and realized his father must have gone back inside. Two deep breaths and one wish later, and Troll-Son was gently pressing the eyeball into the empty socket in the middle of his forehead.

At first he thought he had made a mistake. The eye was in place, in the socket, and fitted perfectly, but he couldn't see a single thing. However, he soon noticed that the darkness he had known for three weeks had suddenly changed. Instead of being black, it had a brown appearance, and as he kept blinking, this brownness became lighter and lighter.

Of course, after being left in the ground for so long the eyeball was completely covered with earth, and as the troll boy kept blinking, the eyeball was gradually becoming cleaner. Pretty soon, Troll-Son could see light once more. He could see the glorious stars shining above the trees – the thousand little holes in the darkness that made sure even a troll's life could be blessed with beauty.

Troll-Son looked around. He saw the empty

rabbit pen. He saw the chopping table, stained with dry blood. He saw the stone cottage where he and his family lived; the square wooden door and round window he hadn't seen for such a long time.

He remembered the day Samuel Blink had run through that door when he was escaping the evil huldre-folk. He remembered the first time he'd heard the exotic name, which sounded quite delicious on Troll-Son's tongue. He said it again now, to feel its flavour once more.

'Samuel Blink.' And he kept saying it: 'Samuel Blink, Samuel Blink, Samuel–'

Then he saw the door open and his mother step out of the house. Having spent so long without an eyeball, he had forgotten quite how scary she looked. With her wild and matted black hair, her bulbous red nose with hairs dangling out of her nostrils, and the wonky grey teeth that stuck out of her mouth even when it was closed, she looked quite a monster even by troll standards. But it wasn't her looks that frightened Troll-Son the most. It was the appointment she had in store for him tomorrow. With the Betterer.

'Troll-Son?' she shrieked.

'Yes?' said Troll-Son quietly.

'What you be doing? Your father be calling you in for your bath a whole minutes ago, be he not?'

'Yes.' Troll-Son blinked and rubbed away the last of the dirt from the eye.

'Be you scratching your socket?'

'No, Mother, I be not.'

'Be you lying to me, son? My ears be hearing a socket-scratch from fifty paces away. Now, don't be lying.'

Troll-Son thought for a moment about what he should do. He knew that now was the time to declare that he had found the missing eyeball. Surely Troll-Mother wouldn't be cross with him once she knew they would be able to catch rabbits again.

He made his way across the grass to the open door where his mother was standing.

'I . . . I . . . I be fi–' As he stared up at his mother's confused and angry face, and the empty eye-socket that blinked away in the middle of it, Troll-Son struggled to get his words out: 'I be . . . there . . . be . . . a hole . . . it . . . be . . .'

Troll-Mother screwed up her nose and shook her head crossly. One of her giant hands swept wildly through the air towards where she guessed Troll-Son was standing. But Troll-Son saw it coming and ducked quickly away.

'Where you be?'

Troll-Son hesitated. 'Here,' he said.

'Right, well, be getting yourself inside ready for your bath, you stinking little fugwap!'

And so Troll-Son went into the house without saying a word about finding the eye – the eye that was now looking once again at the wooden dinner table, at the stone walls and kitchen, and at his sister, miserable and wet, fresh from her bath.

She started chanting angrily at her brother: 'Bath! Bath! Bath!'

'Troll-Son,' Troll-Father said, 'the bath be ready. Don't be upsetting your mother, now.'

Troll-Son shuddered at the thought of the bath, but what he especially hated was the way his mother enforced it so strictly when she was the grubbiest troll in Trollhelm.

A year ago Troll-Son had found the courage to ask her: 'Why you and Father not be washing if we be?'

'You be young. And we be wanting you to be getting into good ways. Now, every good young troll has a yearly bath, you be knowing that. If it be up to me you'd be having one every month but your father says that would be cruel.'

Today, Troll-Son was careful not to cause any more

trouble. After all, this little bathtub and its gentle soap was going to be nothing compared to what lay in store for him in the Bettering Tower, and so he walked silently into the bathroom. When he had shut the door behind him, he heard his mother and father's dull voices through the cracks in the wood.

''Tis most strange,' said Troll-Mother.

'What be strange?' said Troll-Father.

'He be walking himself straight into the bathroom.'

'I be missing your point, Troll-Mother.'

'Well, normal times he be banging into the door before he be opening it.'

There was a long pause, during which the troll boy pressed his ear to the door to hear better. He heard his father's voice, soft and confused:

'No, I still be missing your point.'

Then his mother's: 'Troll-Son, I be opening this door if you don't be coming out.'

The troll boy panicked and looked around the room, desperately trying to find a place to hide the eyeball. The windowsill? The bathtub? The toilet-hole?

As Troll-Mother pushed the door open, he poked his fingers into his socket and, with a little effort, pulled out the eyeball. By the time the door was open and his mother was standing right in front of him, Troll-Son had it cupped in his hand behind his back. Which meant, of course, that he couldn't see Troll-Mother's red and angry face lean in towards him.

'Let me take the feel of you,' she said, and Troll-Son felt one hand grab the back of his head and another pat around his face.

'Open your socket!' she ordered him. 'Open it!'

Troll-Son duly obeyed, and opened his eyelid for his mother to press one of her filthy fingers inside the socket.

'Hmm,' she said in a puzzled tone as she realized the eye wasn't there.

'Come on, Troll-Mother, don't be getting all hipperty, let him be having his bath.'

Troll-Son felt comforted to hear his father's voice, but knew it would have no effect.

'Sit down, Troll-Father. The boy be hiding it! He be making fools of us, hipperty or not!'

She was shouting so loudly that Troll-Son knew this was his opportunity to get rid of the eyeball. So, with a quick flick of his wrist he threw the eyeball behind him.

Just at that moment Troll-Mother stopped shouting.

Then:

Plop.

The eyeball landed in the bath water and sank to the bottom.

'What be that sound?'

Troll-Son gulped. 'There be no sou–' But before he could finish his sentence he felt a hard slap against his head. Then came another order.

'Hold out your hands!'

Troll-Son did as he was instructed and held out both his empty hands for inspection.

'Hmm,' grumbled his mother again, before pushing her son aside and heading towards the bathtub.

'Ugh,' she said. 'Oh, I do be hating wetness.'

In the blind darkness Troll-Son heard the sound of a hand entering water. Searching, searching, searching. He knew that it was too late. He knew that any moment now his mother's hand would happen upon the eyeball, and he would find himself in the worst trouble of his life. It would be worse than the time he accidentally let a rabbit out of the sack when they were hunting. Or the time he drank some of his mother's hurgleberry wine by mistake. Or the time he stubbed his toe against the door and shouted 'Flenk!' Or the time he snored. Or when he wet the bed. Or when he got caught talking to a tomtegubb. Or when he sneezed at Troll-the-Weaver's house. Or when he said he wished he lived with Samuel Blink.

And what punishment would be inflicted this time? Would he be sent for *two* weeks with the Betterer?

'If I be finding the eye,' Troll-Mother was saying as her hand kept searching, 'you'll be having such a punishing as will never leave you – unless you be owning up to it before it be found.'

This was Troll-Son's chance. He could confess to finding the eye and maybe everything would be all right. After all, everyone would surely be so pleased to see again that they would forget about him keeping it a secret until he got in the bathroom. And yet he knew he would still be sent to the Betterer, and so when he tried to speak, he found it hard to get the words out.

'I . . . I . . . I . . . ' he mumbled.

'Eye . . . eye . . . eye . . . what?' his mother snapped back.

He couldn't say it. He couldn't bring himself to confess. While the secret was alive, he still had hope. What it was precisely he was hoping for he didn't know, but Troll-Son had never been very good at knowing things. All he had was a *feeling* – this hopeful feeling that told him to keep his mouth shut and not to breathe another word. And so he didn't.

But then, just as this hope was beginning to turn itself back into dread, something happened. There was a knock at the front door. Troll-Mother heard the knock and her hand shot out of the bathtub. She cried out: 'The door! Be the door, Troll-Father! Someone be a-knocking!'

She stood up and Troll-Son could feel his heart lighten with relief as he realized he was about to be left alone.

'Now, you get yourself clean,' she said. 'And then you can be showing me where you be keeping that eyeball.' Troll-Son could feel her lean closer, her nose sniffing the air around his head as she whispered sharply: 'And you'll be showing me, Troll-Son, be sure you will.'

Troll-Son heard his mother leave, and heard her happily address the guest who had just arrived. The guest was Troll-the-Wisest, the leader of the Troll Council, and he was going around the village checking who was going to be at the Troll Council meeting tomorrow night.

Troll-Son searched around in the disgusting water until he found the eyeball. He quickly placed it back in his socket as he heard his father's voice beyond the door.

'Don't worry, I'll be there, Troll-the-Wisest.'

'Good, good,' said Troll-the-Wisest (who, even by troll standards, wasn't very wise). 'Good, good. And be there any issues you be wanting to be raising?'

Troll-Son never heard his father's answer. He was too busy pulling himself up and out of the window with the hot, wet eyeball lodged in place, viewing a forest of dark trees and imagining the freedom that might lie beyond.

OUT OF THE WINDOW

Troll-Son fell to the ground with a soft thud, and ran along the side of the cottage. After a few steps he heard a voice behind him. Two voices at once, in fact.

'Troll-Son?'

It wasn't his mother and his father, he realized as he turned round and saw a giant two-headed figure standing in the pale moonlight.

It was Troll-the-Left and Troll-the-Right. Troll-Son said nothing. He didn't move, but they carried on staring at him.

'What you be up to, Troll-Son?' asked Troll-the-Left.

'He be running away,' said Troll-the-Right, showing little gratitude for having been found.

'I be asking Troll-Son.'

'Well, it be obvious, be it not? Why else would someone be climbing out of a bathroom window when there be a perfectly good front door he could be using. We should be telling his parents. We should be grabbing him and taking him inside.'

Troll-Son was doubly frightened now. He thought about running away. After all, he had the eyeball, and even in the dark he could see roughly where he was going. But the two-headed troll had *four* eyeballs, and much longer legs.

'Be this true? Be you running away?' asked Troll-the-Left, with a much kinder expression than that worn by the newly stitched head to his right.

'They be sending me to the Betterer.'

Troll-the-Left went pale. 'The Betterer? Oh, my poor boy . . .'

Troll-the-Right was less sympathetic. 'Well, if they be sending you to the Betterer, they must be having good reason.'

'Why be they sending you to the Bettering Tower?' asked Troll-the-Left.

Troll-Son thought very carefully as he looked up at both bearded heads. At the kind and gently frowning face of Troll-the-Left, and the sterner face of Troll-the-Right.

Any minute now someone would realize he was gone and would start searching. He didn't have long. He had to act fast, but had nothing to offer the two-headed troll except the truth.

'I be in trouble about what I be saying to you.'

'To *us*?'

'Mother be not liking nobody knowing about us having no rabbits and eating worms.'

'But that be silly,' said Troll-the-Left. 'We be helping, not judging. If we be not catching any rabbits, we be wanting folks to give us all the rabbits they can be affording to give. That's what neighbours be for . . . She be sending you to the Betterer just for that?'

Troll-Son nodded.

'He be lying,' said Troll-the-Right.

This made Troll-the-Left cross. 'You be the most ungrateful fluglump, you really be. If it not be for this lad here you'd be still stuck on that path where I be leaving you.'

'That be beside the point. There be a principle here. Parents be knowing best even when they be' – Troll-the-Right took a second to consider – 'even when they be not knowing best. We can't be letting a boy out into the forest. It be dangerous.'

'I be going to Samuel Blink. He be a human boy. He be not dangerous.'

'Well, there might be other humans who *be* dangerous,' said Troll-the-Right.

'Oh, and the Betterer be not, I be supposing?' scoffed Troll-the-Left. 'And besides, be you not hearing? The forest be safe now.'

'That be beside the point. Parents be knowing best.'

'You would be saying that,' said Troll-the-Left as sad memories of his childhood tugged down at his mouth. 'You be always Mother's favourite.'

'I be doing as I be told, that be why.'

'You be a creep and a cold-blooded do-goody tell-tale and you be one all your life.'

'We can't be helping a runa–'

Just at that moment they heard the door open and saw Troll-the-Wisest come out of the house. They shrank back against the wall of the next-door house as he went past and back to his house.

Troll-Son waited for the inevitable, and then it came. His mother's scream, from inside the house: 'TROLL-SON???!!!' *She must be in the bathroom,* he realized. *She must know I've climbed out of the window.* 'TROLL-SON? WHERE BE YOU GONE?!'

The two heads of the troll were looking at each other, wondering what to do. Troll-Son could see in Troll-the-Right's face that he was itching to tell Troll-Mother that her son was right here. Then he saw something even more worrying. *His father.* Out of the house. Walking down the thin path towards them with his hands outstretched, feeling along the wall.

'Troll-Son?' he was saying. 'Be you there?'

A moment later he saw his mother too. A wild hairy silhouette in the dark.

'He be he–'

Before Troll-the-Right had time to inform the two blind parents of the location of their son, Troll-the-Left quickly slapped his hand across his mouth. Troll-the-Right then tried to use the hand *he* was in control of to yank the left one away.

'Who be there?' asked Troll-Father.

'It be only us neighbours,' said Troll-the-Left as he struggled to keep his hand over Troll-the-Right's mouth, feeling teeth bite into his palm. 'Just the–*Argh* . . . Just the two-headed – ow – troll . . . Troll-the-Left and Troll-the-Raaargh!' Then he looked over his shoulder at Troll-Son. He mouthed a word that the troll boy couldn't understand, so he converted it into a whisper.

The whisper was:

'Go!'

Troll-Son stepped slowly and silently backwards. When he was finally at the end of the passageway, he took one last look at the figures standing in the dark. He felt a pang of guilt as he saw his father talking in a concerned voice to Troll-the-Left. But when he saw the large, wild outline of his mother, guilt turned back into fear.

And this fear swiftly pushed him through the wooden gate and into his back garden. Past the chopping table. Past the empty rabbit pen. Past the hole where he had found the eyeball.

The voices of his parents and Troll-the-Left faded as his walk switched to a jog and then a run. Within moments he was out of Trollhelm, dodging trees as the forest sped past. On and on he kept running, down the eastern slopes, past the little cabin that belonged to a truth pixie, past the furry forms of sleeping slemps, dodging fast and feathery calooshes, then through a quiet village where houses with pictures of the sun carved on the doors sheltered harmless huldres. He kept on. Not stopping even as the sun came up. Never stopping.

Eventually he slowed to a walk and saw the forest

as he had never seen it before. A thousand browns and greens, humming with secret life. It was beautiful, but he had no time to stop and appreciate it. He had to keep on until he had made it out of the forest, where he could be free, and in the meantime he tried not to think about the worry he'd heard in his father's voice.

BREAKFAST WITH THE MYKLEBUSTS

Cornelia's father, Mr Magnus Myklebust, was a very important man in Flåm. You see, he was a land developer and was always buying land on which to build houses and ski lodges and hotels. Whereas other people would look at the landscape around Flåm and marvel at the highland pastures and majestic mountains, Mr Myklebust would only ever see *opportunities*. This is why he had also become the head of the tourist board. After all, the more people he could get to visit the area, the more valuable the land and properties became. And so he loved making the area look nice and welcoming for visitors.

You know the type of thing – posters of mountains . . . A gift shop selling tea towels . . . Pleasant forest walks . . .

Well, actually, pleasant forest walks were something Mr Myklebust had a problem with. After all, the only area of woodland in his district was Shadow Forest. And for years, people had been too scared to even set foot in the place.

'Trolls? Pixies? Huldre-folk? Tomtegubbs? Never heard such nonsense!' he always used to say.

'Well, if it's such nonsense, why don't you go into the forest with your camera and prove it once and for all?' This was Mrs Myklebust's standard reply, usually delivered while lying on her gigantic sofa as she filed her nails or watched their cinema-sized TV.

Mrs Myklebust was a very beautiful and glamorous lady, who wore very expensive clothes that she bought on shopping trips to Oslo. She was *so* beautiful and *so* glamorous that she didn't feel the need to worry about the things other people worry about. For instance, she didn't care if people *liked* her. As with her daughter, it was far more important that they should be *jealous* of her. Which is why she had chosen to marry the richest man in Flåm. She knew her husband looked like a big, fat, balding pig in a suit, but he was a *rich* big, fat, balding pig in a suit – and that was what mattered.

Oh, and did I mention that she was a bad mother? No? Well, she was. Terrible, in fact. She wasn't evil or anything like that. And she didn't clout Cornelia around the head or make her eat worms and grass. She just didn't *care.* If you asked her when Cornelia's birthday was, she would take about a minute to answer and have to work it out on her fingers and then would *still* get it wrong. And every single day she would be late to pick Cornelia up from school, which Cornelia didn't mind at all as it meant she could read books or learn new places in the atlas or browse the dictionary for really difficult words.

But anyway, we're not meant to be talking about Mrs Myklebust because she's not that important to the story. Far more important is Mr Myklebust, as he's the one who's obsessed with Shadow Forest. That's right, *obsessed.*

'It's such a waste!' he used to say, sitting in bed, while Mrs Myklebust read one of her fashion magazines. 'All that forest and no visitors. Imagine if no one was scared! Imagine how much money I could make. We could buy the land – it would be easy . . . And we could chop down the trees and turn it into a theme park – "Shadow Forest", it will say as people drive in. "The place where your dreams become reality."

It would be the biggest theme park in the whole of Scandinavia and there would be people dressed up as trolls everywhere. I could make so much money. After all, I know the right people . . . I could get a very good price – who else would want it? It would be perfect . . .'

But then his voice always faded, because he knew it was no good. He didn't believe in trolls and pixies, but he did know that something wasn't quite right about the forest. A long time ago, before he had grown fat and lost his hair, Magnus Myklebust had been a great skier, and his hero had been a ski jumper called Henrik Krohg, a man he ended up hating more than anyone in the world. (I will tell you why, but not quite yet.) Anyway, as far as Mr Myklebust knew, Henrik had disappeared into that forest years ago, never to be seen again, and greedy as Mr Myklebust was, he was also a nervous type who was too scared to face any kind of danger.

But one day – that is, *today* – something changed.

Over the evening meal, Cornelia told him about an English girl she had met at school.

'Oh, where does she live?' he asked, as he thought it was important to know where someone lived before they could be approved of.

'In a house next to the forest,' said Cornelia.

Mr Myklebust was shoving handfuls of cold meat into his mouth as he received this information. 'Next to the forest?' he asked. 'What? Shadow Forest?'

Cornelia felt sick looking at his open mouth and the mashed-up meat inside, and wished for a more sophisticated father. A father who loved books. A father who could take her to the theatre to watch plays. A father who didn't eat like a pig. Mind you, at least he was *there.* Not like her mother, who was still at the beauty parlour, having her legs waxed. And anyway, meals with her father were very good ways of making money.

'Yes,' said Cornelia, staring down at her plate. 'She lives as close to the forest as you can get, with her brother Samuel, her Aunt Eda and her Uncle Henrik and–'

When Mr Myklebust heard the name 'Henrik', he choked with shock, causing the mashed-up meat to splatter all over the tablecloth and over Cornelia's dress.

'Ugh! *Daddy.*'

'I'm sorry, Cornelia.'

'*How* sorry?'

Mr Myklebust knew what his daughter was

hinting at, and pulled a ten-kroner note out of his wallet for her.

'Apology accepted,' Cornelia said, suddenly not bothered about the pink spots of ready-chewed cold boiled lamb sprayed over her clothes.

'Henrik? You said he was called Henrik, her uncle? And he lives with a woman called Eda?'

'Yes.'

Mr Myklebust's small piggy eyes gleamed with excitement. 'Very *interesting* indeed. Now, my little princess, I want you to try your best to make friends with this Martha.'

'But I don't really want to be friends with her. She's not my type of person, to be honest with you, Daddy. She just chatters away about nothing in particular and hums silly little songs when she thinks I'm not listening.'

'Oh,' said Mr Myklebust sadly. 'That's no good. No good at all. We must change that . . . Now, I wonder . . . what would it take to make her *your type* of person. A new pony?'

Cornelia – who was now wiping the splattered meat off her dress with some kitchen roll – considered the offer. 'No. *Two* new ponies.'

'For that, you must become her *best* friend. You must

do it tomorrow. At school. And find out everything you can about her aunt and uncle.'

Cornelia smiled mischievously. 'Easy. Leave it with me.'

SOMETHING CONFUSES SAMUEL

Samuel was confused on his second morning at school. It wasn't the geography lesson that was confusing him. After all, Mrs Sturdsen had spent a while crouched by his desk, calmly explaining in English what precisely he was expected to write in his exercise book.

No. What was confusing him was Martha. You see, all yesterday he'd had to listen to her go on and on about how horrible Cornelia was, yet now, there she was talking and giggling with her non-stop.

'Honestly,' said Mrs Sturdsen, whose voice could go from calm to cross in a second (and therefore nearly deafen Samuel, who was right next to her), 'I didn't very much know that the geology of a volcano could be quite so amusing.'

Later on, Samuel was outside, sitting by himself on the school bench. Voices he couldn't understand filled the air around him. Boys laughed as they played and their laughter was as foreign to Samuel as the words they spoke.

If it wasn't for Martha, he thought to himself, *I would run away. Not to the forest, but home. I would get on a boat and sail to England. And I would walk back to Nottingham. I wouldn't have anywhere to live, but it wouldn't matter. It would be better than being here and feeling like an alien.*

It was then, amid these bleak thoughts, that Martha appeared in front of him holding Cornelia's hand.

'This is my brother, Samuel,' said Martha, smiling. 'And Samuel, this is Cornelia.'

'I know,' said Samuel, in a voice he knew didn't sound very friendly.

He stared up at Cornelia. She looked nice enough, with her pretty face and her silky blonde hair. In fact, she looked too nice, too smiley, to be completely trustworthy.

'Yes,' she said. 'Everyone knows who I am. You see, my father is a very famous man in Flåm.'

'Oh,' said Samuel. And inside he thought, *Who cares?*

'And another thing,' said Cornelia.

Samuel looked suspiciously at his sister, wondering what she had done now. 'What?'

'Guess who's coming to stay at my house this Friday night?'

Samuel's heart sank with dread. 'Who?'

'Your sister.'

'No, she's not. She can't be.'

'Yes, she is. I checked with my father this morning and it's fine.'

Samuel couldn't believe it. He turned to Martha. 'But you haven't even asked Aunt Eda or Unc–' He stopped himself just in time. 'You haven't even asked Aunt Eda,' he said again.

'Oh, she'll be pleased,' said Martha.

'I'm not too sure about that,' said Samuel, staring straight at Cornelia's face as if it were a puzzle he couldn't quite work out.

Samuel thought something about this whole conversation was rather odd. And then he realized what it was. What had Cornelia said? *She had checked with her father this morning.*

But Martha had hated Cornelia before school started this morning. And from what Samuel had seen yesterday, the feeling had been mutual. Cornelia hadn't been friendly to Martha until school today . . .

Yes, it was definitely odd. And he turned to his sister to say as much: 'But it's a bit weird–'

'What's a bit weird?' Martha asked, smiling.

Samuel remembered her screaming awake in the middle of the night and stared at that smile the way a vet might stare at a puppy he didn't want to put down. 'Nothing,' he said. 'Nothing's weird.'

THE BETTERER'S RULES FOR BETTERING

The Betterer was on the top floor of the Bettering Tower, preparing a giant tub of Itch Water. Itch Water was made of normal hot water but with a variety of herb soaps so strong it made you itch. The water was already itchy, but he wanted it even itchier, because only when it was really, really itchy would it make a troll child as clean as a human. You see, that was the first thing that happened when a troll child was sent to the Betterer. They were forced, in their grubby clothes, into a cage that was hoisted up on a rope then lowered into a vast tub full of Itch Water. Then they'd be hung out to dry with strong iron pegs clipped to their sleeves so they couldn't scratch their itches.

'To itch and not scratch – that is the art of betterment,' the Betterer would always say.

And while they were forced to hang there, the Betterer would recite how a troll child must behave if he were to be bettered. These were known as the Betterer's Rules for Bettering.

1. You must itch but never scratch because humans never scratch their itches.
2. You must know that itching from Itch Water is better than smelling from dirt, because humans know this.
3. You must close your mouth unless I ask it to be opened, and learn the human art of silence.
4. You must never pick your nose or ears or eye-socket, because a human would never do these things.
5. You must never laugh, especially if you find something funny, because humans never laugh.
6. You must never play, especially if you are bored, because humans never play.
7. You must never swear, because humans never swear.
8. You must put words in the right order at all times the way humans do.
9. You must learn human manners, washing methods and hair-combing techniques.

10. You must start each day by saying 'I wish I were better' one hundred times because humans always strive to be better.
11. You must expect to be punished every day, whether you break the rules or not, just for being the disgusting creature you are.

THE ROOM OF THE UNBETTERED

And the Betterer was whispering these rules to himself now, as he added the various forest herbs and flowers that ensured the Itch Water would be as uncomfortably cleansing as possible. He thought of the strict lessons he was going to teach and the punishments he would take pleasure in inflicting, such as the time spent in the Room of the Unbettered, a thick-walled, heavy-doored room so silent it drove young trolls to despair after only a few hours. Still, it was an essential part of their betterment, on their journey towards human dignity and refinement – silence was a human thing and against a troll's nature, and anything that went against a troll's nature had to be a good thing.

'It is late,' said the Betterer. 'It is very late. Where is

the disgusting creature? He should be here by now.'

At first he was not too worried. After all, lateness was common among trolls. Along with scruffiness, smelliness, rudeness, laziness, ugliness and general ignorance, lateness was a key characteristic of the troll species. Indeed, the Betterer had worked hard to fight these things inside himself and worked even harder still to fight them in others. Because the truth was, he *hated* being a troll. He hated it so much that if he ever caught sight of a reflection of his lumpy nose or boil-covered face, he was immediately sick.

Sometimes, after a long soak in his tub (using only the very mildest Itch Water), or after eliminating all the creases in his clothes with a rock press, he imagined himself so bettered that he wasn't a troll at all. It was quite easy for him to imagine this, because for the first ten years of his childhood this is what he had believed to be true.

You see, to understand the precise nature of the Betterer's hatred of trollish manners you need to know that his parents tried to tell him he wasn't a troll at all but someone rather like you. That's right. Throughout much of his childhood the Betterer believed himself to be a human. As his parents lived quite a way from Trollhelm, deep in the darkest part of Shadow Forest, there was no one on hand to correct his mistake. His parents certainly didn't.

'You are the finest of all the humans,' his mother used to tell him.

'So much *better* than those vile trolls,' his father would add.

It was only when he found a troll boy fishing in Still Lake that he discovered the truth, as the troll boy had told him to look at his reflection.

'You be not a human with a face like that. You be a troll.'

And even though this had happened many, many years ago, the memory of that horrendous day stayed with him. It had eaten away at him, and had given him many hatreds. He hated his parents for calling him a human name, and hadn't shed a tear when they never returned home after a truth pixie's dinner party. He hated humans too, although he had never met one. He hated them because he wanted to be one, but knew he never could. But most of all he hated trolls. Hated their lumpy faces, their shaggy beards, their unkempt hair, their deformities, their bad grammar, their bodily smells, their table manners, their scruffy clothes, their rotten teeth, their stupid beliefs, and just about everything else that came with being a troll.

And he hated his own troll blood, just as he hated living in Trollhelm.

The only thing that kept him going was his knowledge that he was better. He lived in a better house. He spoke better sentences. He had better clothes. And, of course, he loved to better others. To take noisy, stinky lumps and quieten them, and make them hate their dirtiness, was surely a worthy service that would benefit the whole community.

Which is why he'd been a bit sad lately. After all, it had been a while since any troll parents had sent their troll children for bettering. It wasn't his fault if some troll children reacted badly to his punishments. And now, as the Betterer looked over towards the heavy black door and the Room of the Unbettered that lay beyond, he thought of those horrendous troll twins and wished he'd never met them.

They were the noisiest, stupidest troll children the Betterer had ever encountered and it was no wonder they hadn't been able to cope with being silent for so long.

For weeks he had gone without seeing the look of effort on a troll child's face as he forced them to recite the tralphabet (the troll alphabet, which is exactly like the human one except it has two 'g's and no 'x') while holding two heavy rocks. It had been so long since he'd made a troll use, in the human style, a knife and fork to eat their Bitter Bettering Bread, or since he had lowered the Dunking Cage into the Itch Water.

'It b-b-b-be itchy,' they always used to say.

To which he would reply, 'It *is* itchy. *Is*, not *be*, you disgusting little troll.'

Oh, it had been so long! But now – the Betterer thought to himself – now, at long last, the wait was finally over! Another vile troll child was coming to stay. And this one really *was* going to be vile, if his mother was anything to go by. That pathetic empty eye-socket blinking away in the middle of her forehead. *Eugh!*

Where *were* they?

He looked at his watch. (The Betterer was the only troll in Trollhelm who could tell the time.) His watch told him: 'TROLL-SON IS LATE.'

'Oh, this is no good. No good at all. I will have to dunk him for longer in the Itch Water to punish him for his lateness.'

Then came a knock on the door.

'Aha, he's here! The eyeless cretin has arrived!' And so he stirred the water with a large wooden stirrer, left the Bettering Chamber, and ran down the spiral staircase to reach the ground floor. Then he had to unlock the thirteen locks on his front door.

'I am coming,' he said. 'I am coming. Your child is about to be saved from his own stinking bad manners. Do not worry, the Betterer is at your serv–'

When the door was finally opened, the Betterer didn't like what he saw. Troll-Mother was there, which was to be expected. But where was her son?

'Hello, Mr Betterer, sir,' she said, in her politest voice.

The Betterer felt sick at the sight of her. In his excitement he had forgotten quite how hideous she was, with her wild hair and boils and empty eye-socket.

He managed to squeeze a 'Hello' out of his mouth, before asking, 'And where, if I may enquire, is your son?'

'Well, this be what I be coming about.'

The Betterer rolled his eyes in disgust, but resisted the urge to correct her grammar. He was too eager to understand why Troll-Son wasn't with her.

'Well?' he said. 'Can you explain?'

Troll-Mother took a deep breath. 'He be missing.'

'Missing? *Missing*?'

'Yes. One moment he be there and then the next moment he be not there.'

'Not *there*?'

'We be thinking – his father and me – we be thinking that he be running away.'

The Betterer shuddered with hatred at the word 'father'. He had known Troll-Father for many years, and had hated him so much that he couldn't even look at him or answer back when he said, 'Hello.' (Troll-Father had always been confused as to why the Betterer ignored him, but Troll-Father wasn't a very bright troll and spent most of his life confused about one thing or another, so he didn't think too much about it.)

'Running away?' The Betterer began to feel the anger rise inside him, speeding up his heart and heating his blood.

'Aye. His father be out in the forest looking for him now, so he be.'

'He is meant to be *here.* He is meant to be bettered.'

Troll-Mother nodded and opened her mouth in an apologetic smile – a smile that revealed a grim graveyard of teeth. The Betterer winced as he caught the smell of her breath. The smell conjured up a concoction of rotten fish guts, unwashed armpits and unwiped behinds. It was a smell that seemed to be designed to induce instant vomiting. But he was too angry to be sick.

'Oh dear,' said the Betterer, trying not to sound angry. 'You must be *so* worried. You poor dear. Where has he gone?'

'We be not knowing. He could be gone anywhere. I be in a most terrible funkle about it all. We be not knowing what to do . . . It be my fault, you see. I been so terrible hard on him.'

'You can never be too hard on an unruly child, my dear. "Hardness helps, softness spoils" – that's my motto.'

As Troll-Mother kept talking, the anger inside the Betterer reached such a level that he was trembling with it. He had half a mind to shove her in the Dunking Cage just for the sake of it. But no. He knew he had to try and keep his anger under control because already in his mind a plan was forming. A plan that was so delicious he could almost taste it.

'Oh, Mr Betterer, you be so much better than we be. What should we be doing if Troll-Father be coming home with no Troll-Son?'

The Betterer took a moment to consider, although he already knew precisely what he was going to say. 'You know what day it is, don't you?'

'Yes, it be Moon Day.'

'No. That was days ago. It's Thor's Day today, you stupi– you stupendously concerned and understandably confused mother.'

'Oh yes, so it be . . . so it be . . . My head be in such a muddle with all this wotsit, I don't be knowing if I be here or there.'

'Well, you know that every Thor's Day the Troll Council meets in the meeting hall, don't you?'

'Yes,' said Troll-Mother, remembering Troll-the-Wisest's visit the previous night.

'Well, if Troll-F–' He couldn't bring himself to say the name. 'If your *husband* comes home without Troll-Son, you must tell him to see Troll-the-Wisest as he's the council leader. He'll know precisely what to do. So don't worry, I am sure that everything will be resolved, my dear – don't you worry.'

The Betterer smiled his most cruel smile, knowing that Troll-Mother's lack of an eye meant she couldn't see the smile or the cruelty it contained.

'Right, I be thanking you humbly, Mr Betterer, sir. Most humbly indeed. I'll be telling Troll-Father just that if he be coming back empty-handed.'

'Very well, goodbye,' said the Betterer, watching as Troll-Mother stumbled blindly away. 'And good luck, although I'm sure you won't need it. Don't worry – once Troll-Son is bettered he won't be doing this again. That's a certainty, my dear. An absolute certainty.'

And with that he shut his front door, climbed back up the stairs and pulled out his Bettering Box from under the floorboards.

'Now, what do I need?' he said to himself. There was a lot of choice. You see, for years and years the Betterer had made use of the magical herbs, plants and other substances that could be found around Trollhelm. He had experimented in his Bettering Chamber, and come up with various ointments, soaps, sweets, fruits and potions that made the task of bettering so much easier. Itch Water was only one of several strange things that a pupil of the Bettering Tower could come into contact with. There were hundreds of others, and some were going to prove very useful now that Troll-Son had gone missing. So this is what the Betterer decided to put inside the many, many pockets of his overcoat:

A SMALL JAR OF SLEEPING SALTS. Made with the dried saltwater from Still Lake. Guaranteed to send trolls into the darkest, most dreamless sleep for hours and hours. The Betterer always made sure his pupils smelled these before going to bed, so they were too tired to escape.

LERTWICK ROOT. Does the opposite. One lick would keep you awake for hours. He never used lertwick on pupils, but it was the perfect thing to keep him awake when he trundled through the forest.

SILENCING SWEETS. Made with fendrake, a herb that makes your tongue so heavy you can't speak.

POOKLEBERRIES (OR STOMACH STUFFERS). One berry will fill you up for a week.

STINGING NETTLES. The Betterer didn't realize these existed in the Outer World as well.

GRIPGRASS JUICE. This clear jar of dark green liquid was his favourite medicine of all – it came in very handy for bettering. One toe only has to touch this strong blend of different herbs and tree resins and your feet will be planted to the spot for a day.

THE BETTERING BRANCH. A long thin piece of wood, rather like a whip, which curls around anything it touches and squeezes it tight. Even though it lets go when the Betterer says 'Stop', he still finds it a lot safer to keep it rolled up in a special pouch.

'There,' he said finally as he grabbed one last item – a booklet on human habits he thought might be useful; it had been handwritten by a human professor and the Betterer had picked it up on his travels around the forest. He had always assumed it had been blown in on a gusty wind from the Outer World. 'That should be plenty.'

And then, after a little rest, he damped down the fire, unplugged the bath, climbed down the stairs, unlocked his thirteen locks, and headed through the village towards the meeting hall.

THE LIGHTER PATH

As Troll-Son walked on through the forest, he noticed that it was lighter one way than the other.

'Light,' he said, and pointed towards it.

Every time the path broke off in two directions he followed the lighter path. And these paths grew lighter and lighter until he stopped and noticed something.

He realized that the final path he had chosen stopped a short way ahead. And where the path stopped, so did the trees. He felt happy and scared all at once. He was nearly there. He was nearly at the Outer World.

Of course, he didn't know what exactly lay in store for him beyond the forest. He had tried to imagine what it might be like, but he could only picture grey stone cottages like the ones in Trollhelm. He wondered if anyone evil could live in the Outer World. Samuel Blink wasn't evil. If it was a world full of Samuel Blinks, he would be fine. And even if it wasn't a world full of Samuel Blinks, at least the Betterer didn't live there.

He looked back over his shoulder at the thick shadowy darkness. Even if he'd wanted to go back home, he doubted if he would remember the way now. It was so dark in that direction, and the path curved and split in so many places.

So, realizing he had little choice, the troll boy continued as the earth path beneath him grew lighter and lighter and eventually turned into grass. Then, when he was at the very edge of the forest, he saw it all. The fjord. The distant mountains. And the white wooden house at the foot of the grassy slope, with two humans standing outside the door. A fat, bald man and a fair-haired girl. They looked so smart, and so different from trolls, that Troll-Son felt ashamed of his own scruffy appearance. He wondered what they would do to him if they saw him, so he stepped back into the shade. But then the door to the house opened, to reveal a human boy in the doorway.

'Samuel Blink,' whispered Troll-Son under his breath. The fat man and the girl entered the house,

leaving the door open, and Troll-Son wondered what to do.

This was it.

This was the Outer World.

This was his chance.

And so, with a racing heart Troll-Son stepped out from the trees, felt the soft grass beneath his feet and the full expanse of the sky above him. A sky that was now blushing with the raw pinks and reds of evening.

'Samuel,' he said quietly, his eyes fixed on the open door. 'Samuel Blink.'

PLAYING BLACKJACK (AND OTHER SECRETS)

It was Thursday evening. The evening before Martha was meant to sleep at Cornelia's house. Samuel was sitting on the stairs, bored, listening to Aunt Eda and Uncle Henrik talking to each other in the bedroom. He couldn't understand everything they were saying, but Aunt Eda sounded very worried. He heard Martha's name mentioned, and Cornelia's, and 'Myklebust' at least seven times. Then Uncle Henrik said something and Aunt Eda switched to English, as she sometimes did when she was about to see Samuel and Martha again, and said, 'Yes, you're probably right, Henrik. I'm sure there is nothing to worry about. And Martha does seem so much happier than she's been all summer. It's only one night after all.'

At this point Martha ran upstairs. 'What are you doing sitting here?'

'I'm bored,' said Samuel.

'Well, I've got to see Aunt Eda and find out what she's decided about tomorrow night.'

'Don't worry,' said Samuel miserably. 'They're going to let you stay with Cornelia Superia.'

'Really? Wow! That's so cool. I'm going to check.'

She ran past him and into Aunt Eda's room, squealing with delight when she found out it was true. She stayed chatting with her aunt while Uncle Henrik came out and wondered what Samuel was doing on the stairs.

'I don't know,' said Samuel glumly.

Henrik smiled – Samuel's sitting on the stairs was a problem he knew how to solve.

'Well, I know living here might not be the most exciting thing in the world but I promise there are more interesting ways to pass the time than sitting on the stairs.'

'Like what?' asked Samuel.

Uncle Henrik's voice dropped to a whisper. 'Follow me – I'll show you.'

Intrigued, Samuel followed his uncle into the living room, where he produced a pack of playing cards.

'Now,' said Uncle Henrik as he sat down and started to deal, 'the aim of Blackjack is to get cards close to twenty-one but without going over. If you have two cards and they add up to sixteen, and then you are given a six, you lose, but if it's a *five*, you will be very hard to beat . . . You see, Blackjack is really much like life – the difference between total success and total failure is often very slight. The tiniest thing. But that tiniest thing is everything.'

'Why are you whispering?' asked Samuel.

Uncle Henrik looked up at the ceiling, as if it were a stranger in the room who wasn't to be trusted. 'If your Aunt Eda caught me teaching you Blackjack, she might be a little cross with me.'

'Why? It's only a card game.'

Uncle Henrik laughed and nodded. 'Yes, it *is* only a card game. You are right, Samuel. You are very right. But when I used to be a ski jumper, me and the other skiers in the team, we used to sometimes play this game for money . . . And, well, I was never very lucky with cards and I would lose money every night. Your aunt wasn't very happy with me.'

'Can *we* play for money?' Samuel asked.

Uncle Henrik laughed so loud he had to cover his mouth in case Aunt Eda heard. 'I'll tell you what.

We'll bet on washing up. If you can beat me, you don't have to help with the washing up for a month. But if your aunt comes downstairs, let's just pretend we are playing Snap, because people don't normally bet on Snap. Agreed?'

'Agreed,' said Samuel, smiling. And as he began to play, he felt rather strange – his head seemed lighter than normal. He had felt like this before, but not since his parents were alive. And then he realized what this feeling was. It was happiness. Sitting there that Thursday evening, as he beat his uncle at Blackjack, all the sad and heavy thoughts began to evaporate.

And just at the moment he realized this, there was a knock at the door.

Uncle Henrik looked a little uneasy when he heard the knock. He looked over towards the stairs and wondered if he should hide. No. He would be all right in the living room. It was out of sight of the front door.

'Oh dear – where is Eda?' he said.

There was a second knock.

'It's all right,' said Samuel. 'I'll get it.'

'Whoever it is, don't let them in,' said Uncle Henrik.

'I won't.'

And so Samuel went out into the hallway and opened the front door to see Cornelia standing in front of a very fat man in a suit, smoking a large cigar. The man, who Samuel rightly assumed to be Cornelia's father, looked disappointed, as if he had expected someone else to answer the door.

'This is Samuel,' Cornelia said, curling her lip in disgust. 'The brother.'

'Hello, Samuel,' said Cornelia's father, peering over Samuel's head and into the house. 'Is your aunt around?'

The man had tiny eyes, Samuel noticed. Or maybe they weren't tiny. Maybe his cheeks were so fat that his eyes could hardly open. He sucked again on his cigar before throwing it behind himself onto the path.

'Er . . . no . . . she's not here at the moment,' said Samuel.

'Well, I am afraid that is no good. I really can't let my poor little Cornelia stay in a house without meeting the people who own that house. Anything could happen to her!'

Samuel was confused. 'But Cornelia's not staying here. Martha's going to *your* house.'

Mr Myklebust pretended not to hear. 'Now, if no

one is here, then we will have to come in and wait for them to *get* here.'

'No,' said Samuel. 'I think it's best if–'

But it was no use. Cornelia had already pushed him aside and was walking down the hall, with her oversized father following close behind.

A MYSTERIOUS SHADOW

Forgetting to close the door, Samuel ran after the intruders. 'Wait, you–'

It was too late. Cornelia and her father were already in the living room, staring at Uncle Henrik, who had quickly fanned the deck of cards in front of his face to try and disguise himself.

But of course, Mr Myklebust knew *exactly* who he was looking at. Indeed, it was the reason why he had driven over.

'Henrik?' he said, faking surprise. 'Oh my goodness, Henrik, is that you? It *is*, isn't it? It is you.'

Henrik lowered the cards he had been cowering behind and offered a weak smile.

'You don't recognize me, do you? It's me. Magnus. Magnus Myklebust. I have put on a little bit of weight since I last saw you – you remember, don't you? That skiing race on Mount Myrdal? When you cheated . . . yes . . . yes . . .' He tapped his highest chin, as if he were only just now remembering it.

'I didn't cheat,' said Uncle Henrik quietly.

'But wait a minute . . . I heard . . . I heard you went missing . . . Yes – your wife Eda, she told the whole village. She said you disappeared into Shadow Forest and never returned . . . That is why all these years people have been so scared of the place. They said you must have been kidnapped by trolls or murdered by pixies or some such nonsense. Of course, I never believed these stories.' He laughed wildly at this point and Samuel had absolutely no idea what he was laughing about because he had been saying all this in Norwegian.

'So,' said Mr Myklebust, 'tell me, Henrik. What does live over in that forest? What happened to you?'

'Er . . . It is wonderful to see you, Magnus, truly . . . but I am afraid that really there is not much to say–'

'You disappeared into the forest for nearly ten years and there is not much to say?! That seems mighty strange, Henrik, my old friend. Come on, you must know something.'

Uncle Henrik sighed. He felt very awkward indeed.

You see, he was as bad at lying as he was at playing Blackjack, and any secret that stayed inside him for too long always ended up turning his face bright red.

'Yes . . . well . . . it's a long story. I will have to tell you about it another time.'

Mr Myklebust looked around the room. His small piggy eyes scanned over the rocking chair, the sofa covered with the multicoloured woollen blanket, the dining table, the fireplace, the rugs, the shelves full of glass vases and ancient-looking books, the framed paintings of mountains and fjords on the wall. His eyes lingered when he reached the empty dog basket.

'You have a dog?' he asked.

Uncle Henrik hesitated. 'Yes . . . No . . . We did have a dog called Ibsen . . . but he died.'

'And you keep the basket?'

'Eda was very fond of him. We keep the basket for sentimental reasons . . .'

'Oh, it's just that my little princess hates dogs, you see. Don't you, Cornelia?'

'Yes,' said Cornelia, giving the dog basket the same look of disgust that she had previously used on Samuel. 'They are descended from wolves. And give me a rash.'

'Well . . . there is no dog here now,' said Uncle Henrik.

It was at this point in the conversation that Samuel heard something, or *someone*, out in the hallway. And Samuel wasn't the only one to hear it either.

'What was that?' said Mr Myklebust.

'What was what?' asked Uncle Henrik, who had been too busy working out what to say about the forest to notice anything.

'That noise. It sounded like a dog coming in through the door.'

'I didn't hear anything,' said Uncle Henrik, putting the fan of cards down on the dining table. And then, in English, to Samuel: 'I will have a look in the hall and see if there is anything there.'

'No, it's OK,' Samuel said. 'I'll go.' After all, the last thing he wanted was to be stuck having to talk to Cornelia.

So he left the three of them talking Norwegian while he headed back out into the hallway. He looked right, towards the front door that he hadn't had time to close after Mr Myklebust barged in. There was no immediate sign of anyone. He looked left, and just for a second thought he saw a shadow slide and disappear at the top of the stairs.

It was probably just Aunt Eda, he said to himself. *Or Martha.*

Maybe they had been about to come down when they heard the voice of Mr Myklebust, and backed away.

Maybe.

But it did seem rather unlikely.

It was probably nothing. I'm probably just seeing things.

Samuel went to close the front door but then, glancing outside into the fading light, he noticed something on the path. He decided to nip out and inspect it.

It was cold out this evening, under that blushing sky. Aunt Eda had told him and Martha about the wind that travels from the east, getting cooler as it soars over the mountains, then gains speed over the fjord. And it greeted him now, that wind, as he stepped out onto the path in his socks. Like a warning he couldn't translate.

He looked at the giant jeep parked behind his aunt and uncle's battered white car. *They must be rich,* Samuel thought. *And I bet Cornelia's spoiled rotten. I bet that's why she's so annoying.*

He crouched down and studied the path. There was dirt on it. Footprints. Not shoe-prints, *foot*prints.

Someone had been walking with muddy bare feet along the path.

'Strange,' he muttered.

As he studied them, he thought again. Maybe it wasn't footprints at all. They weren't really shaped like feet. They were wider, shorter, rounder. There weren't enough toes.

Samuel looked towards the forest, knowing no creature would have escaped. After all, it was a paradise now. No creature would ever risk venturing out into this world.

He went back into the house, closed the door and saw some dirt on the floor. *Probably off Cornelia's shoes,* he thought. *She probably made them muddy on purpose.* But what was that cabbagey smell? When he got back into the living room, Martha was there, talking and giggling with Cornelia. Aunt Eda had also come down, a sour expression on her face as she observed Mr Myklebust.

'Oh, it's a lovely house,' Cornelia was saying, as if auditioning for the World's Biggest Creep contest. 'It must be so great living here.'

'Yes,' said Martha. 'It's OK. I like the views out of the windows of the mountain and the forest.'

Samuel wondered how his sister could be so stupid.

Not only was she mentioning the forest; she was trying to impress Cornelia. Why couldn't she see how stuck-up the girl really was? Then again, why did Cornelia only pretend to be nice when Martha came into the room?

Mr Myklebust, meanwhile, was still sniffing for information. 'Listen, Henrik . . . if you ever want to tell me a story – a true story – about what lives beyond those trees, then I will pay a good price to hear it, be assured of that. A very good price. In fact, I would pay you ten thousand kroner right now if you could tell me the truth about that place – and what happened to you.'

And to prove his point he pulled his wallet out of his pocket and drew out a hefty wad of crisp blue notes.

Uncle Henrik was momentarily hypnotized. 'Ten thousand kroner? Wow, that's a lot of money for a story.'

'I have to ask you,' interrupted Aunt Eda. 'Why are you *really* here?'

Mr Myklebust frowned and pushed out his bottom lip, as if thinking very hard about this question.

'I am a man who cares about this area. It is indeed my job to do so. I want as much of the district of Flåm as possible to be enjoyed by visitors and tourists. And so it would be good to know the truth about the forest. But that is not my main reason. You see, my dear little princess was really looking forward to having her friend to stay tomorrow night. But unfortunately it is not very appropriate. You see, there is some very important work being done on the house . . . One of our jacuzzis has broken . . . So I was wondering if the sleepover could take place here instead?'

Aunt Eda eyed him with suspicion. She had only just heard, from Martha, that there was to be any kind of sleepover at all. But to have one *here*, in this house? No. It wasn't a good idea. She looked at Cornelia, who was making sure she looked as innocent as possible. And as Aunt Eda looked at those innocent eyes, she began to weaken. What harm would it really do? It wasn't fair to punish a girl for what father they happened to have. And there was clearly no point trying to hide Henrik any more.

And then she turned to Martha and remembered the terrible state she had been in the night before, when she had cried out in the night. 'Oh . . . all right . . . yes – the sleepover can happen here.

Mr Myklebust clapped his hands. 'Good,' he said, and he threw Henrik a triumphant look, as though he had just won a prize no one else knew existed. 'I'll drop her off tomorrow.'

Yes, I know what you are thinking.

If Mr Myklebust was worried about the forest, why would he leave his only child staying in a house so close to it?

It's a good question, and I'm glad you asked it. Well, what can I say? Mr Myklebust was obviously greedy enough to take the risk. If Cornelia came back with any information from Martha, it would have been worth it. And Cornelia was, of course, getting paid, so she was more than happy to brave the danger. And besides, she was far too sensible and clever to believe in such things as trolls and pixies. She knew everything there was to know about science and so she knew such creatures couldn't possibly exist. But if her father was silly enough to pay her to be a spy, then who was she to try and stop him?

Just as Mr Myklebust and Cornelia were leaving, Samuel heard a noise coming from upstairs. A kind of scraping noise. *Weird*, he thought to himself. And he was about to investigate when Aunt Eda closed the door and asked him and Martha to help with the supper.

TROLL-MOTHER'S SUGGESTION

'He be not there,' Troll-Father told his wife. 'He be not nowhere.'

'You flenking useless lump,' she said, torn between anger and desperate worry. 'You be gone for hours and you not be no closer to finding him than when you be leaving.'

'I be sorry, Troll-Mother. I be sorry.'

'Sorry? You be sorry?'

Troll-Daughter, who was seated on the floor with a wooden doll cradled in her lap, said nothing. Even she seemed sad her brother was missing.

Then Troll-Mother remembered what the Betterer had told her. 'You be knowing what to do,' she said hurriedly.

'And what be that then?'

'You be telling Troll-the-Wisest. At the council meeting. You be going there and you be sorting it out.'

Troll-Father nodded anxiously. 'Yes. It be a good idea. I be going. I be going right now to sort it out.' And then he hesitated. 'But won't you be worried about what everyone be thinking of us?'

And Troll-Mother stood there for a moment, unsure. 'No,' she said in a softer voice than normal, before snapping out of it. 'No! What kind of mother be you thinking I be?! Go on, Troll-Father. You be late for the meeting!'

'Bye, Troll-Mother,' said Troll-Father.

'Be finding our son,' she said. 'Please . . . be finding him.'

Troll-Father left the house without further objections, and made his way to the village hall to tell Troll-the-Wisest the news.

THE NOISE UNDER THE BED

Samuel couldn't sleep.

There was a strange, slightly cabbagey smell to the room this evening, but that wasn't the problem. The problem was the thought of school tomorrow. He just lay in the dark looking at the silhouette of his sister in the next bed. It was all right for Martha. She was a singing chatterbox who *always* managed to make friends. Back in England, she seemed to have a different best friend every day. It was like she was a friend *magnet.* She only had to turn up at school – at *any* school – and stand in the yard, and friends would fly towards her like iron filings.

Why was it never like that for him? Sure, he'd had one best friend in Nottingham, but that was different. That was someone he had something in common with. Joseph had lived a few houses away and hated girly pop songs as much as Samuel did. Sometimes after school they had bike races down the street. It had been fun, but it was in the past now.

He had thought of writing Joseph a letter, but what was the point? Joseph wouldn't want to know him now that he lived in Norway. He'd be having bike races with someone else.

No. Samuel had to face facts. He was just a friendless loner who had to live in a strange country with his aunt and uncle. *And* wear woolly jumpers like the one Aunt Eda had bought him the other day, which was far too big. If only it had never happened. If only his parents had listened to him when he told them to stop the–

What was that?

He had heard something.

Definitely, he had heard something. At first he thought it was Martha in the next bed, having another nightmare.

'Martha?'

But she didn't answer. She was fast asleep.

It was a strange creaking from underneath the bed. And now that he was concentrating, he noticed another sound too. It was a kind of *breathy* sound, and it was getting louder.

Yes, there was no denying it. The sound was of someone snoring.

'Martha? Stop snoring.'

But the snoring wasn't coming from her side of the room. And Martha didn't snore.

Maybe it was Uncle Henrik. Yes, that was who it must be. Mind you, there was a bathroom between Samuel and Martha's bedroom and their aunt and uncle's. He must be a very *loud* snorer for it to sound so close through two closed doors. And Samuel couldn't remember hearing him snore any other night.

He tried not to think about it. He closed his eyes and sank back down in his bed, trying to fall asleep. He counted backwards from a hundred, which was a trick his mother had once taught him when he was younger to help him drop off.

One hundred, ninety-nine, ninety-eight, ninety-seven, ninety-six, ninety-five, ninety-four . . .

There it was again.

Louder, now. And closer too. That *definitely* wasn't Uncle Henrik. Unless Uncle Henrik was sleeping under the bed, which was rather unlikely when he had a perfectly good bed of his own to sleep in.

It was probably just his imagination, Samuel told himself. The dark can play funny tricks on you. That's what his mother had always said. Like when he was little and had been convinced that a monster lived in the wardrobe.

So once again he tried to go to sleep and ignore the sounds.

. . . *ninety-three, ninety-two, ninety-one, ninety, eighty-nine* . . .

But then there was something else.

'A-a-a-atchoo!'

Now *that* wasn't his imagination. Someone had sneezed. He sat up and looked over at Martha, but she was still asleep, and besides, he would have known if it had been one of her sneezes.

No.

It was someone else. Not himself and not Uncle Henrik. But someone who was very real, and currently lying right under his bed.

AN EYE AMID THE DARKNESS

Samuel's heart was racing. He knew he couldn't just lie there with someone – or some*thing* – under his bed. What if it was something evil? What if it was something out to kill them?

He was about to wake Martha up when he changed his mind. Hadn't he managed to survive a whole forest full of deadly creatures? Surely he could handle whatever was under the bed.

Slowly he peeled back his covers and hung his head over the side. He couldn't see anything *by* the bed, so he lowered his head further until he could get a view *underneath.* At first he could see nothing. It was too dark. Then, as he lay hanging half upside down, his eyes began to notice something a bit more worrying.

The darkness seemed to have two shades. There

was the same airy grey darkness that filled the whole room, and then there was something blacker, more solid, in the foreground. A shape that moved slowly in time with the snores.

Samuel hung there for a moment while fear pulsed inside him. Maybe he should wake it, whatever it was. His arm reached under his bed, his hand and finger pointing into the darkness. It was going to pass right through, he was sure. It was just in his mind. But then his finger touched something. Something that felt like skin, but rougher and more lumpy.

His finger jerked back in shock. And, just as it did so, something appeared amid the darkness. Something light and round that had just blinked open.

An eye. And only one eye at that.

Then, around the eye, Samuel started to make out a face. An ugly but strangely innocent kind of face. A troll's face, and one he vaguely recognized.

'Samuel Blink.'

Troll-Son's whisper surprised Samuel, and had the same waking-up effect on him as if someone had flicked water in his eyes. Samuel's head stayed hanging upside down as he whispered to the troll. 'It's . . . it's *you.* The troll boy. I've seen you before. I . . . I ate at your house. Your mum and dad gave me food when I was looking for my sister. It's you. Isn't it?'

'Yes, Samuel Blink,' Troll-Son said, in a voice that was tense with excitement. 'It be me, Samuel Blink. I be your friend, Samuel Blink.'

'*Sssh!*' said Samuel as Martha rolled over and mumbled in her sleep. 'Don't . . . don't . . . speak.'

So. He'd been right. There *had* been a bare footprint on the path. And he *had* heard someone upstairs.

'What are you doing here?' Samuel whispered more quietly.

Troll-Son didn't answer.

'I said, what are you doing here?' And then Samuel remembered he'd ordered the troll boy not to speak. 'You can tell me – but keep quiet.'

'I be running away from the forest, Samuel Blink.'

'You must go back – it's not safe for you here.'

Troll-Son seemed to panic. Samuel could hear his breath quicken. 'No . . . no . . . here . . . not forest . . . I be here, Samuel Blink.'

Of course, Samuel had met Troll-Son before. But that was in the forest. Having him right here in his own bedroom was completely different. It was like spotting a polar bear in the middle of the desert.

'You have to go,' Samuel whispered, noticing again the cabbagey smell that Troll-Son had brought with him. 'You can't stay here.'

Martha rolled over again, but stayed asleep.

'I be staying here. I be staying under the bed. I be hiding, Samuel Blink.'

Samuel wondered how living under the bed for ever, face pressed into the carpet, could be better than returning to the forest.

And then he heard something out on the landing – Aunt Eda shuffling sleepily along as she headed for the toilet. And again, Martha mumbled something in her sleep.

Samuel put his finger to his lips and hoped the troll would understand this meant 'Be quiet', which he seemed to, because he didn't say a word as they lay there, listening to Aunt Eda flush the toilet and then wash her hands.

It was almost funny.

All evening everyone had been worried Mr Myklebust might find out something about the forest, and all that time a real live troll had been hiding in Samuel's bedroom.

Yes. *Almost* funny. But Samuel was nowhere near laughing.

'Listen,' he whispered over the fading sound of the toilet flush. 'Whatever it is you're scared of in the forest, you have to believe me that it is no safer here . . . Seriously, you've got to go back – if humans find out about you, they'll send you for tests and they'll chop you up or someth–'

But he stopped. He saw a tear glisten in Troll-Son's eye, shining like a jewel in the dark.

'All right,' he said, remembering how this troll's family had once saved his life. 'All right, don't cry . . . Just stay still – and stay quiet until I speak to you in the morning. Then we'll work something out.'

THE TROLL COUNCIL

Troll-the-Wisest was the head of the Troll Council because he was widely considered to be the wisest inhabitant of Trollhelm. That is why he was called Troll-the-Wisest. Everyone knew he was wise because he had a very long beard, the longest in the village, and such a beard could only be a sign of supreme wisdom. Of course, there was a time when his beard hadn't been so long, and back in those days Troll-the-Wisest had to contend with the name Troll-the-Quite-Clever. Then, one day, it was noted in a council meeting that his beard had grown longer than that of the then Troll-the-Wisest, and so, after a vote in Troll-the-Quite-Clever's favour, he became the new Troll-the-Wisest.

(In case you are wondering what happened to the

previous Troll-the-Wisest, I should tell you that he took very badly to this news and tried for months to stretch his beard. It didn't work. And soon he became so depressed at being known as Troll-the-Once-Wisest he took to drinking gallons of hurgleberry wine day and night, until eventually his name had to be changed *again* to Troll-the-Crying-Drunk.)

Anyway, where was I? Ah yes, the Troll Council. Well, the first thing to mention is that by the time Troll-Father turned up at the hall the meeting had already been going on for over three hours, and was no closer to ending than when it had started.

You see, Troll Council meetings weren't known for their shortness. Indeed, they would often last whole nights and include numerous debates and votes on subjects such as whether or not they should scrap the Annual Washday or clamp down on rabbit thieves. Today, though, they had even more to talk about. News had reached Trollhelm that the evil overlord who had once ruled the forest was now dead, and so all the creatures he had once made deadly – the truth pixies, the slemps, the huldre-folk – were peaceful again.

'Now that the forest be a safe place again, and now that the Changemaker be dead, there be no reason for us to be staying in just the troll places. We can be going after rabbits anywhere we please, be we not?' said one troll.

Another hand went up, a bit slower this time as it belonged to Troll-the-Weaver, who was rather old. 'And why must we still be coming out only after dark? Surely it be safe for us to be going out in the light hours. The Changemaker be dead and his Shadow Witch be up in the north, be what I hear, and all them creatures they made evil be back being good now. No one be trying to steal our shadows and make us evil. I be missing the sunshine something terrible, you see.'

Troll-the-Wisest was quiet for a while, and seemed to chew on the suggestions as if they were unknown food that he didn't know if he liked.

'These be most interesting suggestions,' he said as Troll-Father found himself a seat on the back row. 'The question be whether we be wanting to change our whole way of living just because things be safe again. Some of us be so used to the darkness, we be worried the light might blind us. You might be missing the yellow sun, but some of us be having most soft feelings for the holes the humans cut out of the sky for us. The holes that let in the white stars and the moon. Now, I be not saying that one way be better than the other, but if we be having a vote on this, we be needing to consider all such matterings.'

There were two votes. A vote on whether to revert to daylight hours, and another to decide if they should head deeper into other territories on hunting expeditions. As usual, they voted for things to stay precisely the way they were.

'Now,' said Troll-the-Wisest, stroking his beard, 'be anyone else having something they be wishing to say?'

And so Troll-Father slowly raised his hand.

'Yes? You. Yes, you at the back.'

The whole room fell into deep silence, which was very unusual at troll meetings, and made Troll-Father feel very nervous.

'Well, it be my boy, Troll-Son,' he said.

Troll-the-Wisest nodded. 'Yes it be, yes it be,' he said, as if he knew what the matter was. And then, realizing that in fact he had no idea what the matter was, he said: 'Your boy?'

'Yes, he be missing.'

Everyone gasped.

'No,' chuckled Troll-the-Wisest. 'He won't be missing.'

'We be looking everywhere but he be gone.'

Troll-the-Wisest still looked unconcerned. 'Troll boys be small and easy to lose. He be somewhere.'

'No,' said Troll-Father, and there was another collective gasp of shock. No one ever spoke in such a way to Troll-the-Wisest. 'No, no. I be sorry. I be knowing my beard be not so long as yours and that my wiseness be of the shortest type, but I be saying with stone certain truth that my son be missing. He be running away, I know he be. I be searching all last night and all today, risking the light of the sun. But I be not finding him nowhere. And I be thinking he be leaving the forest.'

Troll-the-Wisest was shaking his head and closing his eyes. 'Trolls don't be leaving the forest. I been in this village all my life – that be seven hundred and thirty-eight years – and I never be hearing of no troll running away. We be not knowing what be out beyond them trees, be we? Even when the Changemaker be at his worst, no troll be ever tempted to leave the forest, so why be we thinking that, now the Changemaker be gone and the forest be safe, there be a runaway? Who'd be wanting to leave Trollhelm now? Now, I be wise and my wiseness be telling me that Trollhelm be not a place no troll be wanting to leave.'

The whole hall muttered its agreement.

'But he be scared–'

'Scared?'

'His mother be most dreadful cross with him, you see. Most dreadful cross. And she be going to send him to stay at the Bettering Tower but he be not wanting to go, see? He be sick with worry, so he be.'

The Betterer, who was also sitting in the meeting, shook his head with disgust.

At the front of the hall Troll-the-Wisest was tugging gently on his beard, as though it were the switch to a light that might go off inside his head. 'A lot of young trolls be not liking to be bettered, but they don't be running away, not out of the forest at any rate. No one be knowing what be out there, be they?'

Troll-Father gulped, realizing he had to reveal the secret his family had been keeping. 'He be having a better idea than most be, Troll-the-Wisest.'

Everyone in the hall joined the Betterer in looking at Troll-Father as Troll-the-Wisest put the question: 'A better idea than most? How that be?'

'Well, you see, it be like this. There be a human boy, a boy called Samuel Blink, who be running into our house one day to escape from some huldres. This be many nights ago now, and before the whole forest be peaceful again. Anyhow, we be giving this human some rabbit casserole and he be telling us his sister be in the forest and that he be looking for her. He be seeing her in a prison wagon. Them huldres be taking her to the Changemaker.'

There was an excited commotion in the hall at this point.

'A human?' cried one voice.

'Never in all my years . . .' cried another.

'Nonsense!' cried a third.

'Burp,' burped Troll-the-Crying-Drunk.

'No,' said Troll-Father. 'I be telling you the truth, so I be. I be seeing a human with my own eye – which my son be taking – and this human be as real as any troll. And ever since he be staying with us he be Troll-Son's hero. And he be knowing Samuel Blink be living in a house just outside the forest. He be telling us that when he be visiting. And so I be betting that be where he be.'

The entire hall fell into complete silence. No one had ever heard anything like this in a council meeting before. Troll-the-Wisest's mouth kept opening, but with no reason, like the door to an empty house flapping in the wind.

And then, when the silence had stretched out as long as it could without snapping, another hand was raised. And this hand belonged to the two-headed troll. Specifically, to the half of the two-headed troll we know as Troll-the-Left.

'Yes?' said Troll-the-Wisest. 'What be you saying about this story?'

'I be saying I know a lot of it be true.' Troll-the-Left's voice was slow and solemn, and had to compete with the grumblings of Troll-the-Right as he proceeded. 'We be in that prison wagon with the human girl. Samuel Blink's sister. When we be caught chasing rabbits in huldre territory, we be put in prison with the girl and then sent with her to the Changemaker. There then be a snowstorm, then all the prisoners be escaping, including the girl. Me and Troll-the-Right be staying and fighting the huldres and that be when Troll-the-Right suffered his little mishap.'

'Mishap?!' cried Troll-the-Right. 'Mishap? My head be chopped off. Some flenking mishap!'

'Well, my point be, we be supporting Troll-Father's story. We be knowing there be humans in the forest and we be knowing . . . we be knowing . . .'

The two halves of the two-headed troll were now engaged in a physical struggle. Troll-the-Right had his hand over Troll-the-Left's mouth, while Troll-the-Left was trying to push Troll-the-Right's arm away so he could speak. You see, although Troll-the-Right had been the one who wanted to stop Troll-Son running away, he didn't want to get himself into trouble. Troll-the-Left, on the other hand (and head), didn't mind getting into trouble and had been worried he'd made a mistake in letting Troll-Son escape, especially after hearing what Troll-Father had just said.

Troll-the-Wisest looked sternly towards Troll-the-Right. 'Now, you be letting your other head finish what it be saying.'

And so Troll-the-Left's mouth was free again to deliver the information. 'We be seeing Troll-Son leave his house. We be asking him where he be going and he told us he be running away to live with Samuel Blink. He be scared of his mother. And the Betterer. And I be having no heart to be stopping him.'

'I be trying!' shouted Troll-the-Right. 'I be trying! Blame this flenking idiot. Not me!'

Troll-Father was standing up now, his empty eyelid blinking in excited agitation. 'You be seeing my son? He be telling you that? He be telling you he be off to find Samuel Blink?'

'Aye,' said Troll-the-Left. 'I be sorry, neighbour, I didn't be telling you earlier. But the boy be so terrified and so wanting to escape.'

And after that the whole hall fell into another unusual silence as everyone turned to examine the face of the eyeless father on the back row. The silence stretched on and on, too strong to snap this time, as Troll-Father felt dry, invisible tears well up inside him.

THE SEARCH PARTY

Troll-the-Wisest didn't know what to do. Normally it was enough for him to suggest a vote and then stroke his long beard, just to remind everyone of how wise he was, but the issue of this missing troll boy seemed to require a different kind of leadership. The trouble was, what kind?

'Er . . . yes . . .' he said. 'I be in the most sympathy with Troll-Father. It must be a most terrible happening, for a son to go missing. But your beard don't be needing to be as long as mine to be knowing it makes no sense to be going looking for him. If he be inside the forest, then he be most likely safe and coming home. And if he be *outside* the forest, then . . . well . . . there be nothing much to be done. There be not a troll in this room who has ever been outside the forest, and that be the way it should stay.'

Troll-Father felt a heavy feeling descend on him. What hope was there now of finding his son?

'Well,' he said nervously, 'I be going to look for Troll-Son. And if that means going out of the forest then I be going out of the forest.'

Everyone muttered their surprise. They had never heard Troll-Father disagree with anyone, least of all Troll-the-Wisest.

Up until this point, the Betterer had sat silently in the crowd. Normally he avoided Troll Council meetings altogether. The idea of sitting there, in a single room full of a hundred unwashed and dim-witted trolls, filled him with horror.

But today was different. Today he had a reason to be there. And that reason was the same as Troll-Father's. He wanted to find the runaway troll boy.

So he pinched his nose and put up with the odorous stench until he found the perfect moment to speak up, which was right now.

'I will go with you,' he called out into the hall. 'I will go and help you find your son.' And soon, as he had expected, there were other voices too.

'And we be going too!' Everyone looked to see

the two-headed troll's left head staring defiantly at Troll-the-Wisest.

'We? We?' said Troll-the-Right. 'I don't be thinking so. It be not our business.'

'Yes, it be,' said Troll-the-Left. 'We be the last to see Troll-Son. We should be stopping him. And if you be wanting to argue I be pulling your stitches out.'

Other voices were raised, and more trolls agreed that there should be an organized search party sent out to look for Troll-Son.

'A search party!'

'Find the missing troll boy!'

'Think of the poor parents!'

'Custard!' added Troll-the-Crying-Drunk, for no reason whatsoever.

'Thank you,' Troll-Father kept saying. 'Thank you, Betterer. Thank you, Troll-the-Left. Thank you, everyone. I be thanking you all for kindliness, I be really.'

Troll-the-Wisest scanned his audience with dismay, and realized he had to change his mind. After all, if the Betterer was going to look for Troll-Son, there was probably some point to it. But of course, Troll-the-Wisest could never let anyone know he was changing his mind.

'Yes,' he said. 'As I be saying only a few moments before, it be my job as leader of the council to be keeping trolls safe. So it be better to be having a whole village go looking for him than to be leaving him out there alone in any kind of danger. I be sorry but there be no vote on this matter. I say that we be organizing a search party. As I be saying, if that means some trolls be going out of the forest, then there be some trolls going out of the forest. And that be that.'

Everyone looked confused for a moment, but Troll-the-Wisest spoke in such a wise voice and had such a very long beard that everyone (or everyone apart from the Betterer, who knew this would happen) thought this must have been what he had been saying all along. And so it was agreed that a search party should be formed, and that this search party – if the need arose – should be allowed to leave the forest.

Even though he couldn't see any of the faces in the hall, Troll-Father noticed a sudden chill in the atmosphere as soon as this realization sank in. And he understood why. After all, no one knew for sure what type of world lay beyond the forest. Not even Troll-Father himself had any idea. Sure, he had met a real-life human called Samuel Blink, but that was in the forest. He had no clue what a human adult might be like, or a whole *village* of human adults. How would they react to seeing a troll? He silently prayed for his son's safety, and tried to feel a bit more hopeful. If all the humans were like Samuel, there shouldn't be very much to worry about, should there?

'Now,' said Troll-the-Wisest, 'any men trolls of beard age who be wanting to be in the search party stay in your chairs. The meeting be now most fully over so the rest of you be leaving.'

Troll-Father waited in the blind dark as chairs scraped back across the floor and heavy feet left the hall. He wondered how many were still staying there and who they would be.

Not so many as he had hoped, that was for sure. There was the Betterer, obviously Troll-the-Wisest, the two-headed troll and Troll-the-Crying-Drunk. Troll-the-Crying-Drunk, it turned out, had fallen asleep and realized his mistake as soon as he woke up.

'No, no . . . I be – hic – I be meant to be somewhere that not be right here,' he said, with a look of sad confusion. 'And if the hall be stopping moving I be swimming myself out. But I – hic – I think it be good to be in a search party . . . Troll overboard! . . . It be just that I be doubting you be finding anything till we get out of the custard . . .' He staggered out of the hall, banging into far more chairs than Troll-Father managed to even without his eyeball. 'I be having a date.'

'I be betting,' muttered Troll-the-Right. 'A date with a bottle of hurgleberry gin.'

Once Troll-the-Crying-Drunk had left the room, the two-headed troll began to argue between its selves.

'We be going!' said Troll-the-Left.

'We be not!' said Troll-the-Right.

'We be going!'

'We be not!'

'Listen,' interrupted the Betterer in his crisp, clear voice. 'Perhaps Troll-the-Right might be right. That is to say, perhaps Troll-the-Left should be left.'

'But I be wanting to come,' said Troll-the-Left. 'I be feeling so guilty for poor Troll-Father.'

The Betterer nodded. 'Yes, yes, yes. But think very carefully. When we leave the forest – if indeed that is what we will do – we will need to be well hidden. To blend in. To be inconspicuous.'

None of the other trolls knew what inconspicuous meant, but they weren't going to admit it.

'Yes,' said Troll-the-Wisest. 'We must be inconsipulous.'

The Betterer nodded and stroked his shaved chin.

'And having an arguing, two-headed, medium giant troll in the search party punching its own heads is going to get us noticed, and that is not helping anyone.'

Troll-the-Left was confused. He glared at the Betterer and wondered what he was up to. 'The more trolls there be, the more chance we be having of finding Troll-Son, no?'

'Yes,' said Troll-Father. 'You be quite right.'

'No,' said the Betterer. 'He's not.'

'Yes,' said Troll-the-Wisest. 'That be what I be saying. He be quite wrong. The Betterer be right. It be for the best. Troll-the-Left, you and Troll-the-Right should be staying in Trollhelm. Leave it to us – we be finding Troll-Son.'

'But don't you be getting it? This be why the boy be running away! He be scared of going to the Betterer,' said Troll-the-Left.

'Just be leaving it,' said Troll-the-Right, wondering why Troll-the-Left was so bothered.

'But don't you see,' said the Betterer, determined not to lose the chance of finding his new pupil. 'That is why I need to be *outside* the forest. Then he will realize there's nothing to be scared of *inside* the forest.'

'But–' said Troll-the-Left.

'*Be leaving it*!' said Troll-the-Right, so loud in Troll-the-Left's ear that Troll-the-Left got a headache.

The other trolls had a headache too, trying to work out the Betterer's argument.

'Trust me, if you meet humans you will need someone who can put all his words in all the right places.'

Troll-Father wondered why someone who had always ignored him was trying to help him. In fact, the Betterer wasn't interested in *helping* Troll-Father at all. Quite the opposite, actually, as I'm sure you'll find out. But he was a very good liar. Just listen to this:

'Do you be meaning it, Mr Betterer?' asked Troll-Father.

'Yes, don't worry. I have devoted my life to the care of troll children. I would never sleep again if I let you – or that confused troll child – down. We'll find him, I assure you. My nose can smell a grubby troll child a mile away.'

Troll-Father felt such relief that he wasn't going to be alone in his search. 'Oh thank you,' he said. 'Thank you all. I be so grateful. Thank you.'

'It is a pleasure,' said the Betterer, feeling like a conductor in charge of a small but rather gullible orchestra that would play any note he asked for. 'Now, let's bring your poor boy home.'

TROLL-THE-ALLERGIC

It was a Friday.

Samuel was due to go to school.

Troll-Son stayed quiet, as he had been instructed. It was only when Martha got up, took her school clothes from the back of the chair and went to the bathroom that Samuel looked under the bed again.

'Do you need the toilet?' asked Samuel.

'No,' said Troll-Son, from under the bed. 'I be doing toilet last week.'

'Last *week*?'

'Yes.'

'Trolls only go to the toilet once a week?'

'Yes.'

'Listen,' Samuel said, realizing there were more

important matters than toilet habits to discuss. 'If my Aunt Eda or Uncle Henrik see you, they'll make you go back to the forest. Do you understand?'

'I be understanding, Samuel Blink.'

'And if my sister Martha sees you, she'll find it hard to keep a secret. She's not good with secrets. She talks a lot and tells people things. OK?'

'Yes, Samuel Blink.'

Samuel heard his sister's footsteps leave the bathroom. Now it was broad daylight in the room, he had a new worry. He quickly rearranged his top blanket so that it was hanging down to the carpet, thereby concealing Troll-Son from Martha's view when she came back.

'What's that smell?' enquired Martha, fully washed, dressed and ready for school.

'What smell?'

Her nose twitched. 'I don't know. It's weird. It smells like . . . earth . . . No. Like school dinners.'

'School dinners?'

Samuel suddenly noticed Troll-Son's three-fingered hand sticking out from under the blanket. He quickly sat up and reached down to cover it before Martha saw. 'What are you doing?' she asked.

Samuel kept his hand over Troll-Son's, and couldn't

help noticing how warm it was. (Trolls, dear readers, have a lot hotter blood than you or me, which explains why they can go hunting at night in a Norwegian forest without needing a coat. Indeed, only one troll has a coat, and that's the Betterer, but he only wears it so he can carry all his bettering medicines, so that doesn't count . . .)

Martha repeated her question. 'What *are* you doing?'

'I dropped something,' Samuel said.

'What did you drop?'

'My . . . er . . . watch.'

'But it's on your wrist.'

'Oh yes,' said Samuel, sliding Troll-Son's hand back behind the blanket. 'So it is . . . Anyway, what were you saying?'

He was sure he heard the faintest of whispers coming from under the bed – 'I be sorry, Samuel Blink' – but it was so faint Martha didn't seem to notice.

'The smell. It's like school dinners. Like vegetables. Boiled vegetables. Something disgusting. Like cabbage. Or swede. Or broccoli. Or–'

'I get the picture. But I can't smell anything.' Samuel made a show of sniffing the air and pretending not to notice the trollish odours that filled his nose and clogged his throat. 'Nope. Not a thing.'

Troll-Son sneezed *again.* Like all trolls he was allergic to carpet, but as he'd never been on a carpet before he'd never known this fact.

'What was that?' asked Martha.

'I sneezed.'

'But your face didn't move.'

'Faces don't need to move if they sneeze.'

'Yes they do. You need to close your eyes, at least. If you have your eyes open when you sneeze, your eyeballs pop out because they move at seven hundred miles an hour or something, and don't say "Like your mouth" because it's not funny.' Martha knew she talked a lot, and talked fast, but she couldn't help it. She had been quiet for a long time recently – long enough to know that silence was a hole, letting sadness in, and she wanted to keep that hole filled as much as she could.

'I won't. And I know about sneezes. I was the one who told you that. But I did close my eyes. I just didn't move my whole face.'

Troll-Son was not only allergic to carpets; human blankets made him feel sneezy too. Now that the blanket was directly in front of his face, the dust was proving too much for nostrils used to pure forest air. But the second time he sneezed, Samuel had warning.

'A-a-a-a-atchoo!'

Samuel did the required face at the required time, and did it just about well enough to ease Martha's suspicions.

'I think I'm ill,' he said. 'I think I've got a cold.'

Martha's face fell. 'Don't make me go to that school on my own. It's not fair. I promise I won't sing in the car.'

'What are you on about? You love it. You'll be with your new best friend, Cornelia.'

'Well, I'm sure you'll make friends too.'

Samuel felt angry suddenly. 'I don't *want* friends,' he said. 'I *had* friends. At home. And proper friends. Not like the weirdos you get here.'

'They're not weirdos,' said Martha as she sat on her bed with her hands together, fingers interlocked and resting on her knee. Their mother used to sit in precisely the same way, Samuel remembered, whenever he and Martha were upset about something.

Samuel felt strange. As if he weren't just facing his sister but his mother as well. As though his mother were still alive in some way, and looking out for him from a secret watchtower behind Martha's eyes.

'No, I know,' said Samuel. 'They're not weirdos. But all I'm saying is I might not be going to school today.'

'What are you going to tell Aunt Eda?'

'The truth. That I'm ill. Or even better, you could do it for me. Please, Martha.'

'Erm, I doubt it,' said Martha teasingly as she left the room. Then she poked her head back round the door to say: 'Good luck. You'll need it.'

She was right, of course. Aunt Eda wasn't the sort of person who let you have a day off school just because you asked for one. No. Aunt Eda required proof that you needed – truly *needed* – to stay at home.

And as Samuel wasn't the slightest bit ill, it was going to be something of a challenge convincing her.

When Martha went downstairs for her breakfast, Samuel hopped out of bed and opened one of the windows. Then he waved his arms about, trying to get rid of the smell, before closing the window again but this time leaving a tiny crack open. Then he jumped back into bed and popped his head behind the blanket hiding Troll-Son.

'Now, in a minute, Aunt Eda's going to come

upstairs and that means you've got to be extremely quiet. If you feel like you want to sneeze, just hold onto your nose and press really hard. OK?'

Troll-Son's eye looked sad and worried. 'I be sorry, Samuel Blink.'

'It's OK. But you don't have to call me "Samuel Blink" all the– Sssh, it's Aunt Eda. She's coming.'

SAMUEL GETS A TEMPERATURE

As Aunt Eda climbed the stairs and creaked her way along the landing, Samuel made sure the blanket was still hiding Troll-Son. Then he lay back in bed and tried to look as ill as possible. He even coughed a few times before Aunt Eda entered the room, for extra authenticity. He tried to look pale, and wondered if he should have gone into the bathroom to put some talcum powder on his face, but he didn't have time. Anyway, he didn't need to try and whiten his skin. The moment he saw Aunt Eda appear in the room holding a *thermometer*, the colour drained right out of his cheeks.

'Now,' said Aunt Eda, 'Martha tells me that you aren't ferry well.' She flicked the thermometer upright at the end of the sentence, as if it were an exclamation mark.

'No,' croaked Samuel. He knew Martha would help him out, despite her teases. 'I've got a headache, and a cough, and a sore throat, and I keep sneezing.'

Aunt Eda's nose wiggled slightly, like a mouse detecting cheese. 'What's that smell?'

'I don't know' – cough – 'maybe it's because I'm ill.'

The curtains billowed slightly as a breeze made it through the narrowly open window.

'Why is the window open?'

'Martha opened it,' Samuel said. 'I asked her to' – cough – 'it helps let the germs out.'

Aunt Eda stood there for a while, saying nothing. Samuel tried to read her expression, but she wasn't giving much away. It wasn't just her cardigan that was buttoned right to the top. That's how Samuel always saw his aunt – as a person buttoned up to the top. He knew she was kind and loving underneath, but on the surface she was quite intimidating, especially with a thermometer in her hand.

'I want you to put this thermometer under your tongue for two minutes,' she said stiffly. 'If you haff a temperature, you will stay at home. If not, I am afraid you must go to school. And you will haff plenty of time at the weekend to recuffer. Now, open wide and lift up your tongue.'

Samuel knew he didn't have a temperature. But he also knew he couldn't leave Troll-Son in the house all day without him getting caught. What could he do?

So he opened his mouth and felt the prod of the thermometer as it went under his tongue.

'All right, Mr Infalid, let us see if it's a day in bed. Two minutes and we will know.'

Samuel faked a cough, and pulled the thermometer out of his mouth. 'I think I need a drink,' he said. 'Some fruit juice.'

Aunt Eda nodded. 'Ferry well. I will go and fetch you a juice from the kitchen. And when I come back, I will read your temperature. If it is ofer thirty-seven degrees Celsius, then you will stay at home.'

Samuel put the thermometer back under his tongue and nodded. Then, once Aunt Eda had disappeared out of the room, he searched around frantically. At home, when he had wanted to avoid rugby, he had once placed the thermometer on a hot radiator to convince his mum he had flu.

But there were no radiators in this bedroom. 'Something hot . . . something hot . . . something hot . . .' he whispered as he looked around. Then he remembered how very warm Troll-Son's hand had felt when he had covered it earlier, and hung his head upside down by the bed, before pulling back the blanket.

'There,' Samuel said. 'Put it in your mouth.'

Troll-Son's face recoiled in fear. So Samuel quickly put the thermometer in his own mouth to show it wasn't dangerous. 'See, just like that. But don't bite it. Quick.'

Samuel shoved the thermometer in Troll-Son's mouth, trying to ignore the grubby face, the greenish-brown tongue covered with ulcers, and the grey, rotten teeth. 'And remember, stay still and quiet when Aunt Eda comes back.'

He waited until he heard the creak of floorboards on the landing, then whipped the thermometer out and put it back under his own tongue.

Ugh.

It was disgusting.

Now, for any of you who might not have shared a thermometer with a troll, I should point out that it is a rather unpleasant experience. You see, as well as being very warm, troll saliva has the most vile taste you can think of. Imagine sucking on a stale, sweaty sock stuffed with boiled cabbage, foot fungus and rotten fish.

But of course, Samuel had to act completely normal.

'Now,' said Aunt Eda, returning into the room and putting Samuel's drink on the small cabinet by his bed. 'One glass of cloudberry juice.'

She leaned over him, took the thermometer out of his mouth, and looked at it. 'Good Heffens! It's at forty degrees.'

By this point the taste of troll saliva was making Samuel look quite a pale shade of green.

'We will haff to call the doctor.'

Samuel panicked. 'No, it's all right. I'm not *that* bad. I get like this sometimes. I always have very short fevers. I'm sure I'll be feeling much better by this afternoon.'

'Ferry well. We will see. But for now you must stay in bed. You haff some cloudberry juice and I will make you some hot lemon and ginger. And you must make sure you are warm in bed. I will tuck in this blanket. Look, it is hanging down. No, we must tuck you in like a caterpillar in the chrysalis. That is what your grandmother used to say to your mother and me, when we were young. Effery night she used to say it. "My two little tucked-in caterpillars, ready to become butterflies in the morning." And your mother said, "But if we are butterflies we will fly away," and of course she was the one who did fly away – when she met your father and moofed to England.' Aunt Eda stood for a while as fond memories glazed her eyes. 'Anyway, where was I? Ah yes, I was going to tuck in this blanket.'

Samuel gulped, but could think of no words to stop his aunt kneeling down and pushing the loose blanket under the bed, leaving Troll-Son exposed.

'Are you all right, Samuel? You look scared.'

'No, I'm fine. Just ill, that's all.'

The blanket was fully tucked in by now and so Aunt Eda stood up and started to leave the room.

Don't turn round, prayed Samuel. He knew that if she turned round, she would have a clear view of the troll under the bed. She stopped at the door but didn't look back. 'I will come back up with the lemon and ginger – and some tablets.'

And then she was gone, leaving Samuel desperately searching for a new place to hide the runaway troll.

Which was tricky, as Troll-Son kept whispering questions up through the mattress.

'Be she Samuel-Mother?' said Troll-Son.

'No. She's my aunt.'

'Where be Samuel-Mother?'

Samuel tried to ignore the questions, but they kept coming.

'Where be Samuel-Mother? Be she with Samuel-Father? Be she here in the house, Samuel Blink? Samuel Blink?'

It was too much. '*Shut up*,' Samuel said, in a whisper that had the force of a shout. '*Just shut up*.' Then, after a moment's silence: 'Why are you here? Why have you run away from your mum and dad?'

Samuel remembered Troll-Mother as quite a strict woman, who had scolded Troll-Son over the smallest things, but she *was* his mother. And if you were lucky enough to have a mother, you didn't run away from her.

You see, Samuel's mother hadn't been perfect. She hadn't been one of those mothers you saw in those movies they show on Christmas Day. She didn't always smile and say the right thing, but she was his mother and it was only when she was gone that he realized her hugs and smiles had been so special. Only now did he understand how her love had kept everything together, in place, where it should be. And the truth was, Samuel had loved her, just as she had loved him, and he would rather have gone back in time to hear his mother in her very worst mood than live another moment in the present without her.

He was thinking this as Troll-Son gave his explanation. 'It be the Betterer.'

'The what?'

'The Betterer. Troll-Mother be making me go to be bettered.'

'Bettered? What do you mean?'

Troll-Son told him about the Bettering Tower, and all he had heard about what happened there. The strict lessons, the Dunking Cage, the medicines, the silent room so quiet it drove you mad.

As he listened, Samuel understood. After all, hadn't his own sister once sought to escape her misery by entering the forest. Wasn't this the same thing, but in reverse?

'All right, I will help you.' And as the words slipped out of his mouth he wondered what, precisely, he was letting himself in for.

A SILK HANDKERCHIEF

As I already mentioned, the Betterer hated the company of Troll-Father and Troll-the-Wisest. For the time being, he could do nothing about Troll-Father. After all, Troll-Son was far more likely to be caught without a struggle if his father were there. But what was the point of having Troll-the-Wisest tagging along?

The Betterer made a mental list (because the Betterer loved lists) of all the reasons Troll-the-Wisest should, indeed, tag along. The list consisted of one reason:

1. Because he is the leader of the Troll Council.

Now, this was quite an important reason. Having the leader of the Troll Council on his side was certainly going to help when they got back to Trollhelm.

But then he made a list of reasons why Troll-the-Wisest should *not* be tagging along and it was considerably longer.

1. He is 738. Even by troll standards, this is old, and it means he slows them down to the pace of an athletic snail.
2. He is too noticeable. He has a hideously lumpy forehead, tattered clothes and a grey beard that reaches down to his knees, all of which would make him stand out in the Outer World.
3. His breath, which was almost as bad as Troll-Mother's, who has the stinkiest breath in the whole of Trollhelm.
4. His annoyingly slow voice.
5. His stupid belief that he is wise just because he has a long beard.
6. His dry, flaky lips, which make the Betterer feel sick.
7. He hasn't had a bath for at least 700 years.
8. He is a weak-minded troll, just like all the others.

9. He is getting too friendly with Troll-Father.
10. He is proving to be unreliable with promises.

It was number 10 in the list that was a particularly pressing problem. You see, after the council meeting the Betterer had had a quiet word with Troll-the-Wisest, suggesting that Troll-Son should stay in the Bettering Tower for the rest of his childhood, to ensure that he didn't run away again. Although the Betterer had specifically made Troll-the-Wisest promise not to mention anything about this until they found Troll-Son, he was already making Troll-Father suspicious.

As Troll-the-Wisest led Troll-Father by the arm, the Betterer hovered quietly behind, listening to their conversation.

'I be missing him so much,' said Troll-Father.

'That be natural,' said Troll-the-Wisest.

'I be thinking of all the times his mother be most awful cross with him and I be doing nothing to be sticking up for him. If . . . *when* we be finding him, I be going to be unmistaking myself.'

'Yes, but–'

'I be going to be doing good fathery things with

him. I be going to take him fishing at Still Lake like I be doing when I be a boy. And he will be having no reason to be running away again.'

'Oh,' said Troll-the-Wisest, who had only been half listening to Troll-Father. 'He won't be running away, not after all that bettering.'

Troll-Father's empty eye-socket narrowed in confusion. 'Bettering?' he said. And then he whispered, so the Betterer couldn't hear (although the Betterer *could* hear every word, as he unplugs his ear-wax every morning): 'Oh, Troll-the-Wisest . . . when we be finding Troll-Son, we won't be sending him to the Betterer. If you be asking me, that be the reason why he be running away in the first place.'

Troll-the-Wisest looked worried, and scratched his beard. 'Well . . . er . . . bettering can be good for a child. It might be what he be needing. P'raps if he be bettered, he be not running away again.'

The Betterer, who was still walking quietly behind, was listening very closely to every word. And as he listened, he pulled a purple silk handkerchief from one of his inside pockets.

'I be hearing what you be saying, Troll-the-Wisest,' said Troll-Father. 'And you be very much wiser than a humble short-beard such as me, but I be knowing my son and I don't be thinking that a bettering be the right thing for him.'

Now it was Troll-the-Wisest's turn to whisper. 'Well, Troll-Father, seeing as you be feeling so strongly on this matter, there be something you should be knowing . . .'

The Betterer kept listening as the hand that wasn't holding the purple handkerchief felt in another inside pocket to find the appropriate medicine.

'Something I should be knowing?' asked Troll-Father, more confused than ever. 'What be that, Troll-the-Wisest?'

'Well,' continued Troll-the-Wisest in the same whisper, 'it might . . . you might . . . the thing be . . . I might be agreeing to something I shouldn't be.'

'I still not be following you, Troll-the-Wisest.'

'You see,' said Troll-the-Wisest, 'the Betterer be telling me that when we be getting back to Trollhelm it be better . . . to . . . kee–'

Troll-the-Wisest felt something cover his face. It was something that felt firm and silky all at once. He could see nothing but purple, and he instantly forgot what he had been saying to Troll-Father. All of a sudden he felt extremely sleepy, as if standing up and talking required the most preposterous amount of effort. He lost hold of Troll-Father's arm and had a vague sensation of someone catching him as he fell backwards to the ground. After that, he was lost in his usual nightmare, where he imagined his beard was shrinking.

'Troll-the-Wisest? Troll-the-Wisest? Where be you?' Troll-Father was feeling blindly to his side, searching the space that only one moment ago had been occupied by the old troll.

The Betterer put his silk purple handkerchief back in his pocket, along with the small jar of Sleeping Salts that he had just used on Troll-the-Wisest.

'Mr Betterer, sir, what be happening to him?'

The Betterer cleared his throat. 'He appears to have collapsed.'

'Collapsed? Oh, flenk! Do pardon me, sir, I be not meaning to swear . . . It be just I be worried about Troll-the-Wisest.'

'I can assure you, Troll-Father, I am very worried myself,' lied the Betterer. He then crouched down and had the pleasure of slapping Troll-the-Wisest on the face. 'Can you hear me? Oh, wise one, can you hear me? Wake up! Wake up!' The Betterer kept slapping the old troll, knowing very well that the salts would ensure he wouldn't be wake up for at least a day.

'Oh no,' said Troll-Father in a most worried voice. 'Be he dead?'

'Dead? Why, no. He's not dead. Listen, you can hear him snoring.'

He stopped slapping to let Troll-Father hear the loud snores.

'I be hearing but not understanding. He be only talking to me one moment and then, right in the middle of a sentence, he be falling to the ground and sleeping. It be making no sense.'

The Betterer looked at Troll-Father and knew he was going to have his work cut out: Troll-Father was growing more suspicious by the minute. 'He is a very old troll, and he has walked a lot further than he's used to. And it's broad daylight, which he's never seen for years. Perhaps it's had a funny effect on hi–'

He stopped because Troll-Father was now crouching down and tapping Troll-the-Wisest's shoulder. 'Troll-the-Wisest?' he said, in a much gentler voice than the Betterer had used. 'Troll-the-Wisest? Be you all right?'

Troll-the-Wisest snored his answer.

'He's all right,' said the Betterer. 'He's just having a nap.'

'Well, we should be staying here until he be waking up.'

'Well, Troll-Father, yes, that is one possibility.'

'And what then be the other? We can't be just leaving him.'

'Now, I'm as worried about him as you are. But he is clearly very tired, and is in such a deep sleep that I don't think he'll wake up at least until nightfall. By which time it might be too late.'

Troll-Father's mouth and eye-socket both opened so wide that if there hadn't been a nose between them they would have formed a figure eight. 'Too late? What be your meaning, Mr Betterer?'

'I would rather find your son alive than–'

'*Dead?*'

'Oh, Troll-Father,' whined the Betterer, pretending to be on the verge of tears. 'Don't even think it! Please, it's too much for me to imagine what might happen to him if we wait any longer . . . But of course, if you want to wait for Troll-the-Wisest to wake up, then I perfectly understand. And I'm sure your wife will as well when you return home empty-handed.'

It was working, the Betterer realized as he watched the colour drain from Troll-Father's cheeks. Troll-Father could only imagine how many clouts he

would get from his wife if he was unsuccessful again.

'But . . . but . . . but . . . we can't be leaving him here.'

'Why not? The forest is perfectly safe. In fact, he's far safer here than he would be in the Outer World. And if we can find Troll-Son and come straight back, then he'll probably be snoring away, right in this spot.'

Troll-Father considered for a while. The Betterer did have a very good point, and even though it seemed strange that someone who once couldn't even say hello to him was going to such lengths to save his son, he supposed he should be thankful. He was reluctant to travel without Troll-the-Wisest, but what could he do?

'Yes, Mr Betterer. You be right. We should be keeping on going without him.'

The Betterer smiled as he heard these words. *You're even more stupid than you look*, he thought.

He grimaced and bit his tongue as Troll-Father's grubby hand took his arm. They carried on walking, letting Troll-the-Wisest's snores fade behind them.

THE ART OF HIDING TROLLS

Samuel had once enjoyed having days off school. To be at home on his computer, or watching TV, when he knew he should have been suffering the many tortures offered by the rugby field on a frosty January morning, was a pleasure like no other. Even on those days when his mother was home and he had to stay in bed, it had been quite lovely to glance at the clock by his bed and wonder precisely which teacher's lesson he was managing to avoid.

But staying off school with a troll to hide was an entirely different matter. Especially as both Aunt Eda and Uncle Henrik were in the house the whole time. A house that had the creakiest floorboards in the whole of Norway (which, as they don't tell you in the guidebooks, is the land of creaky floorboards).

Indeed, there were quite a few more close shaves that day. Five, to be precise:

CLOSE SHAVE NUMBER ONE – THE WAR-DROBE

The blankets were tucked in. Troll-Son was exposed. Samuel needed to move him before Aunt Eda came upstairs with the hot lemon and ginger.

'Quick, the wardrobe,' Samuel hissed. He could hear his aunt talking to Martha as she finished her breakfast downstairs.

'War-drobe?'

'Yes, the wardrobe.'

Troll-Son was confused. He had no idea what a wardrobe was, as trolls only have one outfit that they never change. When they grow out of it, they simply sew on more sackcloth. Troll-Son had worn the same tunic since he was a baby, and it now had a variety of patches that he had stitched on himself.

'That thing over there,' Samuel explained. 'Follow me.'

Slowly Troll-Son crawled out on his elbows and stood by the bed, facing the human he thought would be his friend. He was roughly the same height as Samuel, though with a wider head and larger nose and ears. (While we are on the subject of ears it is worth noting that they weren't in any way symmetrical. I should probably have mentioned this earlier, but I was too distracted by the fact that he had only one eye. Anyhow, I will mention it now. Troll-Son had very mismatched ears, by human standards at least. His left ear was very small, and high up, while his right one was larger and lower down. In fact, the whole shape of his head was rather odd. It was a lopsided, round-cornered, triangular head.)

'Quick . . . in there . . .' said Samuel, pointing to the wardrobe.

Aunt Eda was climbing the stairs as Troll-Son squeezed into the wardrobe. 'It's all right,' Samuel said, noting the fear contained in the eyeball that peeped out from behind the clothes. 'I promise you'll be OK.'

As he hurried back into bed, Aunt Eda opened the door. 'Right, one hot lemon and ginger . . .'

CLOSE SHAVE NUMBER TWO – MARTHA GETS HER COAT

Five minutes later, Martha finished all her gjetost cheese and flat-bread and went upstairs to fetch her coat. But not the coat she'd left hanging by the door. No, it was so cold outside she needed her big, thick, padded winter coat. From the wardrobe.

'What are you doing?' asked Samuel as he watched his sister open the wardrobe door.

'I'm getting my coat.'

'No. You can't.'

'What are you on about?'

Samuel didn't know what to say. 'There's a . . . a . . . mouse . . . I mean, a rat . . .'

But Martha was already flicking through her side of the wardrobe, looking for her coat. She turned round to face her brother. Samuel could see an eye blinking at him from the darkness beyond her clothes.

'A *rat*?'

'Yes. I saw it near the wardrobe.'

'Oh well,' said Martha.

'Oh *well*? Aren't you scared?'

Martha shook her head. She had witnessed her parents being crushed to death. She had been locked up in a huldre prison. A witch had turned her into a bird. The Changemaker had tried to murder her. A rat couldn't frighten her now.

Samuel needed a new tactic. 'I'll get it,' he said. 'I'll get your coat.'

He was out of bed, pushing her back onto the landing.

'Hey, what are you doing? I can get my own coat.'

Samuel slipped the coat off its hanger and threw it to Martha. She sniffed it. 'It's that boiled vegetable smell again.'

Samuel shrugged.

'What's going on?' asked Martha, putting on her coat. 'What's up with you? What are you hiding? And why are you pretending to be ill?'

Samuel wanted to tell her. After all, you can lose people through secrets as easily as you can lose them in forests. But he couldn't do it. Martha was too friendly with that Cornelia girl. And that Cornelia girl wasn't to be trusted – Samuel just knew it.

'I'm not hiding anything . . . and I *am* ill,' he whispered.

The words seemed to upset his sister, who suddenly seemed a hundred miles away even though she was right in front of him.

'No,' she whispered back. 'You're not.'

And she turned round and went downstairs, leaving Samuel feeling more alone than ever.

CLOSE SHAVE NUMBER THREE – THE MYSTERIOUS BELCHING (AND SAMUEL'S DRASTIC ACTION)

Aunt Eda had taken Martha to school. Samuel could breathe a sigh of relief. Well, he thought he could.

After all, Uncle Henrik normally just sat downstairs for an hour reading the *Aftenposten* in the rocking chair. But not this morning.

Samuel was just about to get out of bed and see how Troll-Son was coping amid the darkness and the coat hangers when he heard Uncle Henrik coming.

'Samuel?' he called.

'Yes? What?'

'I hear you are having problems with a rodent,' he said, now in the room.

'Er . . .' Samuel cursed his sister. If she thought he'd been lying about the rat, why tell Uncle Henrik?

'Well, I can tell you it is very unlikely to be a rat. Rats are not creatures that like the pure mountain air you find around here. If it is a rat, it must be from Oslo or Bergen. Maybe it has a pen pal here and has come to stay.' Uncle Henrik laughed his gentle laugh. 'A rat with a pen pal! Maybe they write each other letters!'

Samuel realized this was his uncle's idea of a joke, so he tried to laugh with him. But all he was really thinking was: *There's a troll in the wardrobe! There's a troll in the wardrobe! There's a troll in the wardrobe!*

Uncle Henrik was holding a rolled-up newspaper. 'There is of course a species of rat called the Norway rat, otherwise known as the brown rat, but it does not originate from Norway. Did you know that?'

Samuel shook his head, and watched as Uncle Henrik's eyes followed the skirting board around the room.

'No, it is much more likely to be a wood mouse, or even a vole, but I don't know how they would have climbed the–'

Uncle Henrik stopped. He was sure he had heard something behind him, coming directly from the wardrobe. And it wasn't the kind of noise a rodent would make, either. No. It was a belch.

Samuel had heard it too, and couldn't help rolling his eyes. *How hard can it be to stay still and quiet in a wardrobe?* he wondered.

Actually, though, if you are a troll, it is much harder to stay still and quiet than you imagine. Trolls, you see, are much more likely than human beings to belch, or sneeze, or break wind, or make any other noise not normally expected of a wardrobe. They are, in truth, gassier, slurpier, sniffier creatures who are born with no shame of the body and its noises.

'What *was* that?' asked Uncle Henrik.

'What was what?'

'That noise . . . It wasn't a rodent, that is for certain.'

'I didn't hear it,' lied Samuel.

And then – just as Uncle Henrik was about to open the wardrobe door – Samuel knew he only had one option. He sighed, and forced himself to do it.

'Sit!' he ordered. *'Sit!'*

And it worked. Uncle Henrik slipped into a canine trance and followed the command without thinking. He got down on his knees with his hands resting on the floor in canine style, as if he were still an elkhound.

'Come here,' Samuel said, in the same strict dog-owner tones.

And Uncle Henrik stayed in the same trance as he walked over on all fours.

Samuel felt a bit guilty, treating his uncle as if he were a dog, but it was the only thing he could think of. However, he knew the trance was lifting – he could see it in Uncle Henrik's eyes.

'What am I doing?' asked Uncle Henrik, realizing he was on his hands and knees.

'You were looking for a mouse,' said Samuel.

'A mouse?'

'Yes, a mouse. I thought I saw one. But you have searched everywhere.'

'It could have come from the wardrobe.'

Samuel panicked. 'You've looked in there . . . You've looked everywhere. I think I must have imagined it.'

Uncle Henrik stood up. He was clearly confused, but had no memory of the belching wardrobe. 'Right, well, in that case I suppose I will leave you to get some rest. Let me know if you see it again.'

'Yes,' said Samuel. 'I will.'

And as Uncle Henrik left the room, he glanced suspiciously at the wardrobe, just as you might glance at a stranger you thought you recognized. But the wardrobe stayed silent, and Uncle Henrik left the room with his rolled-up newspaper still in his hand.

CLOSE SHAVE NUMBER FOUR – THE ATTIC

Samuel went over to open the wardrobe. When the light flooded in, Troll-Son noticed something in the wardrobe. It was the red sweater and blue jeans Samuel had been wearing when he had stayed in Trollhelm.

'Samuel Blink clothes,' he said.

Samuel ignored this, and tried to think what he should do. The first thing was to work out where Aunt Eda and Uncle Henrik were, so he went onto the landing and tried to listen. After a while he realized Uncle Henrik was doing the washing-up in the kitchen while Aunt Eda was back and getting ready to hang the laundry on the line.

Samuel went back into the bedroom and gasped as he saw Troll-Son, out of the wardrobe – dressed in his red sweater and blue jeans. He was standing in front of the mirror, trying to brush his hair in a side parting – exactly like Samuel's.

'What are you doing?' asked Samuel.

'What . . . are . . . you . . . doing?' copied Troll-Son.

'Why are you in my clothes?'

'Why . . . are . . . you . . . in . . . my . . . clothes?'

'Stop copying me.' Samuel said crossly.

'I be sorry, Samuel Blink.' Troll-Son began to take off the sweater.

'No, there's no time. We need to get you out of this room. They'll find you if you stay in here. You've got to go to the attic.'

'Attic?'

Samuel pointed upwards.

'Be it in the sky?'

'No, it be – *is* up a ladder. Now, quick, while Aunt Eda and Uncle Henrik are both downstairs. Come on. Follow me. But be as quiet you can. No burping!'

So Samuel beckoned Troll-Son towards the ladder that led up to the attic. Troll-Son looked petrified, but agreed to follow Samuel up into the dimly lit room, which was full of dust, cobwebs, old tea-chests and framed pictures of Uncle Henrik from his ski jumping days.

'Right,' said Samuel. 'This is where you're going to stay until we can think of a better option. There's an old mattress over there that you can sleep on, and I'll bring you food when I can . . .'

Troll-Son nodded, but looked scared.

'Samuel? Samuel?' It was Uncle Henrik from downstairs. 'Do you want another hot drink?'

'I've got to go,' Samuel whispered, and headed back down through the hatch. 'I'll be back later.'

CLOSE SHAVE NUMBER FIVE – THE THREE-TOED FOOTPRINT

Aunt Eda was outside, hanging up a pair of her long-johns, when she noticed a strange footprint on the ground. A three-toed footprint, like that belonging to a troll.

'Henrik, come outside and look at this.'

And Henrik agreed. It *did* look suspicious. So they went upstairs to have a word with Samuel.

'No, I haven't seen any troll around here,' he said.

'Well, if you do, you must tell us straight away,' said Aunt Eda. 'We would be in ferry serious trouble if we effer got caught with a troll on the premises. You understand that, don't you?'

'Yes,' said Samuel.

'We must haff nothing to do with the forest. If a creature effer left the forest then we would haff to make sure it went back to the forest. You do understand?'

'I understand,' he said, and added a cough as he remembered he was supposed to be ill.

'All right, Eda,' said Uncle Henrik softly. 'I am sure Samuel is telling the truth.'

And Samuel tried to look as innocent as possible while he pulled his bed-sheets up higher, making sure they covered Troll-Son's discarded tunic.

A LITTLE CONVERSATION

As the two trolls walked through the forest, the Betterer found himself looking around at the scenery. He had never been to this part of the forest and considered it to be exquisitely beautiful.

You see, this was one of the reasons why the Betterer believed he was above the other trolls of Trollhelm. He could appreciate beautiful things. And the late afternoon sunlight twinkling down through the thick pine trees truly was a beautiful thing. It had been so long since the Betterer had been out in daylight. Of course, it had been so long since Troll-Father had been in daylight too, but the Betterer knew that even if he'd had an eye to see with, the beauty would have gone unappreciated. Not that the Betterer minded. He *loved* being better than grubby, dim-witted trolls like Troll-Father. Indeed, he was in such a good mood he even favoured his companion with a little conversation.

'So, Troll-Father, there is one thing I don't understand.'

'What be that, Mr Betterer, sir?'

'Why were you so convinced, right from the start, that Troll-Son had gone to the Outer World? After all, the forest is safe now. He might have gone to live with a pixie, or back there, with the huldres.' He strained his ears and could hear the distant sound of the huldre-folk, singing their hymns to the sun.

'No, he be in the Outer World, Mr Betterer, I be sure of that.'

'Yes, but why? Why did he want to see this human boy again?'

Troll-Father sighed, and scratched his beard. 'I don't be knowing, Mr Betterer, sir.' He could hear the distant singing of the huldre-folk too, and the sound seemed to carry with it a new wisdom that gave Troll-Father a clearer understanding of the situation. 'The thing is, Mr Betterer, if I be being most honest with you, I be having to say that Troll-Son be never a happy boy. He be always wanting something he be not having, and ever since he be seeing Samuel Blink with all his fancy human manners, he be wanting to be something he can never be.'

'I don't quite follow,' said the Betterer as he watched Troll-Father bang his knee against a low branch.

'Ow!'

'Oh, I am terribly sorry, I didn't see it there,' the Betterer said, smiling as he lied. 'Do go on.'

'What be I saying?' asked Troll-Father, rubbing his knee.

'About Samuel Blink.'

'Yes, well, I be thinking that Troll-Son be so impressed by the human boy that he be wanting to be human himself.'

The Betterer went quiet. He remembered that day many, many years ago when he had been told he was a troll. All those happy years believing his foolish parents! The discovery that he wasn't a human had been the most difficult thing he'd ever had to deal with. You would think then, being the kind reader that you are, that he would feel some sympathy for Troll-Son. But he didn't. The Betterer had burned with shame at his own stupidity for believing he was human; and for a one-eyed troll child to imagine the humans in the Outer World would ever accept him was plain ridiculous.

But then something Troll-Father had said echoed in his mind.

Ever since he be seeing Samuel Blink with all his fancy human manners . . .

As it echoed, another plan took hold in his mind and began to grow. Wouldn't he be a better Betterer if he had a human to observe and study and use as an example? Someone he could keep with him, locked in the Bettering Chamber. A human. A clean, unlumpy, well-mannered human. Someone he could question and examine and experiment on. Yes, he would be able to study precisely how humans talk, how they wash, how they dress, how they comb their hair.

Yes. This was it!

The perfect tool for bettering.

A real-life human boy to copy.

Samuel Blink, he thought to himself as the faint melodies of singing huldres vanished into the forest behind him. *Your future is mine.*

THE WEEPING

'I don't suppose you've changed your mind, Henrik?' said Mr Myklebust, the night of the sleepover. 'About telling me what happened in the forest?'

Uncle Henrik shook his head. 'I'm sorry, Magnus.'

Mr Myklebust let out a sigh so long you would have thought he had a puncture. 'I see, I see . . . Then maybe I will have to see for myself.'

Of course, Mr Myklebust was bluffing. He had absolutely no intention of heading into the forest. He was scared enough of the dentist, let alone the deadly creatures people talked about. He didn't *believe* in these creatures, but he didn't *disbelieve* in them enough to see for himself.

And as for Aunt Eda and Uncle Henrik, well, they guessed that Mr Myklebust was bluffing.

'Very well,' said Aunt Eda, her thumb pointing over her shoulder to the forest behind her. 'Take a look. Go on. Go tomorrow. I could make you a packed lunch.'

Mr Myklebust stared over at the dark trees that stood like mysterious soldiers at the top of the grassy slope, waiting for the order to charge. He felt a cold shiver run through him at the thought of stepping into the shadowy darkness between the trunks.

'No,' he said quietly. 'No. I will find another way.' And then he looked at Cornelia, and winked. 'Now, you'll be a good girl, won't you? And when you come home, you'll tell me everything.'

'Yes, Father, don't worry, I'll tell you everything.'

Aunt Eda and Uncle Henrik gave each other a confused frown, as if they had the feeling that something was going on but they weren't sure what. Martha, of course, didn't think anything at all was going on – but then she couldn't understand a word that was being said.

'We'll drop her back home tomorrow,' said Aunt Eda, ushering Mr Myklebust out into the hallway.

'Bye, my princess,' he called as he stepped out of the door.

'Bye, Daddy.'

And when the door closed, Uncle Henrik and Aunt

Eda both took big breaths as they braced themselves for an evening of Cornelia.

Martha and Cornelia were both in the spare bedroom, and directly under the part of the attic where Troll-Son was hiding. The door to the spare room was open, and Cornelia had a foghorn of a voice, so Samuel was able to hear every single word as he lay in bed.

'You do know what people say about that forest?' she said.

'No,' lied Martha unconvincingly.

'They say it's full of strange creatures. Like the huldre-folk, and witches, and trolls.'

There was a silence, which Martha broke by saying something too quiet for Samuel to catch.

As he strained to hear, he thought of his sister's terrible track record at keeping secrets. There was the time, for instance, when she had asked Samuel if he was looking forward to the surprise birthday party.

'Whose surprise birthday party?' he had asked.

'Yours, silly,' she had said, before realizing her mistake.

Or the time she had told their mother about the secret holiday in France their father had booked for them all. Or when she had told her father how much had been spent on their mother's 'Special Theatre Dress'. Or when she had told Samuel that she had eaten his Easter egg after previously blaming it on the neighbours' dog. Or when she told one of her best friends that Samuel used to sing lullabies in his sleep ('Ring a ring o' roses' was his favourite).

'Well,' Cornelia went on, 'a lot of stupid people still believe in these creatures. Some say that trolls arrived in Norway at the end of the last Ice Age. Some people say they are descended from giants. You see, Norwegians used to believe that the world was created from a giant called Ymir, who lived in Jotunheimen – where all the giants lived – and they think that Ymir was killed by Odin, a Norse god, who murdered him with his spear. I read about it in my encyclopaedia, you see. They're meant to have once lived in every forest in Norway, but now people say they just live in *Morke Skog* – Shadow Forest – because that is the darkest of the forests. The trees are so tall and the branches are so close together that there is hardly any light there.'

'It's not *that* dark,' Samuel heard his sister say.

Martha, what are you doing?

'How do you know?' was Cornelia's inevitable question.

'I mean, it doesn't *look* like it would be that dark when I see it from the window, or when I'm out on the grass.'

There was another silence, longer this time, and Samuel could feel that the air – even in his room – was stiff with tension.

'What happened to your Uncle Henrik?' asked Cornelia eventually, and Samuel detected definite menace in her question.

'I don't know,' said Martha, struggling to keep the secret inside her. 'He doesn't talk about it.'

'He disappeared for ten years. That's what my father told me. I think your aunt deserves an explanation.'

'She doesn't want one, I don't think.'

Well lied, thought Samuel.

But Cornelia kept going, trying to weaken Martha with her knowledge. 'Personally, I think trolls are no more than archetypes that people want to believe in so they can project all their fears onto something outside themselves, but really they come from inside their own minds. I read a book about it, by Carl Gustav Jung. Not that you'd have heard of *him*. He was a famous psychiatrist. It would be good, though, wouldn't it, to know what was really in the forest? I'd *love* to meet someone who could tell me what was there. Wouldn't you?'

Martha's chatterbox mouth was weakening under all this pressure. 'Well . . . I . . .'

Both girls suddenly fell quiet, and Samuel knew why. They'd heard something. And Samuel heard it too.

It was a kind of whimpering, which at first Samuel thought was that of a dog. He wondered if Uncle Henrik was having a funny turn. But then he realized: it was coming from the attic.

Oh no, thought Samuel. He even whispered it out loud: 'Oh no. *Troll-Son.*'

'What was that?' asked Cornelia.

'I don't know,' said Martha, because she really didn't.

'It sounded like someone *weeping* . . . Let's go and have a look.'

'No, I don't think we should,' said Martha. But Cornelia was already out of the door.

Samuel's heart was racing. He had to get out of bed. He had to stop Cornelia climbing up the ladder. But then he had another idea.

He took a deep breath and began to cry. They

weren't real tears, of course, but they were loud. Louder than Troll-Son's. And soon they had the desired effect, which was still rather embarrassing.

'Look – it's your brother,' said Cornelia, with a mischievous smile on her face. 'He's *crying*.'

'Samuel?' Martha rushed into the room. 'Why are you crying?'

'I'm . . . just . . . thinking about . . . how I've . . . got no friends . . . and you've got Cornelia,' he said, wishing he'd been able to think of a less pathetic reason to be sad. But he knew he had to carry on pretending to cry, just so long as Troll-Son was weeping in the attic. 'Oh, I'm so sad . . . I'm so sad . . . I can't help it . . . I'm so sad . . .'

And then he felt guilty, and began to feel really cross with Troll-Son, because his fake tears were creating real ones in Martha's eyes.

'Samuel, it's all right,' she kept saying. 'It's all right, don't worry . . . I'm still your best friend. Sisters can be best friends, you know.'

He stopped whimpering for a second, and realized Troll-Son had calmed down. 'I feel a bit better now,' he said.

And then they were called down for their supper.

Cornelia turned as Samuel followed Martha out of

the door. 'What a baby,' she told him, in a voice too quiet for Martha to hear. 'I'd rather not have a brother than a wimp like you.'

'I know what you're up to,' Samuel said, in his normal voice. 'And it won't work. You won't find out anything.'

'Hmm, we'll see,' she said with a mischievous smile. 'We'll see.'

BROTHERS AND SISTERS

Samuel knew Aunt Eda was a little suspicious about how his fever had miraculously disappeared on a Friday evening, but he needed to keep a close eye on Cornelia to see what she was up to. He observed as she charmed her way through their late supper, expressing not only her love of herrings, but also her interest in ski jumping.

'Uncle Henrik won a silver medal at the Olympics,' Martha told her excitedly. 'He was really famous.'

'Well, I wouldn't say that,' said Uncle Henrik.

'What did it feel like, when you used to jump?' Cornelia asked him.

'Yes, what did it feel like?' parroted Martha, ignoring Samuel as he rolled his eyes.

'It felt peaceful,' he answered. 'I heard nothing. I saw

the white snow below me, but that was all. It was the most magical kind of feeling. To be truly free, soaring through the air, imagining you could stay flying for ever. Leaving all your problems on the ground.'

Aunt Eda laughed and pretended to be cross. 'All your *problems*, Henrik? I like that ferry much, I must say.'

Uncle Henrik rubbed her arm to reassure her. 'Not you, Eda. I didn't mean you. If it hadn't been for you, I would never have landed!'

Everyone laughed. Well, everyone apart from Samuel. In fact, he didn't make a noise throughout the whole meal. No one seemed to notice. He just sat there, concentrating on his food, as the darkness fell outside the window. A darkness that rubbed out the grass and the trees and could make you forget anything existed outside the house.

When Martha went into the kitchen to fetch some pickles, she was so excited and happy at having her friend to stay she even *sang* her way there. It was a song she had heard in the forest, from the jolly tomtegubb she had met, but Samuel didn't know this. All he knew was that the song sounded very happy. When she returned to the table, Samuel looked at her. For weeks after their parents died, Martha hadn't said a word. Not a single noise had left her mouth. Samuel had begged and prayed for her to speak – he had badly needed someone to talk to, but she wouldn't.

Now, though, she was talking and laughing and singing as she had done before. And Samuel knew he should have felt happy that she was back in the world of words and laughter, but he didn't.

In a strange way, it made his parents feel further away. As though the shock and sadness he and Martha had felt when they died were a way of keeping them. Now he saw his sister acting normally, he felt as if someone had cut the last string between earth and heaven.

After supper, while Cornelia was in the spare bedroom changing into her pyjamas, Samuel had a quiet word with his sister.

'You haven't told her anything, have you?'

'About what?'

'About the forest.'

'No. Course not.'

'You've remembered what Aunt Eda said? About how important it is that we don't talk about it?'

'Yes. Course. I'm not stupid. There's nothing to worry about. And anyway, Cornelia's nice.'

'Whatever.'

'She *is*. And by the way, jealousy doesn't suit you.'

Samuel coughed, as if something had got stuck down his throat. 'Jealous? *Jealous?* What, you think I'd want to be friends with some stuck-up, two-faced, spoiled brat?'

Martha said nothing. She just stormed upstairs to be with Cornelia. Samuel went into the kitchen.

'What's the matter?' Uncle Henrik was drying up a plate.

'Nothing,' Samuel said, feeling cross with himself. 'It was just . . . nothing.'

Uncle Henrik smiled softly. 'Just brothers and sisters.'

Samuel nodded. 'Yes. Brothers and sisters.'

THE TROLL THAT WENT BUMP IN THE NIGHT

Samuel was the only one still awake. Well, the only *human* still awake. He could hear the odd creak above him, and wondered what Troll-Son was doing. Why couldn't he just lie down on the mattress and be still?

Maybe he should go and see to him. No. It might only wake people up.

'Just be quiet,' Samuel whispered up to the ceiling.

He was beginning to wonder if it would be such a bad thing for Aunt Eda and Uncle Henrik to find out about Troll-Son. After all, what had Samuel got to lose? So far, since Troll-Son had been here Samuel had been forced to lie about feeling ill, share a thermometer with the most disgusting mouth you could imagine, treat his uncle like a dog, give up his favourite jeans and sweater, and cry in front of Cornelia. It was true that he did feel a bit sorry for Troll-Son. And the Betterer certainly did sound rather nasty. But so what? It wasn't as though Troll-Son was a human. Most people don't even *believe* in trolls. OK, so Samuel had failed to make any Norwegian friends, but surely he could do better than a one-eyed troll boy who had to say 'Samuel Blink' in every sentence. No, he would tell Aunt Eda and Uncle Henrik about him tomorrow, when Cornelia had gone home. And then Troll-Son would be sent back to the forest.

So what if Samuel felt guilty? Yes, he probably should never have helped Troll-Son hide. And yes, Aunt Eda had been right: *If we don't effer cause trouble with the forest, the forest won't effer cause trouble with us.*

But now Samuel had learned his lesson. He wouldn't *ever* go back into the forest. And anyway, he was sure he could live with a bit of guilt if it meant never having to taste troll saliva again.

Yet even so, he knew Troll-Son must stay a secret so long as Cornelia was in the house. Who knew what kind of trouble would be caused if she found out? So Samuel winced at every creak above him. He looked around at the room in the darkness. At Martha's empty bed, at the wardrobe, at the mirror, at the vertical rows of flowers on the wallpaper, which in this light could just as easily have been bars in a prison cell.

He imagined for a moment what it would be like to have no one at all. Not just no parents, but no Martha either, and no Aunt Eda or Uncle Henrik as well. And for the present contents of this room to be the contents of the entire world. There would be no point to a life like that, he realized. It would be like a word existing without a language. It would have no meaning. Without other people, he realized, you could never truly exist. Well, you could *exist* – you could carry on breathing, and your heart would carry on beating, but it wouldn't be a life worth having. Life was other people. He realized that now. It was the moments you shared. That's how you got to be happy. That's how you discovered who you were. Not by lying awake in an empty room with a guilty secret creaking above your head. And the sooner he could be free of the secret, the better.

It was precisely then, right at the moment this thought arrived in his mind, that it happened. Samuel heard an almighty thump outside on the landing, as though something had crashed through the roof and onto the floor outside the bathroom.

Troll-Son, was Samuel's first thought.

And he was right.

You see, Troll-Son had been pacing the attic for hours. He didn't like it up there. At sunset he had wiped some dust off the windowpane and worked out how high up he was. His eye had followed the descending slope of the roof to the rich green grass far below – grass that led to the silvery stillness of the fjord. And he had felt terrified. So terrified he had begun to weep.

He knew what Samuel had told him, but he couldn't do it. It simply wasn't natural for a troll to be so high up. That is why, with the exception of the Betterer, trolls only live in one-storey dwellings. They believe a troll's place is firmly on the ground, just as a bird's place is in the sky. Even if they had the brains, you would never find a troll wanting to build an aeroplane or a spaceship. You see, trolls have none of those human cravings for highness. They are low creatures, of earth and stone, who have no understanding of the laws of gravity.

If they see they are high up, they want to be lower down. It's as simple as that. Troll-Son had tried to be brave. And he certainly didn't want Samuel to be cross with him. But it was no good. He couldn't take it any more. He had to go down, back to Samuel's bedroom.

So he had slowly opened the hatch door and stared for a while at the rectangle of light in the floor. He could see the ladder, and the carpet it led down to, but he didn't really know how he should begin his descent.

He wished Samuel were there to help him, but he knew he couldn't call for him to come without getting into all sorts of trouble. So he put a foot on the ladder's top rung. And then, as he lowered his other foot to join the first, he didn't think to crouch or balance himself by leaning on the attic floor.

So needless to say, after about three steps Troll-Son lost his footing and fell the rest of the way down to the landing. He was hurt, but he managed to stop himself from screaming by biting down on his hand.

He saw Samuel in his pyjamas come rushing towards him. He was beckoning madly, and mouthing words Troll-Son couldn't understand.

Samuel grabbed Troll-Son by the sweater – which was of course *Samuel's* sweater – and yanked him into the bedroom. The sweater was ripped at the elbows and back, as it was a rather tight fit, but Samuel had more pressing matters to think about.

'Get back under my bed,' he said in a sharp whisper as he heard Aunt Eda's footsteps out on the landing.

Samuel had another plan. He waited until Troll-Son was under the bed and then he walked out of the room with his eyes closed and his arms out in front of him.

'Samuel!' said his aunt, shaking his arm. '*Samuel!* Wake up! Wake up!'

And so Samuel blearily opened his eyes, as though he had been sleeping. 'I had a dream,' he said wearily. 'I dreamed I was upstairs in the attic and that I fell down a hole . . .'

Aunt Eda looked up at the open hatch door. She checked Samuel for bruises. 'It is a wonder you are not more hurt,' she said. 'It must be to do with your feefer. When you are ill, it can have ferry strange effects on your sleeping.'

Martha, Cornelia and Uncle Henrik were now also out on the landing, having heard the same loud noise.

'What has happened?' asked Uncle Henrik.

'Nothing – it's all right,' said Aunt Eda, catching Cornelia's eye. 'I'll tell you later. Honestly, you can all go back to bed.'

And so they did. Everyone went back to bed,

including Samuel. He lay there, listening to the heavy breathing of the troll under his bed.

'I think you should go back in the wardrobe,' he told Troll-Son. 'Until Cornelia goes. Then I'm going to have to tell Aunt—'

The heavy breathing had become mild snoring. Troll-Son, having spent so long awake, was now eventually drifting off. And the sound of his gentle snores had an almost hypnotic effect on Samuel, dimming the bright worries in his mind, and sending him to sleep.

MARTHA'S DISCOVERY

At ten to seven in the morning Martha went into their bedroom to look for her hairbrush. You see, Martha's hair in the morning was a frightful sight, and she really thought it would be better for her new best friend not to think that she looked like a human palm tree every morning.

So there she was, creeping around the room while Troll-Son and Samuel were asleep, trying to work out where she'd left it. She looked on her side table . . . on top of the chest of drawers . . . And it was then that she noticed that strange smell again. Like school dinners.

Perhaps herrings didn't agree with Samuel's stomach. Anyway, she had a hairbrush to find so she didn't think too much about it. Nor did she think too much about Samuel's snoring, which was certainly unusual – something she had never noticed before. But then she spotted it. The hairbrush. Lying on the carpet between the two beds.

She crouched down, picked it up and, as she stood up again, realized she might have seen something. Something under Samuel's bed, lying on the carpet.

At first she thought it was a bag or a sack of some sort, and she wondered what Samuel was keeping in it. So she knelt down and pressed her cheek against the floor to have a look.

At that moment Troll-Son's eye blinked open.

'Aaaarghh!' screamed Martha, in shock.

'Aaaarghh!' screamed Troll-Son as he woke up to see this screaming human girl.

'What?!' shouted Samuel, sitting bolt upright in bed as the two screams blasted away his dreams.

And then, in no time at all, several pairs of footsteps were running along the landing: everyone was desperate to see what was going on.

CORNELIA THE SPY

Samuel placed a hand over Martha's mouth. 'It's OK,' he said. 'It's just a troll. *You can't tell Cornelia.* Do you understand?'

And during this time – during those thirteen words issuing from Samuel's mouth – Aunt Eda had arrived, wearing her long white nightie. She was closely followed by Uncle Henrik in his striped pyjamas, rubbing the sleep out of his eyes.

'What is the matter?' asked Aunt Eda, switching on the main light. 'Samuel, what on earth are you doing to your sister?'

Uncle Henrik sniffed the air. 'I can smell cabbage,' he said.

Samuel took his hand away from Martha's mouth.

'It's nothing,' she said, turning to her aunt. 'I was

just looking for my hairbrush and I . . . and I . . . banged my toe against the bed. That's all.'

Samuel looked at his aunt and uncle, and prayed for their eyes not to lower. If they saw what was under his bed it would surely lead to even more of a commotion, and instantly alert Cornelia.

Actually, while we are on the subject of Cornelia, I should tell you that she was already awake at this point. In fact, she had woken five minutes earlier. She had been in the middle of a very strange dream in which she was the youngest ever Queen of Norway, and she was sitting on a throne in the royal palace of Oslo in front of two guillotines. 'Yes, they have kept secrets from me – off with their heads,' she had said to the executioner, who released the blades. Then, a moment later, the heads of Samuel and Martha had been chopped off, falling into two baskets to the applause of thousands of people, who took to throwing banknotes at the young queen. 'All hail our wise and beautiful queen!' they shouted. And Cornelia just sat there, gloating, staring at the two heads, and thousands and thousands of kroner rained down on her.

This was the exact point the dream ended and Cornelia woke up to see Martha slip out of the door. She looked at her watch, which had glow-in-the-dark hands, and saw it was only a quarter to seven.

I wonder where she's going?

Cornelia waited in bed for a couple of minutes but didn't hear the toilet flush. Then, ever so quietly, she peeled back the covers, slipped out of bed and went to the door. Peering out onto the landing, she saw that Samuel's door was open, and remembered that it had been closed when they went to bed.

So, that's where she is, thought Cornelia.

And as soon as she realized that, she decided to investigate. So she tiptoed out onto the landing, and made her way towards the open door. The floorboards were very creaky, as she had discovered in the middle of the night when she had gone to the toilet, so she made each step as slow and light as possible.

And then she heard it.

The scream.

'Aaaaarghh!'

It was Martha.

Cornelia froze. She wanted to know what was going on, but didn't want to risk her life. (It had sounded like a life-in-danger sort of scream.) So she stood perfectly still out on the landing and watched Martha's aunt and uncle appear from their room and rush to see what was happening.

Neither Aunt Eda nor Uncle Henrik had noticed Cornelia standing behind them on the landing. So, once they had entered the bedroom, Cornelia waited a moment, then thought of all the ponies her father would buy her if she discovered something important. And she knew there *was* something important to discover. She knew it because Martha was a particularly bad liar, who wasn't at all convincing when she said: 'I don't know anything about the forest.'

No. Cornelia was convinced Martha *did* know something about the forest. And she also had a sneaking suspicion that the scream she had just heard had something to do with it.

And, now she came to think of it, the scream had sounded rather strange. Yes. In fact, it hadn't been one scream at all. It had been two.

She reached the end of the landing, and spied the whole scene through the crack in the door.

She saw Samuel with his hand over Martha's mouth. She saw Aunt Eda and Uncle Henrik standing by Martha's empty bed.

She heard Aunt Eda: 'What is the matter? Samuel,

what on earth are you doing to your sister?'

She heard Uncle Henrik: 'I can smell cabbage.'

She heard Martha: 'It's nothing. I was just looking for my hairbrush and I . . . and I . . . banged my toe against the bed. That's all.'

Which leads us, dear reader, to precisely where we were. Yes, to Samuel desperately looking at Aunt Eda and Uncle Henrik, unaware that there was one more observer standing just behind the door.

'It's nothing,' Samuel said. 'Honest. Nothing.'

'He's right,' said Martha, hurriedly sitting down on Samuel's bed so her legs hid Troll-Son's face. 'It's nothing.'

Aunt Eda knew something was going on. She could sniff a secret, along with cabbage, in the air. 'Now, children, I do not want to get cross with you . . . but if you are hiding something, you must tell us. We haff no secrets in this house. Not any more. Secrets start ferry small, but they grow and grow and sometimes turn into something monstrous. Secrets are ferry much like dangerous animals. It is best to handle them when they are newly born.'

Samuel nodded. He knew his aunt was right. He didn't want to keep a secret from her, especially not one about the forest. And he was going to tell her.

As soon as it was safe. As soon as Cornelia had gone home. Well, that is what he told himself.

'Now, I will ask you both again – is there anything you want to tell me?'

Martha went red.

Samuel avoided his aunt's gaze and prayed Troll-Son wouldn't sneeze or say another word.

But then he noticed something happening to Uncle Henrik's face. His eyes were widening. His mouth was dropping open. And then Samuel watched as he raised his arm to point right under the bed.

'What is it, Henrik?' asked Aunt Eda. 'What's the matter?'

'There . . . under the . . . There's . . . something . . . '

Martha tried desperately to rearrange her legs over the side of the bed, but there was no way she could completely hide Troll-Son. 'Don't be silly,' she said, in such an unconvincing voice that Samuel prayed for her to be quiet. 'What would be hid–?'

'Yes,' said Aunt Eda. 'I see it. There's something under the bed.'

'No,' said Samuel. 'There's not.'

Aunt Eda gave him a rather stern look. 'I think there is, young man. Now, Martha, get up off the bed so me and your uncle can haff a closer look.'

As you can imagine, Cornelia – who was still peeping in through the crack in the door – was most intrigued by this point. What was hiding under the bed? She strained to see but Martha's bed was blocking her view.

She watched as Martha did as she was told, standing up so that her Aunt Eda and Uncle Henrik could have a look.

Uncle Henrik was first, crouching down. 'Well, I never,' he said.

Then Eda also peered underneath and Samuel's heart sank as he heard her gasp. 'Good Heffens abuff!'

A SCIENTIFIC IMPOSSIBILITY

'He won't hurt you,' said Samuel.

'No,' said Uncle Henrik. 'He looks more scared of us than we do of him.'

'How long haff you kept him here?' asked Aunt Eda, in a sharp and serious voice.

'He came on Thursday,' said Samuel. 'When Mr Myklebust was still here. I heard him come into the house but I didn't see him until later. In the night.'

Aunt Eda scratched her forehead in frustration. 'So why on earth didn't you tell us then?'

'I was going to tell you later. When Cornelia's gone home.'

Aunt Eda nodded. 'Samuel is right. We must not let Cornelia know. No, no. That would be no good.'

'No,' agreed Uncle Henrik. 'If Cornelia knew we

had a troll in the house, we would get into all kinds of trouble.'

Troll.

Cornelia could hardly believe what she was hearing as she stood there, watching it all through the thin crack in the door.

But trolls don't exist, she thought to herself. *They are a scientific impossibility.*

She had read very big and very in-depth books on animal biology and evolution, and never had she come across trolls. Trolls were what stupid people believed in. Like the brainless dimbats who lived in the village.

But right now she found herself wanting to believe in what the brainless dimbats believed in. After all, if that really was a troll under Samuel's bed, then her father would be so pleased with her. He wouldn't have to have people dress up as trolls when he bought Shadow Forest and turned it into a theme park. He could have the real thing. And this would also mean he could get Henrik into trouble. You see, Cornelia knew her father hated Henrik more than anyone, although she didn't know why. Not that she cared very much about making her father proud. After all, he was scarcely any better than all the other brainless dimbats. Except, of course, he had money. Lots and lots of money. And she knew that fatherly pride meant daughterly presents. If she could get proof of a real-life troll, she could get anything she asked for.

So she turned and went back along the landing to the spare room.

I will act as if I know nothing, she silently told herself. *And that way, I'll get to know everything.*

'What was that?' Aunt Eda asked.

'What?' said Samuel.

'I heard something. A creak. Out there on the landing.'

'I heard it too,' said Martha.

'I will look,' said Uncle Henrik.

And so Uncle Henrik went to look, but Cornelia had already disappeared back inside the spare room.

'No,' said Uncle Henrik, shutting the door. 'There's no one there.'

Aunt Eda beckoned Troll-Son to come out from under the bed. 'Come on, young fellow. There's nothing to be afraid of – we're not going to hurt you.'

So Troll-Son pulled himself out and stood in front of them.

'He's only got one eye,' said Martha, who could

hardly hide her surprise at seeing such a grubby, cabbagey, funny-eared creature standing in front of her. Not in the forest, but right here in her bedroom.

'I'm sure it is perfectly sufficient,' said Aunt Eda. 'So, tell me, young fellow, what's your name?'

Troll-Son looked at Samuel.

'It's all right,' said Samuel. 'You can tell her.'

Troll-Son's eye blinked nervously. 'I be . . . I be . . . Troll-Son.'

Meanwhile, at the other end of the landing, Cornelia was on her gold-plated mobile phone, talking to her father.

'What is it, my little princess?' said Mr Myklebust.

'A troll,' whispered Cornelia.

'A *what*?'

'There's a troll. In the house. In Samuel and Martha's bedroom.'

'Now, Princess, are you teasing your father?'

'I'm not teasing. I swear on my *Encyclopaedia for Gifted Girls* that it's true.'

'Oh, my dear girl, how can I live with myself? I should never have put you up to this . . . Run! Run for your life! Run, Princess, run!'

'No. It's safe. They're talking to it now.'

'It hasn't . . . eaten them?'

'No.'

'It hasn't . . . bitten off their noses?'

'No.'

'Or vaporized their flesh with its breath?'

'No. It's *scared* of them.'

Mr Myklebust paused, his heavy breath crackling down the phone. 'A troll? Scared? An *undangerous* troll? Oh . . . this . . . this . . . is . . . *incredible.* Henrik Krohg is harbouring a troll in his house. He'll be in such trouble! Oh . . . I'll finally get him back for what he did to me on Mount Myrdal!' There was another pause. More excited heavy breathing. Cornelia had no idea what had happened on Mount Myrdal but she could almost hear the ticking of her father's brain. 'What if all the creatures are like this? I could finally get my hands on the forest because there'd be nothing to be scared of . . . What if . . . what if there are hundreds of trolls like this? We could put them in cages for people to get up close to. We could even force them to operate the rides if they really aren't dangerous! They could even *be* the rides! Have a piggy-back on a troll! Then eat dinner at the Troll Tavern! A hundred kroner each! My theme park would be the tourist attraction to end all tourist attractions! Never mind the biggest in Norway, it would be the biggest in the world! A real-life troll . . . Oh, Cornelia, you are a miracle of a daughter. Have you seen it?'

'No, but I know it's there.'

'Right, well, you must make sure it stays there. And I will come as fast as I can. You mustn't let anyone know you know I know – or that I know you know. Do you understand?'

'Yes, Daddy.'

'And I must think of a way we can get proof of what's going on without Eda and Henrik and those pesky children interfering . . . '

Cornelia knew her brain was much faster and cleverer than her father's, so she quickly put it to work. 'I've got it!' she said. 'Call Mr Thomassen. Bring him with you.'

'Er . . . I don't know, Princess. We can't waste Tomas's time. He is a very busy man . . . '

Mr Myklebust sounded a little worried, and Cornelia knew why. You see, Mr Tomas Thomassen was the local police chief in Flåm and Mr Myklebust liked to keep him on his side. After all, if you were the richest person in the area, and owned lots of land full of houses and hotels and restaurants and shops, it helped to be friendly with the police.

And as many of the villages had been complaining about the horrendous noise being made building one of Mr Myklebust's newest developments – the Flåm International Five-star Luxury Peace and Tranquillity Spa Getaway Hotel and Mountain Resort Complex – he knew he needed Mr Thomassen on his side now more than ever.

'But think about it,' said Cornelia. 'When Mr Thomassen finds out that they have been hiding a troll here, he will get his photo in the paper and become a celebrity and a local hero. He'll surely ignore all those stupid villagers and their silly complaints.'

'You're right!' said Mr Myklebust, out of breath. 'You're a genius. We'll be there in half an hour . . . But you are *absolutely* sure there's a troll in the house?'

'Absolutely.'

'Good, well, keep them all there, Princess. And remember – you know nothing. Oh, Henrik Krohg, I have waited years for this day.'

THE HUMAN SNOWBALL

M*any years previously* . . . Mr Myklebust hadn't always been the kind of man who got out of breath from a phone call. No. At eighteen years of age he was six foot six and had muscular legs the size of tree trunks and the kind of blond hair that girls wanted to run their fingers through.

In those days he was exceptionally strong, and did two hundred press-ups every morning, before running around the fjord with a goat across his shoulders. Or, if he was feeling particularly strong, a pig.

Magnus lived on his father's farm, you see. He didn't like it though. It bored him senseless. But what he hated most was the thought that he'd end up like his father, who was also called Magnus Myklebust.

After all, who wanted to be a bald, overweight farmer struggling for money?

No. The younger Magnus Myklebust was going to be different. He was going to be famous, and he was going to travel the world.

Magnus had a special talent. He was a brilliant skier. So brilliant, in fact, that he believed he could make it into the Olympic team. Every afternoon, once he'd had all he could take of cows' udders and manure, he would drive in his father's car up to Mount Myrdal and practise on the slopes.

In particular, he loved to race. He loved the feeling of overtaking, and being in front, while his skis sprayed snow into the eyes of those behind him. And the biggest race in the Flåm skiing calendar was the annual giant slalom event held on Mount Myrdal, which he had not yet been old enough to enter.

This year, though, he had turned eighteen, and had made sure he was the first to put his name down. After all, he couldn't afford to miss the opportunity. This was his one chance to impress the Norwegian Olympic skiing coach, who travelled every year from his home in Lillehammer to watch the race and select members of his Olympic squad.

'Just you wait and see,' he told his father. 'I'll be spotted and never have to work on your stinking farm again.'

'Whatever makes you happy,' said the older Magnus Myklebust, who was a kind and gentle man.

So Magnus spent every spare hour on Mount Myrdal practising for the race. He skied the exact course on his own hundreds of times and tried to make it as difficult as possible. He went down it on one ski, then blindfolded, then with a goat across his shoulders.

At night he dreamed of winning the Olympics, stepping onto the podium as a gold medal was placed around his neck. 'I did it for Norway,' he would mumble in his sleep, while imaginary crowds roared all around him. 'My beautiful country. I love this whole land.' (Of course, he didn't like Norway at all, but he knew how to get the biggest cheer.)

A lot of the time, though, he couldn't sleep. He was so excited about the race, especially after he was interviewed for the local newspaper, the *Flåm Chronicle*.

'So, you are the favourite,' said the reporter, a pretty lady called Ingeborg who had a bit of a crush on Magnus.

'Yes. I certainly am.'

'I bet you are ever so excited to race in front of the largest crowd the Mount Myrdal annual giant slalom has ever seen.'

'The largest crowd?' asked Magnus.

'Yes, haven't you heard? Henrik Krohg has agreed to take part.'

'Henrik Krohg? The ski jumper?'

'Yes.'

'I thought he had retired – and besides, he doesn't do races – he was a ski jumper.'

'Well, he competed in the slalom in his younger days before concentrating on ski jumping – and he's agreed to do this one race to help his favourite charity, Save the Forests.'

'Save the Forests? Why would anyone want to save the forests? But still, it is good news. I'm looking forward to the race even more. This is my chance to beat an Olympic medallist! Yes, I will do it for Norway. My beautiful country. I love this whole land.'

'Apart from the forests?' said Ingeborg, whose crush was melting faster than snow.

'Er . . . yes . . .' said Magnus, flexing his arm muscles. 'Apart from the forests.'

He was so excited.

Now he had a chance to race against a real Olympic medallist! And not just any Olympic medallist – Henrik Krohg.

When Magnus was twelve, Henrik had been his hero. He had seen him ski jump and spend what seemed like whole minutes in the air. When Henrik was entered for the Olympics, Magnus consoled himself with the thought that next time he would definitely win gold.

Yet Henrik never did win gold. Indeed, he never even entered the next Olympics. Magnus couldn't believe it when he heard the news. Henrik Krohg – *the* Henrik Krohg – was moving near Flåm with his new wife to be a . . . a . . . *goat farmer*.

After that, Magnus decided he hated everything about his former hero. Why would anyone *choose* to give up the chance of a gold medal to farm goats?

But Magnus was looking forward to the big race because to beat a skier with a silver medal in ski jumping – the scariest and hardest of all ski events – would surely get him into the Norwegian squad.

'And when I win the race,' he told his kind and gentle father (who was kindlyand gently cooking Magnus gammon soup for supper), 'I will go to the Olympics and I will never give up until I win a gold medal. And even then I won't live on a farm near Flåm.'

'Oh, Magnus, there are worse things than working on a farm, you know.'

'Like what? Breaking your legs?'

'Magnus, do you know what your mother used to say when she was still alive? She used to say, "It's not what you *have* that makes you happy, but who you *are.*"'

'Yes, I know,' said Magnus. 'And I will be a gold medallist living in the sunshine.' *Not a fat farmer living in Flåm like you*, he nearly added. 'But first I will win the race and turn *myself* into a hero.'

However, Magnus wasn't leaving anything to chance. He knew Henrik was the only person who might beat him because Henrik and snowy mountains went together like bread and jam. And so he knew Henrik had to be stopped.

So he went to Anders, a skinny young boy who worked on the farm.

'Anders, do you want to earn yourself two hundred kroner?'

Anders's eyes widened to the size of saucers. Magnus knew his answer would be 'Yes' because Anders was poor and looked after his mother, who was dying of a disease with a long name that Magnus could never be bothered to remember.

'Two hundred kroner? That will be enough to send Mum to the clinic in Oslo,' said Anders, his eyes wide with hope.

'Good,' said Magnus. 'All you have to do is . . .'

The day of the race arrived. Magnus tried to ignore the crowds chanting, 'Henrik! Henrik! Henrik!'

Henrik, of course, was quite embarrassed about the chanting and went bright red.

'In one hour I will be back at home with my Eda,' he told Magnus as they stood at the start with the vast snowy slope below them.

Magnus said nothing. What could he say to a man who didn't want crowds to chant his own name? *I will beat you*, he thought to himself. *I will beat you and everyone in this race. And then the crowd will chant* my *name, not yours.*

The starting pistol went off.

The race was under way.

Magnus and Henrik were neck and neck, speeding ahead, turning all the other skiers into shrinking dots behind them. They skied faster and faster and faster. As they swept down the mountainside, Magnus looked in vain to see if he could spot Anders in the crowd. Henrik was now slightly in front. *Not for long,* thought Magnus. *Not for long.*

Henrik saw Eda and returned her smile. But then, suddenly, Eda wasn't smiling. She was screaming something:

'Watch out!'

She was pointing too, and Henrik followed her finger to see a tall skinny boy running out onto the track. 'Henrik! Henrik! Henrik!' the boy was shouting, as he had been instructed. His mother was struggling through the crowd to reach him, but it was no good. She was too weak and frail.

'Move!' Henrik was shouting. 'Move out of the way, boy!'

But the boy wasn't moving. He would let Henrik smash into him if he had to. After all, he needed the money Magnus had promised to give him.

'Henrik! Henrik! Henrik!' he kept shouting, but his voice was full of fear as he stood there, eyes closed, blocking Henrik's path.

'Move! Move! Move!' screamed Henrik, the frozen air whipping past him.

'Stay, stay, stay!' whispered Magnus, who could see Anders now.

It was all going perfectly to plan. Henrik would swerve to the side rather than risk crashing into any of the skiers. Indeed, that's what he seemed to be doing right at that moment.

But then something happened.

Anders's sick mother had finally made it through the crowd, and was now on the course, running towards her son.

'Anders,' she coughed. 'Anders, my baby, get off the track.'

And Anders opened his eyes and saw his mother running closer and became scared for her. After all, if she got hit by a skier travelling at eighty miles an hour, it would surely kill her.

'Mother, no! No, Mother! Stop!'

As he ran towards her, Henrik knew he had to change direction to avoid hitting them. So instead of turning into the barrier, he was forced to go the other way. And that is when he clipped Magnus's skis.

'Hey!' shouted Magnus, who suddenly lost his balance. 'You were meant to go the other waaaaaaaaaaargh!'

Henrik reached out to stop Magnus falling but it was too late. Magnus lost both his poles as he landed, and began to roll down the slope.

The crowd gasped.

'Aaaaaaaaaaaaaaaargh!' wailed Magnus, and he heard his bones crunch.

You see, unfortunately for Magnus, Anders had decided to run out at the very steepest part of the course, so once Magnus had begun to roll, there was no stopping him.

'In all my years,' said Henrik to Anders and his mother as they stood watching, 'I have never seen anything like this before.'

Indeed, no one had ever seen anything quite like this before. Magnus had fallen on the far side of the course, where the snow was deeper. And he wasn't simply rolling *over* the snow, he was taking it with him.

On and on he rolled, and the snow covered him now, turning into a kind of snowball. A *human* snowball.

'Aaaaaaaaaaaaaargh!' continued the wail, but there was nothing anyone could do.

The snowball held Magnus inside it like a bun holds a hot dog, and grew so big and so fast that it couldn't be stopped.

It ploughed past the finish line at record speed. And even as his head spun round faster than a spin dryer, Magnus was aware of the bitter fact that he had just achieved his ambition. He had finished the race in the fastest time ever. He had broken every record. But still Magnus the human snowball didn't stop.

He rolled towards a ridge and was rocketed higher and faster than Henrik had managed even in his Olympic days.

The snowball flew so high that Magnus had a panoramic view – a view that was spinning so fast he was nearly sick. He could see the whole fjord swapping places with the cloudy sky several times a second. And just beyond the fjord he could see the white wooden house where Henrik lived, and the grass slope that led up to the forest.

'Aaaaaaaaaaaaaargh!'

The snowball landed again, and rolled on down Mount Myrdal, with Magnus's head sticking out of one side.

By the time the snowball splashed into the fjord, Magnus was so bruised and frozen and dizzy he didn't know who he was.

'Who are you?' asked one of the fisherman who sailed out to rescue him.

'I'm . . . brr . . . I'm . . . brr . . . the King of Norway.'

'The King of Norway?' said one of the fishermen

– a man with a whiskery, ratty face who sat staring at the floating human snowball that was slowly melting in his boat. 'Then I'm the Queen of Sheba.'

They took Magnus to hospital, where a doctor told him that although, given time, he would eventually walk once more, he would never be able to ski again.

Magnus would wake up in the middle of the night and discover he was shouting out, 'Henrik Krohg – you will pay for this! You will pay! I'll get my revenge!'

But by the time Magnus was out of hospital, Henrik had gone missing. It was all over the *Flåm Chronicle*: HENRIK THE SKIING HERO GOES MISSING. Apparently Henrik was convinced that trolls were stealing his goats and taking them back to the forest, so he went to investigate but never returned.

'Now I will never get my revenge,' Magnus grumbled to himself as he lay in bed, staring at the legs that had been in plaster for months. 'He disappears a hero, and I am a laughing stock. Everyone calls me "the human snowball". I will never win a gold medal and it is all his fault. Oh, I hate him. I hope the trolls have boiled his brains!'

And so Magnus became a very unhappy man. A man determined to make all those people who had called him 'the human snowball' respect him again. He decided he would become rich. And he did. He became rich, but he stayed unhappy. People still called him 'the human snowball'. Indeed, he was beginning to look more and more like a snowball as the years went by – paler, balder, fatter – because he guzzled more and more food for comfort. He built houses and hotels, and bought shops, and made a fortune promoting the area he had always wanted to escape. He got married and had a beautiful daughter, but in his heart he knew no one would ever respect him the way they had respected Henrik.

'He ruined everything,' he used to say to his wife, who never listened. 'Oh, I hope he's still alive. I hope he comes back out of that forest so I can ruin everything for him!'

But of course, he never really believed he would get such a delicious opportunity.

Until now.

And one thing was for sure: he wasn't going to let it disappear again.

A SIMPLE PLAN

It had been a long journey for the Betterer and Troll-Father. Unlike Troll-Son, they'd had various obstacles slowing them down. Even without the weary legs of Troll-the-Wisest, they still had the problem of Troll-Father's eyelessness and the other small matter of *not actually knowing the way*.

Troll-Father knew the southern section of the forest a lot better than the Betterer, but without an eye he navigated at less than half the speed his son had. However, they had encountered two other creatures en route and had asked for directions. First there was a truth pixie, who truthfully told them he didn't know, not having ever left the forest. Then there had been a tomtegubb, who *had* left the forest but could only sing the directions in a rhyme:

'The forest is a giant place,
With all its paths so hard to trace,
But if you walk this way first,
Then turn left when the path gets worse,
You'll realize you are heading where
The humans live and the light does glare.'

They trekked on without sleeping, licking Lertwick Root to keep them awake and Stomach Stuffers to stop them feeling hungry. Once they reached the edge of the forest, the Betterer stopped.

'Why we be waiting?' asked Troll-Father.

'We'll move in at night. We'll stay here until it's dark. We can't let the humans see us before we see them.'

'But Troll-Son be out there. He be getting further away.'

The Betterer looked at the grass beyond the trees, and saw small, heavy, three-toed footprints leading towards a white wooden house with a grey slate roof. 'No,' he said. 'He's not going *anywhere.*'

The plan was simple.

Samuel was to wait in his bedroom with Troll-Son until Cornelia went home. Cornelia had said that her father was going to pick her up at ten in the morning.

That was nearly three hours away. And although three hours of having to make conversation with Troll-Son did not fill Samuel with joy, it was better than having to listen to Cornelia talk about how rich and clever and pretty she was over breakfast.

Aunt Eda had brought some flat-bread and gjetost cheese up for Samuel and Troll-Son to share, along with two glasses of orange juice, because she knew Samuel preferred orange juice to cloudberry juice. It tasted more like home.

'Now, young fellow,' she said, putting the tray down on the chest of drawers. 'Remember what we said – you try and be as quiet as you can while we wait for Martha's friend to leave. Do you understand?'

Troll-Son nodded. 'I be understanding.'

'Good. And then, later on, we can work out what we are going to do with you.'

'I be not wanting to go home. I be wanting to stay here with Samuel Blink.'

'Well, we'll see about that later,' said Aunt Eda. 'Right, I had better go and see to the girls before Cornelia gets suspicious.'

After she had left the room, Samuel lay back on his bed. He wasn't hungry. But why wasn't the troll eating when his stomach was rumbling so badly?

'You can eat, you know,' Samuel said. 'It's *food*.'

Troll-Son looked nervous and scratched his lumpy cheek. 'Samuel Blink be eating, Troll-Son be eating,' he said.

'I'm *not* hungry,' said Samuel.

But Samuel realized that if Troll-Son didn't eat soon, his rumbling stomach would probably give him away. So he sat up again, laid a piece of cheese on his flat-bread, then popped it into his mouth. Troll-Son watched him do this very closely and then he did the same, but he hated the taste. Yet he was going to make an even worse discovery when he copied Samuel with the orange juice. He screwed up his face and spat it back in the glass.

'Eugh! Eugh!' he kept saying, rubbing his hand over his tongue to try and get rid of the taste.

'Sssh!' said Samuel. 'What's the matter? It's only orange juice.'

'Be it poison?'

'No. It's orange juice. From oranges.'

'Oranges,' said Troll-Son. He kept saying the word. 'Oranges, oranges, oranges . . .'

'They're fruit,' said Samuel, rather crossly.

'It be worse than worms, Samuel Blink.'

Now it was Samuel who nearly choked. 'You eat worms?'

Troll-Son nodded, and looked at the carpet. He was clearly ashamed. 'I be eating worms and grass.'

All of a sudden the strange Norwegian foods Samuel had been eating didn't seem so bad. 'But what about rabbits?'

'We be running out of–'

Samuel was waving for Troll-Son to be quiet. He had heard something – a car – and he headed over to the window and spotted the same red jeep he had seen yesterday. It was Mr Myklebust, driving fast towards the house. *Three hours early.* And not *just* Mr Myklebust, either. There was someone with him. A man, Samuel thought, although he couldn't see clearly.

He quickly shut the curtains. 'Back under the bed!' he told Troll-Son. 'And stay there. Stay quiet!'

Once Troll-Son was back in his hiding place, Samuel went out onto the landing. He could hear the voices of his aunt and uncle and the two girls rising up from kitchen.

'No,' he heard Cornelia say. 'Let's not go for a walk by the fjord. Let's stay here. We can talk in your room until my daddy comes.'

Then there was a knocking at a door: three hard, steady raps against the wood.

'Who can that be at this hour?' said Aunt Eda.

'It must be the postman,' said Uncle Henrik. 'Yes, it must be Johannes. I will go and apologize to him for my funny turn the other day.'

And Samuel stood at the top of the stairs, listening to his uncle go and open the front door. He peered out through the wooden railings of the banister.

It was Mr Myklebust, standing there with a policeman.

A POLICE VISIT

'Magnus,' said Uncle Henrik to Mr Myklebust, 'we weren't expecting you until later. We are in the middle of breakfast.'

'Well, Henrik, I'm afraid I'm here now. And so is my very good friend Mr Thomassen, the chief of police.'

The chatter and clanking of cutlery stopped.

'Henrik?' said Aunt Eda. 'Is something wrong?'

'No,' said Henrik. 'I am sure there isn't. Now, Mr Thomassen, how can I help you?'

Mr Thomassen was quite old, with the kind of crinkled and sour mouth that made you wonder if he was always sucking lemons. His tired and creased face was a contrast to his neat and perfectly ironed uniform.

'I have a warrant to search these premises, Mr Krohg,' he said, taking off his hat.

'Whatever for?' called Aunt Eda, who was now coming out into the hall.

'Oh yes,' said Mr Myklebust. 'I should have told you, Tomas. They are very good at keeping secrets.'

'How dare you!' said Aunt Eda.

'Now, now, Eda,' said Uncle Henrik. 'I'm sure there has been a misunderstanding of some kind.'

Mr Thomassen came into the house without being invited; he had such a cross and sour look on his face, no one dared to object. He went into the living room and began looking around, his eyes sharpening as they scanned the vases, the paintings, the table, the rocking chair, the empty dog basket, the two girls.

'I am sorry, Henrik,' said Mr Myklebust, trying not to smile, 'but I couldn't let my daughter come to any danger. I hate to get the police involved, but as a concerned parent I have no choice.'

'A concerned parent? What are you on about? And Mr Thomassen, why are you opening all my cupboards?' said Aunt Eda.

'There are many ancient laws in this country,' said Mr Thomassen in a slow and careful voice. 'Many laws formed in less scientific times that have never been updated.'

'I don't understand,' said Uncle Henrik.

'There is a law, for instance, against harbouring illegal creatures.'

'Illegal creatures?'

'Yes, illegal creatures.'

Mr Myklebust decided to help out. 'Pixies . . . tomtegubbs . . . huldre-folk . . . *trolls* . . .'

Mr Thomassen turned to give him a sharp look. You see, in common with most people his age who lived in Flåm, Mr Thomassen had never really liked Mr Myklebust. Mr Myklebust would indeed be for ever known as 'the human snowball' – and that is how Mr Thomassen still saw him: as a man who rolled over anyone who got in his way, growing bigger and more powerful and not caring about what or who he crushed in the process. But still, if Mr Myklebust were right and Eda and Henrik *were* concealing a potentially dangerous creature, then he had to do something.

'And if anyone was caught hiding such a creature on their premises, they would face a very serious punishment,' said Mr Thomassen.

'A life in prison,' said Mr Myklebust.

Uncle Henrik and Aunt Eda both went pale, and looked at each other.

'Yes, thank you, Magnus – I think I can tell them the facts,' said Mr Thomassen.

Aunt Eda tried to sound as if she found this funny, but her laugh was unconvincing. 'Well, I don't know how we can hide a creature that doesn't exist!'

'Nice try,' said Mr Myklebust. 'But my daughter is not a liar.'

Mr Thomassen looked at Cornelia. 'She had better not be.'

Cornelia matched the police chief's cold stare with some frostiness of her own. 'I'm not lying. The troll is upstairs. In the north-facing bedroom. It is hiding under the bed.

Martha was confused. As she couldn't speak Norwegian she hadn't followed a word of the conversation. But she knew that a policeman searching the house wasn't a normal occurrence at breakfast.

'What's going on?' she asked, turning to Cornelia.

Aunt Eda stepped backwards and spoke louder, hoping her words would carry upstairs to Samuel. 'Well, Martha. They think we are HIDING A TROLL. Apparently, you can go to prison for HIDING A TROLL.'

Cornelia was pulling on a strand of her long blonde hair, inspecting the ends, acting as if nothing were the matter. 'I think your aunt and uncle have been putting us in danger,' she said while Eda and Henrik kept talking to the two men.

Martha shook her head, shaking away Cornelia's words like raindrops. 'They wouldn't ever do that.'

Cornelia stopped analysing her hair. 'Well,' she said, in a whisper, 'apparently, there's a troll . . . in the house.'

'What? Who told them that?'

Cornelia shrugged and made wide innocent eyes. 'I have no idea. Why? Did you know there was a troll in here?'

'No,' said Martha. 'No . . . there's not a–'

And then she realized something. 'It's *you.*'

Cornelia pretended to be disgusted. 'Me? *I'm* not a troll, thank you very much.'

'No, it was you, wasn't it? You told them.'

Something hardened in Cornelia's stare. 'So there *is* a troll.'

'I thought we were friends.'

Cornelia frowned, as if Martha were a historical date she was trying to remember. 'Friends? Really? Why would *I* be friends with *you*? *Everyone* wants to be my friend. And *you* – I mean, look at you. You're so . . . *ordinary*. And you live here, with your weird aunt and uncle, and your miserable brother. What do *we* have in common?

'Samuel was right about you,' Martha said.

'Well, that's good. Because when your aunt and uncle are sent to prison, he's all you'll have. And did you know that in Norway they hardly ever let brothers and sisters go to the same children's home?'

Martha couldn't believe that the person who only a minute before she'd thought was her best friend had turned out to be so evil. For once she had absolutely nothing to say.

'Oh, look,' said Cornelia, pointing at the adults leaving the room and heading upstairs. 'It's an old Norwegian custom – a troll hunt.'

Martha watched in horror as Aunt Eda and Uncle Henrik followed helplessly behind Cornelia's father and the police chief. *Oh no*, she thought. *I've done it again. I've ruined everything.* But then, right at that moment, she had an idea. And it was rather a good one.

ON THE ROOF

Upstairs, Samuel had heard his aunt's warning when she responded to Martha.

'*Well, Martha, they think we are HIDING A TROLL. Apparently, you can go to prison for HIDING A TROLL.*'

And as soon as those words reached him, he had run back to his bedroom. 'Troll-Son,' he whispered. 'Troll-Son, come out, come out quickly. We've got to hide you. Somewhere . . . better. They're looking everywhere.'

Troll-Son inched himself out slowly on his elbows.

'Come on, you stupid troll. Quick.'

Samuel looked around desperately. The wardrobe? No, it had only just worked last time. Out of the window? No. The windowsill was too small.

'Quick – the attic,' he said.

Troll-Son's eye gave a frightened look: he remembered how much he'd hated it the first time he'd stayed up there.

'Just follow me. Hurry. And be quiet.'

He led the troll across the landing towards the ladder – the ladder that led up to the small square wooden door in the ceiling. Samuel climbed up first, and beckoned Troll-Son to follow. As Samuel undid the latch and pushed open the door, he heard footsteps coming up the stairs.

Once he was inside the attic he helped pull Troll-Son through the hatch and quickly shut the door. He looked around the room, which was full of framed photographs of Uncle Henrik ski jumping. He saw Uncle Henrik's old skis, and tea-chests full of books and clothes his uncle hadn't worn since before he had gone into the forest.

It was quite dark in the attic, but not dark enough to guarantee Troll-Son wouldn't be found. What little light there was came from the small window caked with dust and cobwebs. Without a second thought, Samuel ran over and tried to open it. It was no good. The long metal latch was stuck.

'What be you doing, Samuel Blink?'

But Samuel didn't have time to answer Troll-Son's

question. He knew that right now they were searching upstairs; any moment they would start climbing up to the attic. There was no way he was going to let Aunt Eda and Uncle Henrik go to prison for a stupid troll. Samuel had already lost his parents; he didn't want to be left alone again.

He grabbed one of Uncle Henrik's old skis and lodged it under the latch. 'Help me,' he said to Troll-Son. 'Push down on this. Now! Come on!'

Troll-Son did as he was told, joining Samuel to push with all his strength on the dusty old ski.

Eventually the latch flew open. Samuel left the ski and beckoned Troll-Son to the window.

'Come on,' he said. 'Climb out onto the roof. You'll be OK – it's not too steep. You can lie down on the tiles. *Come on.*'

Troll-Son didn't move.

'What are you waiting for? If you get caught, they'll probably . . . kill you or something. Come *on.*'

Troll-Son still didn't move. 'Samuel Blink be on roof,' he said quietly. 'Troll-Son be on roof.'

What was with this troll? Samuel wondered. He couldn't eat some bread or drink some orange juice without seeing Samuel do it first. Which was OK when it came to eating bread or drinking juice – *but climbing onto a roof*? Samuel looked out of the window. The roof suddenly seemed a lot steeper now.

'No,' he said. 'I need to stay inside. If I'm not in the house they'll get suspicious. We can't *both* hide.'

Troll-Son nodded, but still looked worried. 'Samuel Blink be on roof, Troll-Son be on roof.'

'*Why?* What's with you? Can't you see this is all your fault?'

Troll-Son was petrified. As we have seen, like most trolls he was exceptionally scared of heights. (Hence the popular troll folk song 'There be no bigger fright than a very big height'.) The main exception, of course, is the Betterer who – we must remember – spent the formative years of his life believing he was a human.

'I be not liking heights.'

No, thought Samuel Blink. *And I be not liking wimpy troll boys.*

And then he heard something. He looked over at the closed latch in the floor. It was rattling.

'Someone's on the ladder,' he whispered. 'They're coming.'

He looked at the open window and knew he had no choice.

'OK, I'll do it.'

Samuel climbed out onto the roof, and helped

pull Troll-Son up after him. Then he quickly shut the window as Troll-Son clung to his pyjamas for dear life.

'Get off me,' Samuel said.

'I be scared. I be never being so high before.'

Samuel looked behind him, towards the fjord and the mountains, and the tiny thin road that led to Flåm. He too felt a little queasy. They weren't *that* high up, but when you are lying barefoot on top of a sloping roof three storeys off the ground with a troll yanking your pyjamas, it starts to feel a little bit dangerous. The wind was making it worse too. That eastern wind was sharper and cooler up here, especially without socks or a nice warm jumper.

'Lie flat,' Samuel said, noticing that some of the tiles were loose. 'Lie as flat as you can on your stomach and don't move.'

Troll-Son nodded and, suddenly wishing his eyeball wasn't in, dug his fingers into his eye-socket and, with a little effort, pulled it out.

'What are you doing?' Samuel asked him.

Troll-Son gripped the eyeball tight in his hand as he lay back against the tiles. 'I be . . . I be . . . I be not liking to look.'

'Well, why don't you just close your eye?'

'It be still there when it be opening. Better in my hand.'

'OK. Whatever.' It was too dangerous to argue. Anyway, what was the point in trying to get any sense out of a troll? These were creatures who thought the moon was just a hole that humans had cut out of the sky.

Samuel lay there, as quiet and still as possible, while Troll-Son clutched his eyeball and nervously hummed the chorus to 'There be no bigger fright than a very big height'.

TROLLEY THE TROLL
(OR 'MARTHA'S NEW BEST FRIEND')

Immediately below them, Mr Myklebust and Mr Thomassen were desperately whipping off all the blankets that were draped over the tea-chests while everyone else stood and watched.

'Excuse me,' said Aunt Eda, 'but these are ferry personal things in these chests. Ferry, ferry personal things.'

'Personal trolls?' said Mr Myklebust, who was holding the sides of his gigantic waist, quite out of breath.

'Oh, don't be so ridiculous,' said Aunt Eda. 'How many times do I have to tell you – there aren't any trolls in this house.'

'She's *lying*,' Cornelia said.

'I am not lying.'

Cornelia smiled, thinking of something. 'Well, where's Samuel?' And to Mr Thomassen: 'Ask them where Samuel is.'

'Who's Samuel?' asked Mr Thomassen, picking up the ski that only moments before had been used to open the window.

'He's our nephew,' said Uncle Henrik. 'And right at the moment he's . . . he's . . .'

'Gone fishing,' Aunt Eda said. 'Yes, every morning he gets up and goes fishing. In the fjord.'

'She's still lying,' Cornelia said. 'Samuel's not gone fishing.'

Mr Thomassen gave Mr Myklebust a doubtful stare, and Mr Myklebust gave that same stare to his daughter. It was a kind of pass-the-parcel of stares, with the music stopping when it reached Cornelia.

'Well, where is he then?' Mr Myklebust asked her.

'He's hiding the–'

'I know where the troll is.' This was Martha, speaking in English. She had stepped forward and was looking directly into Mr Thomassen's sour and suspicious face.

'She's going to tell you where the troll is!' said Cornelia in disbelief (and Norwegian).

Aunt Eda and Uncle Henrik again exchanged

nervous glances, wondering what Martha was doing.

'She is?' said Mr Thomassen. 'Ask her where it is.'

'Tell them where it is,' said Cornelia.

'Can't you see him?' said Martha, pointing to empty space in front of her.

Everyone looked confused.

'Is she saying the troll is in this room?' asked Mr Thomassen, pulling a baton from the holster in his belt, ready to defend himself from troll attack.

'Er, yes, she is,' said Aunt Eda.

'He's waving hello.' Martha kept a straight face because she knew that if she blew this, a Samuel-less children's home would be waiting for her.

Cornelia rolled her eyes, realizing Martha had never had any intention of telling the truth.

Mr Myklebust studied Martha with his small piggy eyes. 'Is this a joke?'

'No. He's right there, next to you.'

Mr Myklebust looked to his left side, then to his right, and saw no troll whatsoever.

'He's my best friend,' Martha went on. 'I call him . . . Trolley. He came to see me after my parents died in a terrible car accident. Uncle Henrik and Aunt Eda can see him, can't you?'

And Martha stared at her aunt and uncle and – with

the eye furthest away from the troll hunters – gave a quick wink to let them know she hadn't gone completely mad.

'Oh yes,' said Aunt Eda, suddenly understanding Martha's plan. 'We can see him. Of course we can.' And then she turned to Mr Thomassen and spoke in Norwegian. 'You see, Mr Thomassen, poor Martha has found it very difficult since her parents died. She has become perhaps a little confused about certain things. But she is a child after all, and if she wants to believe in an imaginary friend, then who are we to stop her? And if Cornelia overheard us all talking about a troll, you know which troll we were talking about.'

Cornelia's face was full of panic, as if Martha's lies were something she could drown in. 'They're lying. Martha's making it up.'

Aunt Eda nodded. 'Indeed she is, Cornelia. But when reality lets us down that is often how we cope with things. We make things up. And if Martha wants to make up a friend who happens to be a troll, well, that's fine with me and her uncle.'

'That's not what I meant. I mean she's making it up that she's . . . making it up.'

Mr Thomassen rubbed his tired eyes. 'Cornelia, did you actually *see* a troll.'

Cornelia looked at her father, whose fat cheeks were turning pink with shame, or anger, or both, and knew she couldn't lie. After all, her father already knew the answer. That answer being the one she gave – 'No, I didn't *see* it. But I know it's there. Can't you *smell* it?'

Aunt Eda chuckled. 'Cornelia, I am embarrassed to tell you that this attic hasn't been cleaned for twenty years. There are bound to be all kinds of smells in here.'

Mr Thomassen nodded and put his baton back in its holster. 'I've seen enough. The only trolls in here exist in the minds of two young girls. This has been a waste of police time, I am afraid, Magnus – and I am suspicious about why you brought me here.'

Mr Myklebust was shaking his head. 'This is what my daughter told me. That's all.'

'Yes, well, maybe next time you should be a little bit less ready to believe what she tells you,' said Mr Thomassen.

Cornelia's father couldn't look his daughter in the eye. So he looked at a framed photograph on the wall. A dusty image of Uncle Henrik flying through the air on his skis. For some reason, this seemed to make his face even pinker. So pink, in fact, that if a pig dressed in a suit had walked into the room on its hind legs, it would have been very hard to tell which would be the better source of bacon.

'Tomas,' he said, 'I am very sorry . . . I don't know what's got into my–'

He stopped to listen to something. A scraping, sliding kind of noise coming from the roof.

And then Martha gasped aloud as she saw something outside the window through the cobwebs and dust.

A foot.

A *three-toed* foot.

Cornelia heard the gasp and followed Martha's stare to the window. She saw it too.

'There! Look! Outside the window! It's the troll!'

And of course Cornelia was right.

It *was* the troll.

But by the time her father and the police chief had turned round, the foot had shot out of sight again.

'I'd better have a look,' said Mr Thomassen, making his way back to the window. 'I did hear something.'

'Go on then,' said Cornelia, in the kind of voice that's best not used on policemen. '*Hurry*.'

SAMUEL HANGS ON

Samuel had told Troll-Son to work his way higher up the roof – they were more likely to be spotted at window-level than above it.

'Put your eyeball in,' Samuel had said as they elbowed themselves up the slate tiles. But Troll-Son knew that if he could see how high they were, he would probably be sick, and he would never be able to live with himself if he was sick in front of Samuel Blink.

'Suit yourself,' Samuel said.

A second later Troll-Son slipped slightly on a loose tile, which caused him to lose his grip on the eyeball. Samuel watched as it rolled down the roof and lodged itself just above the window. And Troll-Son edged lower to try and find it.

'You won't find it, you idiot,' said Samuel. 'You can't see. We'll get it la—'

That was the moment when Troll-Son slipped a second time, and further, so that one of his feet hung down in front of the window. Troll-Son felt for his eyeball, and found it just as Samuel grabbed his hand and pulled him back up.

Once they were safe, they lay against the tiles to catch their breath, and Troll-Son pressed the eyeball back into its socket.

But then – something else.

The window.

Yes.

Someone was opening the window.

'Quick,' Samuel said. 'Higher.'

So he and Troll-Son crawled as fast as they could to the top of the roof. And, once there, Samuel looked behind and below to see the back of Mr Thomassen's head looking out of the window.

'Quick. Over the top!' Samuel whispered his order and tugged Troll-Son over the gable to the other side.

And although they made it just in time to escape notice, there was another difficulty Samuel hadn't predicted: the roof was much steeper on this side. So much steeper that Samuel and Troll-Son slid down and ended up having to hold onto the gutter.

Well, *Samuel* ended up holding onto the gutter. Troll-Son ended up holding onto Samuel.

That's right. Samuel was hanging onto the edge of the roof, high above the ground, with the full weight of a rock-blooded troll boy hanging onto his back.

'Grab the gutter!' said Samuel. 'Get off me! You're too heavy! Grab the gutter!'

'I be trying . . . I be trying . . .' said Troll-Son, whose hand reached out and clenched nothing but air.

The pain was unbearable. Samuel felt as if his fingers were about to snap off. 'Try again!' he told Troll-Son.

This was a mistake. As Troll-Son tried a second time to lean away from Samuel and reach for the roof, he lost his balance, along with his grip on Samuel's back.

And if Samuel's hand had been slower at grabbing onto Troll-Son's wrist, Troll-Son would have fallen to the ground.

Aaaaaaargh!

Samuel kept the scream of pain inside his head, knowing it would be heard inside the house if he let it out.

He looked down and saw Troll-Son staring back up

at him, his mouth and his eye wide open with terror. And then, further below, Samuel saw the hard path they would land on if he let go.

How long could he hang here? Not long. A minute? Thirty seconds?

Maybe he should let go of Troll-Son. Maybe, Samuel thought to himself, trolls don't hurt themselves when they fall. But he couldn't do it. Even though he knew all Troll-Son had done since he'd arrived was cause trouble, Samuel felt responsible. Troll-Son believed in him. He hung on every word he said. Samuel, for some strange reason, seemed to be his hero, and heroes never let people – or trolls – down. So Samuel had to hang on. And besides, if Mr Thomassen came out and found a dead troll in front of the doorstep, Aunt Eda and Uncle Henrik would be in as much trouble as if he found a live troll, and Samuel and Martha would be sent to children's homes.

So he had to keep on holding, and holding, and holding, while he tried to think of a plan. He looked around. He caught a glimpse of the fjord and the snow-covered mountains in the distance. If he let go, he would never see something so beautiful ever again. Or see *anything* ever again.

He was about to scream – and out loud this time.

But right then, below them, the front door opened. He could hear Aunt Eda's voice as she led the guests outside.

'I can assure you, Tomas, if we effer see a troll around here, you will be the first to know.'

And now, biting his lip to stop himself from screaming, Samuel could see the tops of all their heads, and hear their Norwegian voices.

And he knew that any time now it would be too late. He couldn't hold on. He had another ten seconds at most until it was all over. *Ten, nine, eight* . . .

Martha should have been feeling happy. After all, Cornelia had been proved wrong about the troll (even though she had been right) and her father was clearly angry with her.

But Martha didn't feel anything but sad. The first friend she had made since arriving in Norway hadn't been her friend at all. Martha had been using her to get information. And as she stepped out of the house into that cool, sunny morning, she stared at Cornelia with disgust. Not that Cornelia noticed – she was too busy pleading with her father in Norwegian. But Mr Myklebust was ignoring his daughter and talking to Mr Thomassen. And, in turn, Mr Thomassen was ignoring Mr Myklebust and talking to Aunt Eda and Uncle Henrik.

Martha didn't understand the words but could tell Mr Thomassen was apologizing for wasting their time.

I wonder where Samuel is? she thought to herself. *He's probably watching us right now from behind the bedroom curtains.*

When she was sure no one was watching, Martha dared herself to look up at the window, expecting to see Samuel. And of course, she *did* see Samuel, but not where she had expected.

At first the sight of Samuel hanging off the roof and holding onto Troll-Son was so strange that it didn't seem real. But when she saw the panic in Samuel's eyes, she realized it was actually happening.

Her brother was either going to have to scream and let everyone know the troll boy was real. Or he was going to have to fall and, quite probably, die.

No.

Martha couldn't let that happen.

She had saved her brother's life before and she was going to do it again.

She had to think of something. And fast.

Martha stared at Samuel and mouthed two silent words:

Hold. On.

She had no idea how long Aunt Eda and Uncle Henrik were going to stay outside talking to their uninvited guests. And she knew that she couldn't tell them the danger Samuel was in without also telling Mr Myklebust and Mr Thomassen. She also knew that Samuel was too far away from the window to be able to be brought back inside, even if she opened it.

But still she found herself stepping backwards, sneaking back inside, heading upstairs. But instead of going to her bedroom – the bedroom closest to where Samuel and Troll-Son were hanging, she ran into Aunt Eda and Uncle Henrik's room.

Once there, she went to Aunt Eda's knicker drawer and found the small wooden box painted with roses that her aunt had shown her two nights before. She flicked open the lid, grabbed the Hek bracelet, went straight to her bedroom and began to push at the window. It was stiff, but she used all her strength to urge it open.

'*I've got the bracelet*,' she whispered up to Samuel, realizing Mr Myklebust and the others were still below them.

Samuel's face was twisted in agony. He felt

as if his whole body were about to snap in two. 'I . . . can't . . . argh . . . catch . . . argh . . . it . . .'

It was a good point. He didn't have a free hand with which to catch the bracelet, should Martha throw it.

'My . . . argh . . .' he said as he pulled a leg back towards the window where Martha was, but he seemed in too much pain to finish his sentence. 'My . . . argh . . . argh . . . my . . . arghn . . . arghnk . . .'

And then Martha realized what he was trying to say.

Ankle!

Samuel's right foot was now hovering just above the window. If Martha could somehow reach it and clip the bracelet around his ankle, then he would be safe.

But how would she get to it?

She leaned out of the window and stretched her arm as high as she could, but her hand was still too far away from her brother's bare foot.

'I be . . . I be . . . frightified . . .' Troll-Son said.

'Sssssh!' said Martha.

She looked back up at her brother. His face was bright red. Purple veins were bulging in his neck. Even *his* eyes seemed about to pop out with the effort.

But still she couldn't hook the bracelet around his foot.

'I . . . can't . . . argh . . . I . . . can't . . . hold . . .'

Samuel lost more and more of his grip until he was holding on by the very tips of his fingers.

Martha gulped. It wasn't a particularly helpful thing to do but she couldn't help it. When she was scared, that is what she did. She gulped.

And then she did what she had to do in order to save her brother's life. She climbed out onto the windowsill. Onto the *very narrow* windowsill. In fact, it was so narrow that it only had room for Martha's toes, which were what she was standing on as she carefully stood up – facing sideways, legs trembling, not looking down.

She was now as tall as she could be with one hand still holding onto the open window. But it wasn't enough. Even as Samuel stretched his big toe down towards her, it wasn't close enough to reach the bracelet.

So Martha had no choice. She had to let go of the window and straighten her legs as tall as they could go. So she did.

She stood up, and hooked the bracelet around Samuel's ankle. *Oh no*, she thought. *Oh no oh no oh no.*

She was slipping sideways. And she would have fallen completely if she hadn't grabbed hold of her brother's foot.

A moment later she was dangling there, facing Troll-Son's scared eye, as the three of them hung on for dear life.

Why aren't we falling? she wondered. *Samuel can't hold both of us.*

But the Hek bracelet was having the most immediate effect on Samuel. His arms had felt like they were about to snap from the weight, but now they felt strong enough to hang onto the roof for another hour.

And his legs too. The strength poured back into them like water flooding into empty cups. He could hardly feel Troll-Son and Martha holding onto him. They were no heavier than a pair of slippers.

When Martha looked down, she was relieved to see that the guests were leaving. She was less relieved to see Cornelia look back – and up – to see the three of them hanging there.

'Look!' Cornelia said, tugging her father's arm. 'Look – up there, hanging off the roof – it's the troll!'

Mr Myklebust glared down at his daughter. 'Cornelia, stop it! Stop this nonsense! Haven't you caused enough trouble for one day?'

And neither Mr Magnus Myklebust nor Mr Tomas Thomassen looked up to see that Cornelia was telling the truth. Instead, they kept walking and disappeared round the side of the house, along with Aunt Eda and Uncle Henrik.

'They've gone!' Martha said.

'Well, let's wait until they start the car,' said Samuel. 'My arms don't hurt at all now.'

'Well, *mine* do,' said Martha, who after all wasn't wearing the bracelet.

'Oh yes,' said Samuel. 'I suppose they must. Right, I'm going to let go – so hold on tight.'

Martha held on tight to his foot and Troll-Son kept gripping Samuel's hand as they began to fall to the ground.

They fell very slowly – the Hek bracelet made sure none of them hurt themselves. Down, down, down. Indeed, Martha had time to turn her head and see Aunt Eda and Uncle Henrik come back from saying goodbye to their unwanted visitors.

'Good Heffens!' cried Aunt Eda at the strange sight before her.

'What on earth . . . ?' said Uncle Henrik, at exactly the same time.

'It's all right,' said Samuel. 'I've got them.'

'We can see that, but who's got you?' asked Uncle Henrik.

But Aunt Eda could already see the answer wrapped around Samuel's ankle. *The Hek bracelet.* And now she became quite cross.

'Martha, what did I tell you about that bracelet?'

Martha was still in the air, holding onto her brother, her feet now level with the top of the front door. 'I had to get it,' she said. 'Samuel was hanging off the roof.'

'*Hanging off the roof?*' asked Aunt Eda and Uncle Henrik together, although Aunt Eda asked it with a crosser face.

They had to wait for a response as the three fallers were preparing to land. Martha was first, reaching the ground one foot at a time, as delicately as a ballerina. Troll-Son was next, and he landed less like a ballerina. Or like a ballerina with a pair of clumsy, heavy legs that were most surprised to reach the ground. (You may not be surprised to learn that trolls can't even spickle-dance, let alone do ballet.) And last of all was Samuel, who by now was not holding either of his two passengers, and who actually quite enjoyed that last slow downward glide.

'Now,' said Aunt Eda. 'Would you like to tell me how you came to be hanging off the roof?'

THE TOOTHBRUSH INCIDENT AND THE MEETING THAT FOLLOWED (IN WHICH A VERY BIG DECISION WAS MADE)

Samuel was brushing his teeth. Troll-Son stood and watched. It was flattering to be looked up to like a hero, but it was still quite annoying to have someone study him when he didn't want to be studied.

So Samuel spat out the foaming toothpaste, rinsed the brush, and left the bathroom in a hurry. As soon as he was out on the landing, though, he wondered why Troll-Son wasn't following him.

Then he heard the tap running again and sped back into the bathroom. It was too late. Troll-Son was brushing his teeth with Samuel's toothbrush. Samuel felt sick at the thought of the clean white bristles rubbing over those rotten brown troll teeth. And Samuel wasn't the only one feeling sick. Troll-Son was retching at the taste of the toothpaste. It was even more disgusting than the taste of the orange juice. He couldn't believe that Samuel would choose to put something like that in his mouth. He would rather have eaten grass-and-earthworm stew every morning of his life than have to put up with that minty taste.

'Ugh!' said Troll-Son, spitting out the toothpaste.

'Ugh!' said Samuel as he yanked the toothbrush out of Troll-Son's hand. 'Get off! That's *my* toothbrush. Get off it!'

The toothbrush flew into the sink. Samuel kept on shouting as Troll-Son kept retching. He had had enough of being a hero for one day, especially as his only reward was a ruined toothbrush. 'Why do you copy me all the time? It's annoying. *You're* annoying, and you nearly killed us both today! Why don't you just . . . go home!'

Troll-Son was so hurt by these words that for a moment he forgot about the disgustingly clean minty taste in his mouth. 'I be sorry, Samuel Blink.'

Uncle Henrik came upstairs to see what the matter was. 'Hey . . . Samuel . . . Samuel . . . calm down . . . calm down.'

He saw the toothbrush in the sink, its bristles a greenish brown after contact with the inside of Troll-Son's mouth.

'We'll get you a new toothbrush,' said Uncle Henrik.

And something about Uncle Henrik's voice made Samuel feel guilty. He knew he was acting stupidly, and saying things he might not even truly mean, but still he could hear his voice continuing to shout: 'I don't want a new toothbrush! I want . . . I want . . . for him to go back to his parents.'

Uncle Henrik nodded. It was a very wise type of nod, as though he understood more in those words than even Samuel did.

'Yes,' he said. 'Yes, and that is what we are going to talk about, isn't it? We will have a meeting and decide what to do. Come downstairs. Your aunt wants to have it right away.'

Aunt Eda waited for everyone to be seated around the table before she began the discussion.

'Troll-Son, we understand that you are scared of going back home. But we must tell you that you will be safer there than you effer could be here. You see, human beings are a ferry suspicious kind of creature. As a general rule, if something is different, they are scared of it, and if they are scared of it, they will want to get rid of it so they are not scared of it any longer.

And, Troll-Son, I am afraid you will strike many people as ferry different indeed.' And then Aunt Eda picked up her cup of coffee, blew ripples in the surface, then took a sip.

'Now, Troll-Son,' said Uncle Henrik. 'We know you are scared of going to this . . . Butterer–'

'Betterer,' corrected Samuel, wondering how Uncle Henrik thought anyone called the 'Butterer' could be frightening.

'Yes, this Betterer – Samuel has told us . . . But it is only for a week. And I'm sure your parents only want to send you there for your own good. I remember when I was – oh, nine, it must have been – my parents sent me to a winter ski school, and I cried every single night at the thought of being away from home but I ended up enjoying it in the end. And if I had never gone, I might never have become a ski jumper, so sometimes it is worth listening to your parents. They are there for a reason.'

Samuel and Martha caught each other's eye and found the same sadness there. Their parents had been there for a reason too, but now they were gone.

Uncle Henrik noticed their faces and decided to hurry things along. 'I am afraid there is nothing else for it. I will have to take Troll-Son home.'

'Go into the forest?' asked Martha.

'There is no other way,' he said. 'He can't stay here. It is too dangerous. He must go back, and I must go with him to make sure he gets home safely.'

'Oh, Henrik,' said Aunt Eda. 'You can't go back into the forest. You know what happened last time.'

Uncle Henrik nodded as he looked out of the window towards the trees. 'Yes, but the forest is a safe place now. The only danger is Mr Myklebust, or anyone else who finds out that it is safe, and that harmless creatures like Troll-Son live there. They would go in there and ruin those creatures' lives faster than Professor Tanglewood did. No, the threat to that forest is from outside. And the longer Troll-Son stays with us, the greater that danger becomes. So I say he goes back now. Today.'

Troll-Son's face melted with terror. 'No . . . I be scared . . . I be scared . . .'

'Well, Henrik, perhaps we should take a vote on it to make sure we are all agreed,' said Aunt Eda. 'Who votes Troll-Son returns to the forest?'

Uncle Henrik raised his arm, then Aunt Eda. Martha looked at Samuel, made a sad face, then raised her arm. Samuel noticed the tear bulging in Troll-Son's eye, ready to fall. Why was it so difficult to raise his arm? After all, he knew it made sense. If Troll-Son were discovered, all the creatures that lived in the forest could be destroyed. Or locked up. And the forest itself would be chopped down for Mr Myklebust to build a theme park. That's what Cornelia had told Martha. And anyway, how bad could this Betterer be? Yet the fear in Troll-Son's tear-glazed eye seemed very real.

He thought of his aunt and uncle in prison. He thought of living out the rest of his childhood in a children's home a long way from Martha. But as Samuel's arm went up, it felt heavier than usual.

Uncle Henrik nodded solemnly.

'Well, that is that,' said Aunt Eda. 'This is the only solution. Troll-Son, you will have to go back to your parents.'

And everyone turned to look at the troll boy sitting at the end of the table, but none of their ears were sharp enough to hear the nervous whisper trembling on his lips: 'No go, no go, no go . . .'

A THOUSAND FAINT ECHOES

Aunt Eda was writing a list of things that Henrik would need to take with him. Some of these things they already owned but some they would need to buy in the village before leaving, from the hardware store and the grocer's. So far that list included:

One backpack
One compass
Bread (for sandwiches)
Cheese (for putting in the sandwiches)
Emergency blankets
Two camping lanterns
Two sleeping bags
One tent

One power torch
Batteries
One portable gas fire
Meat, for cooking
One Swiss Army Knife

She showed the list to Uncle Henrik. 'Is there anything else you will need?' she asked him.

'Oh, Eda, I won't need any of this. It won't take me long to get to the troll village. I'll go later, when you're back from your trip to the village. I will take a flask of soup. I will wear the Hek bracelet to protect me. That is all I will need. I'm not going to war! Nothing will happen to me. It's not like last time – the forest is safe now.'

'I know, Henrik, I know. But I am so worried. Can't we just let Troll-Son walk home on his own?'

Uncle Henrik chuckled. 'I think there is more chance of his home walking to him!'

Aunt Eda took a deep breath and closed her eyes, as though the rest of the conversation were something she would have to swim underneath. 'All right,' she said. 'I know it is the only way, but–'

It was at this point, or maybe a second later, that Samuel interrupted. He had just come downstairs with his coat on, ready to accompany Aunt Eda on the shopping trip.

'I could go,' he said. 'To the forest, with Henrik.'

Uncle Henrik was shaking his head. 'No, Samuel, that won't be necessary.'

'It will if you don't want to drag him.'

'What do you mean?' asked Uncle Henrik.

But Aunt Eda knew precisely what Samuel meant. 'Troll-Son copies everything Samuel does. If Samuel takes a drink, Troll-Son takes a drink. If Samuel brushes his teeth, Troll-Son brushes his teeth. He'll be more likely to go along with you if Samuel is there too.'

'And I know the way,' Samuel said. 'To Trollhelm.'

Aunt Eda looked worried. 'I don't want to lose *both* of you.'

Uncle Henrik chuckled. 'You won't lose either of us. We'll be all right, won't we, Samuel?' And then, having observed Samuel's nod, he added: 'Good, well, that settles it. You help Eda with the shopping and then we'll take Troll-Son home. By this time tomorrow everything will be back to normal.'

Aunt Eda opened the boot of the car to load her shopping baskets. All three of them. One for her, and one each for the children.

'Samuel! Martha!'

Where were they?

She left the boot open and went into the house to look for them.

'We're coming,' Martha said tunefully as Aunt Eda caught her pinching a pickled onion out of the fridge.

'Where's your brother?'

Martha crunched, then swallowed. 'He's gone upstairs to get his woolly hat and scarf.'

Aunt Eda nodded. 'That is sensible. It is cold today. In Norway there aren't really four seasons. Just four types of winter. That is what they say. So where's Troll-Son?'

'With Uncle Henrik,' Martha said, dipping her fingers back in the jar. 'In the living room.'

Samuel appeared, now warmly wrapped up.

'Right,' said Aunt Eda. 'If efferyone is ready, let's go shopping.'

Samuel, Martha and Aunt Eda had been gone less than a minute when Uncle Henrik stopped reading the sports pages of the *Aftenposten*, and looked around.

'Troll-Son?' he enquired, noting the empty rocking chair.

Then he spoke louder. 'Troll-Son? Where are you?'

Uncle Henrik stood up, went through the hall and popped his head into the kitchen. A half-empty jar of pickled onions sat on top of the fridge. 'Troll-Son?'

Henrik went upstairs, calling the same name and adding the same question mark. 'Troll-Son? Troll-Son? Troll-Son?' All the time his feet were moving faster, and his voice was getting louder as the panic set in. Where was he? One minute he had been there, sitting quietly in the rocking chair, and the next he was gone. True, it had been a particularly interesting article Henrik had been reading about the new ski jump tower that was being built at Holmenkollen, but surely he'd have heard Troll-Son leave the room?

He checked under the beds, in the wardrobes, in the bathroom. Then the attic. *Yes*, thought Henrik. *Maybe he had climbed onto the roof again.*

But no, there was no sign that Troll-Son had been in the attic and opened the window. Uncle Henrik went downstairs and out of the house to look up, but there was definitely no troll on the roof.

He gazed over towards the army of trees that marked the nearest fringe of Shadow Forest. He knew that wherever Troll-Son had gone, it wasn't back towards his home.

'TROLL-SON?!' bellowed Uncle Henrik, and the voice travelled across the fjord and became a thousand faint echoes as it bounced off Mount Myrdal, but received no answer.

BEHIND THE BASKETS

It was almost total darkness in the boot of the car, except for the thinnest slither of light that enabled Troll-Son to see the outlines of the three wicker shopping baskets he was hiding behind.

It wasn't the darkness that scared him, though. After all, Troll-Son had spent much of his life without an eyeball, so one thing he wasn't fearful of was the dark. It was the noise of the engine – a very untrollish noise – combined with the general bumpiness of the road, and the feeling of being trapped in a small space, that caused Troll-Son to tremble as he lay there, mumbling the only thing that gave him comfort.

'Samuel Blink, Samuel Blink, Samuel–'

But even that didn't ease his anxious mind.

The name had lost some of its warmth and flavour the moment he had seen Samuel raise his arm to vote for him to go back home.

Why had Samuel done that? Troll-Son couldn't understand it. So instead of 'Samuel Blink' he began to mumble something else, something drowned out by the sound of the roaring engine.

'No friend, no friend, no friend . . .'

Right at that very moment, as her son lay hiding in the boot of a speeding car, Troll-Mother was unable to sleep. She had gone to bed at the crack of dawn, with Troll-Daughter lying by her side, but today she was strangely restless.

As she currently had no eyeball, she wasn't distracted by the tiny, square, glassless window and the green forest light beyond.

Nor was she kept awake by Troll-Daughter snoring by her side, lost in the dreamless sleep of trolls. After all, Troll-Daughter always snored.

No, it was something else keeping Troll-Mother awake.

Something she couldn't name because she had never felt it before.

But Troll-Mother isn't writing this story. I am. So I

will tell you precisely what Troll-Mother was feeling. She was feeling *guilty*.

As she lay there on that soft pillow, she thought about Troll-Son. 'Where be you, boy?' she whispered. In the blind darkness it was easy to imagine he was there in the room with her.

'I be trying my best and I know I be a clouty mother sometimes and I be not so right in the treating of you. And I be wrong to be giving you the blame for some of the things I be blaming you for. For making you sleep on the stone floor. For being hipperty about eye-hole scratching. And p'raps I be hasty to be sending you to the Betterer, but I be only wanting you to know the manners like I be never knowing . . . I be . . . I be . . .' It took her a long time to find the word because she had never used it before, but eventually it fell into her mind: 'I be . . . *sorry*.'

And she pulled back the covers, and quietly climbed out of bed, or as quietly as an overweight, stone-blooded troll woman can.

Then she picked up her pillow and the top blanket and went through her house to the tiny bare room where Troll-Son had always been forced to sleep. And she was going to say more, but there was no point. Troll-Son wasn't there to hear her.

And nor was he there to watch her, with the family eyeball he had taken with him. But that didn't stop Troll-Mother bending down, ignoring the pain in her knees, and placing the pillow and blanket on the floor, ready for his return.

OUR FRIEND ERIC

Samuel stared out of the window as they drove towards Flåm. The road was empty, except for a lone cyclist up ahead. Samuel remembered one of the Norwegian words Uncle Henrik had taught him: *sykell* – bicycle. It was one of the easiest words to learn. Not quite as easy as *hus*, meaning house, or *kong*, meaning king, but certainly in the top ten. He looked beyond the fjord to Mount Myrdal. There were two words for mountain in Norway. One was *berg* and the other was *fjell*, but he couldn't remember the difference.

Martha was singing quietly next to him. It was a song she had learned from the friendly tomtegubb she had met in Shadow Forest.

'There's nothing wrong
With a little song
When things aren't going your way.

For there's no crime
In a silly rhyme
On the most unhappy–'

Suddenly her singing stopped. 'It's Cornelia.'

And Samuel saw that she was right. The lone cyclist coming towards them was indeed Cornelia, sitting perfectly upright on her bright pink bicycle.

'She hasn't noticed us,' Martha said.

'No,' said Samuel. 'She's *pretending* she hasn't noticed us.'

'Where's she going?' Martha asked.

Samuel shrugged.

'She is a rotten girl,' said Aunt Eda, keeping her eyes on the road ahead. 'A rotten apple fallen from a rotten tree.'

As they came into Flåm, Samuel continued to stare out of the window, watching the blue- and white-painted wooden houses slide past. They passed the church, with its strange short steeple, and the brand new Myklebust Hotel, the tallest building in the village. The Flåm International Five-star Luxury Peace and Tranquillity Spa Getaway Hotel and Mountain Resort Complex. A building that stood out like a gold tooth in an otherwise healthy mouth. It was like a tall curved mirror rising out of the ground, with a billboard in front of it. The billboard featured a picture of Mr Myklebust, smiling in front of painted mountains – mountains that blocked the view of the real mountains behind.

The car pulled onto the high street, passed the bookshop, Old Tor's art gallery, the tourist office and the Myklebust Museet, which was less of a museum and more of a gift shop designed to make Mr Myklebust even more money. They parked outside the *dagligvarebutikk* – the grocer's – where Aunt Eda planned to finish the shopping trip by getting the meat and the bread and cheese for Henrik and Samuel's sandwiches. First they were going to cross over the road and go to the hardware store, the only timber building on the street that was left unpainted.

'Right, come on, children, let's get the baskets out . . . .we don't haff much time before things begin to close. And remember, the willagers are ferry nosy people. If they start asking questions about Henrik, or the forest, or runaway trolls, we don't tell them anything. Do you understand?'

'Yes,' said Samuel and Martha together, in the kind of weary voices used to answer registers or recite prayers. 'We understand.'

And so the two children climbed out of the car and followed their aunt to the boot. They took out the baskets and then, just as they were about to notice the curled-up, trembling figure of Troll-Son, there was a voice. Behind them.

'*Goddag,* Eda.'

They turned round to see an old, decrepit-looking man with a long white beard, wearing a paint-splattered smock. He was holding a bag from the hardware store, full of tubes of oil paint. Samuel recognized him instantly as Old Tor. The man who had once seen a two-headed troll escaping from the forest as he painted a moonlit fjord scene. The man who had been spotted by the huldres pursuing that two-headed troll. The man who had, in his eighties, discovered he could outrun galloping horses with the bracelet he had found – the Hek bracelet he had given to Aunt Eda when she had gone into the forest to find Samuel and Martha.

They spoke in Norwegian for a couple of minutes.

Aunt Eda had to make excuses about why she hadn't returned the Hek bracelet.

'I need the bracelet,' he said. 'I can't sleep without it. I'm so scared. I see things. I close my eyes and I see two-headed trolls, and those evil huldres on horseback galloping towards me.'

'I'll get you the bracelet,' Aunt Eda said. 'Don't worry. But you should know that the forest has changed – it is a—' She nearly said 'safe place' but checked herself just in time. She knew that if it really were considered a 'safe place', then Mr Myklebust would ruin the whole forest within weeks.

As it turned out, it didn't matter. Old Tor wasn't even listening. He was in a stunned kind of trance. He was convinced that, behind Aunt Eda and the two children, he could see a troll. A young, cyclopic troll boy, climbing out of the car boot and walking off down the high street.

He blinked, and blinked again, but it was still there, so he reached into his pocket and took one of the pills the doctor had given him.

Aunt Eda didn't take much notice of this, or of his pale, shocked expression. Old Tor had always been a bit strange. He was an artist, after all. And ever since he was chased by huldres he'd been even stranger.

'Right, well, we had better be getting on. We've a lot of shopping to do. *Morna*, Tor.'

Old Tor didn't say anything. He just stood there like a statue. A statue called *Old Man Sees a Troll in the High Street and Nearly Has a Heart Attack*.

And so Aunt Eda left Old Tor standing there, shut the now empty car boot and led Samuel and Martha into the hardware store.

Samuel and Martha both stayed near the window, looking at a strange-looking boy walking down the high street.

'Is that . . . .?' Samuel gasped.

And Martha saw him too. '*Troll-Son*.' They ran out of the store while Aunt Eda was still deciding which torch to buy.

'We've got to get him before anyone sees,' said Samuel.

'It's broad daylight,' said Martha. 'Someone's bound to see!'

Samuel was first to reach him, and grabbed his shoulder. 'Troll-Son, what are you doing?'

'No forest. No go forest. I be staying here.'

Martha noticed someone stepping out of one of the shops: a man with blond hair and a blond moustache wearing a yellow apron. It was Oskar, the grocer, and he was coming straight towards them to see who the odd-looking boy was who had just walked past his window.

'Quick,' Martha said to Samuel. 'Give him your hat. And your scarf – and your coat.'

Samuel hurriedly put his scarf around Troll-Son's neck and his coat over Troll-Son's shoulders. 'Put your arms through the sleeves,' he told the troll. 'Do it! Quick!' Then he took off his woolly hat and placed it on Troll-Son's head, pulling it down over his eye.

'Now, Troll-Son, listen to me. You mustn't say a word. Do you understand me?'

'I be understanding, Samuel Blink.'

Martha had turned round, doing her best good-girl smile as Oskar approached.

'You,' said Oskar, in a heavy Norwegian accent. 'It's you, the Englanders who went into the forest, isn't it? You who are staying with Eda, *ja*?'

Martha nodded as Samuel adjusted Troll-Son's scarf so that it covered his chin. 'Yes. It is just us, the Englanders, minding our own business.'

Oskar came no closer, clearly concerned about what Troll-Son might be capable of. 'And what is this? Is this something you found in the forest?'

'No,' said Samuel quickly. 'No . . . this is . . . my

friend . . . from England. Eric. He's called Eric.'

'Eric?' Oskar looked suspicious. 'Hello, Eric.'

'He doesn't speak,' said Martha.

'He's shy with grown-ups,' said Samuel.

Oskar plucked up the courage to step forward, and peered at Troll-Son. 'Why does he wear his hat so low?'

'He's . . . er . . . cold,' said Samuel. 'He gets cold . . . er . . . eyes. He likes to wear it like this. He can see through the . . . wool.'

Oskar surveyed the broad, lumpy nose and the warty cheeks. 'He's quite ugly, isn't he?'

'Shhh!' said Martha. 'He's very . . . sensitive. He's been bullied about his nose at school. You'll make him cry.'

Oskar nodded, but his eyes remained suspicious. Samuel and Martha watched in horror as his hand reached towards the woolly hat covering the top half of Troll-Son's face, ready to whip it off. Closer and closer and–

'*Oskar?*'

It was Aunt Eda, coming out of the hardware store with three baskets hooked around her arms – one full of supplies, the other two being those left on the floor by Samuel and Martha when they ran out after Troll-Son.

'*Oskar?*'

The grocer heard his name and the hand that was about to move Troll-Son's hat dropped to his side. And the look of stern suspicion on his face melted suddenly, like cheese in a fire, as he heard the sound of Eda's voice.

'Ah, Eda . . .' he said, standing up and straightening his yellow bow tie and smoothing his blond moustache. 'I'm so pleased to see you. I was just introducing myself to Eric.'

'Eric?'

Samuel and Martha nodded vigorously behind Oskar's back and pointed to Troll-Son.

'Ah yes,' Aunt Eda said. 'Yes, Eric. Little Eric. How could I forget about him?'

Then, in Norwegian, Oskar spoke again. 'I hear Henrik has come back from the forest. Is that true?'

Aunt Eda gave the smallest of nods.

'There will be a lot of people asking questions, you know. Questions about what happened to him in the forest.'

'Well, people really should mind their own business.'

'I could help you, you know. If you wanted to come round and talk about it one evening. It must have been so hard, having a husband run away from you for ten years . . . So if you ever wanted to talk to me, I am here. I would *always* be here.'

'Thank you, Oskar,' said Aunt Eda rather crossly. 'But we really must be getting back. Now, come on, children. Come on, Samuel, Martha and . . . Eric. Let's be getting home. Come on, Eric. It's all right. Come on. It's safe with us.'

And Oskar remained on the pavement as he watched Aunt Eda and Samuel drag Eric back to the battered old car, with Martha following. Little did they know there was another watcher too – Mr Myklebust, who was standing in the doorway of the tourist office.

When the car drove off, he jogged heavily over to where Oskar was standing.

'Who was that third child?' Mr Myklebust asked, out of breath, as he held the sides of his vast belly.

Oskar didn't like Mr Myklebust very much, and had refused about a hundred offers from him to buy the grocer's. 'I don't know,' he said.

'Was it . . . could it possibly have been . . . a *troll*?'

Oskar knew precisely what he was being asked. He knew how much Mr Myklebust hated Henrik. As a young man he had witnessed the infamous 'human snowball' incident on Mount Myrdal. And although Oskar was in some ways a good man, he was weak, and his biggest weakness was Aunt Eda, a woman he had secretly hoped would run into his arms when Henrik disappeared.

'Yes,' Oskar said, after a very long pause. 'I think it was.'

Meanwhile, Samuel was giving instructions to Troll-Son in the back seat of the car.

'Keep your head down! And keep the hat on!'

'I be sorry . . . I be sorry . . . I be sorry . . .'

'I don't understand it,' said Aunt Eda. 'How did you get here?'

Martha stared at the empty basket on her knee. 'The boot. He must have climbed into the boot.'

Aunt Eda nodded. 'Oh, this is no good. This is no good at all. It's happening again. The forest is threatening our happiness. The willagers are turning on us. No good, I tell you. No good at all.'

The car drove as fast as it could be driven out of Flåm. They headed towards the supermarket as they hadn't been able to do their shopping at the grocer's and they still needed to buy stuff for the sandwiches.

'Well, why don't we move?' Samuel said.

Aunt Eda nodded. 'Samuel, I am afraid I think we do not haff the option. Who would buy a house so close to Shadow Forest? Of course, we could tell people it is safe, but then the forest itself would be in danger. Oh, it is a ferry difficult situation.'

The supermarket was tiny compared to the supermarkets Samuel had known in England. And made of wood too, like everything else.

Aunt Eda and Martha disappeared inside while Samuel stayed guarding Troll-Son inside the car.

'The Betterer be bad, Samuel Blink,' said Troll-Son, crouching down in the back. 'He be so bad.'

Samuel gulped. He couldn't be cross with Troll-Son any more. Not really. He wasn't trying to cause trouble. He was just scared. 'I'm sorry,' he said. 'But it's too dangerous for you here. It's too dangerous for Aunt Eda and Uncle Henrik and all of us. You have to go home.'

Troll-Son didn't seem to be listening. 'He be coming,' he said, the words chilling Samuel Blink even more than the cold, unheated air of the old car. 'He be coming for me. You be seeing, Samuel Blink. You be seeing.'

Halfway home, they saw her again. Cornelia. This time cycling back in the opposite direction.

'What on earth has she been doing?' asked Aunt Eda.

'Something evil,' said Samuel.

But Martha said nothing. She just stopped humming the made-up tune that had been in her head and twisted round on the back seat. She stared at her former best friend getting smaller on the road behind, turning to a tiny pink speck amid the vast landscape, and then into nothing at all.

PICKLES AND PREPARATIONS

'Oh yes,' said Uncle Henrik, once he realized Troll-Son had been found. 'Cornelia came round. She came to say sorry. Her dad must have been waiting in the car.'

Samuel shook his head. 'She *biked* here.'

'Biked?'

Aunt Eda sighed her agreement. 'We passed her on the way. Going there and coming back.'

'What did she do when she was here?' asked Samuel.

Uncle Henrik shrugged. 'Nothing. She said sorry. She said she was "deeply, deeply, deeply sorry", or maybe it was even "deeply, deeply, deeply, deeply sorry", and that's all.'

'And then she went?' Samuel said.

'Yes,' he said, before something seemed to cloud his face. 'Well, no. She needed the toilet, and *then* she went.'

Everyone looked slightly worried about this information, and Martha in particular. She consoled herself with a pickled cloudberry from one of the jars they had just bought in the supermarket, and nothing more was said about Cornelia. There were too many other things to discuss, like when Uncle Henrik, Samuel and Troll-Son were going to head into the forest.

'Now, I have been thinking,' said Uncle Henrik. 'And what I have been thinking is that it might be best to wait until it's dark.'

Aunt Eda looked rather dismayed by the prospect. 'Dark? Why? Won't it be more dangerous?'

Uncle Henrik offered a gentle smile. 'Eda, love, it won't be dangerous if we go in the day *or* the night. The forest is *safe*. But it makes more sense to go at night, when fewer creatures will be able to see us, and those that do won't be wondering what a troll is doing out and about in daylight.'

Aunt Eda gave a reluctant nod as she put away the last of the shopping. 'Well, I suppose it will give me time to prepare everything. But you and Samuel must try and get some rest before you go. And Troll-Son too, although it is probably best if he stays down here on the sofa, where we can keep an eye on him. I'll fetch some blankets.'

And so it was.

Samuel went upstairs to lie on his bed, although his mind was too restless (and the room too light) for him to really sleep. He kept hearing Troll-Son's voice echo in his mind. *He be coming.* Who? Who was coming? Surely the Betterer wouldn't be coming here, would he? Trolls never ventured into the Outer World. Well, apart from Troll-Son.

Samuel kept gazing around the room as these worries marched through his mind. He looked at the tall wooden wardrobe, at the chest of drawers, at Martha's empty bed. Pretty, human things crafted from wood. Trees that had been turned into something else yet still contained something of their former life. They suddenly seemed strange to him, these objects. They seemed full of silent warnings that he couldn't interpret but knew were there, craving to be understood.

Downstairs, as Troll-Son lay snoring on the sofa, Aunt Eda and Martha prepared sandwiches. Gjetost cheese and pickles in sourdough bread. Martha, of course, was overseeing the pickles, and for every two that found their way onto the bread, one would find its way into her mouth.

'You really like pickles, don't you?' said Aunt Eda.

Martha nodded, crunched and swallowed. 'Yes, I'm sorry. I can't help it. They're so *pickley*.'

You see, if Martha had a weakness it was this: the inability to resist things. If she thought about something, such as the sharp and wonderful taste of a pickle, and if that pickle was there to be had, then it would be almost impossible for her to resist. But it wasn't just pickles. She could think of something – blinking, swallowing, humming a tune – and the moment she had thought of it, she would have to do it. It was strange, really. Not horrible, but strange. And she never used to be like this, in the days before a giant log thought it would be a good idea to roll off a timber lorry and crush her parents to death. No, in those days she would have been able to think of something and stop herself doing it. But that was before, when everything was different.

'Well, maybe I should give you another job,' said Aunt Eda. 'Why don't you go upstairs and fetch the

Hek bracelet? But remember, try and be quiet. Uncle Henrik will be asleep.'

And so Martha tore herself away from the pickles and headed upstairs while Aunt Eda finished off the sandwiches. She trod softly across the bedroom past a snoozing Uncle Henrik. She reached into the drawer, pulled out the jewellery box, opened it – and gasped. The bracelet wasn't there. She searched the whole drawer, sending Aunt Eda's knickers and long-johns flying behind her. Nope. It had definitely disappeared.

'But it can't ha–' she whispered.

And then she remembered.

She had told Cornelia about the bracelet. It had been a stupid thing to do, really, now she thought about it. But Cornelia had been going on and on about all the things she owned – like the ponies (and Martha had wanted a horse all her life but her parents had never been rich enough). And even though she had probably known, *deep down*, that Cornelia wasn't the nicest sort of person to be around, Martha had felt – and she was ashamed to admit it now – slightly honoured that Cornelia had paid so much attention to her. And when Cornelia told her about her ponies and the million other things she owned, Martha had wanted to impress her too, so that is why she had mentioned the Hek bracelet. She hadn't said it was from the forest but she had explained its magic powers. And had even told her where it was hidden.

'Deeply, deeply sorry? I'll bet,' said Martha as she thought of what Uncle Henrik had told them about Cornelia's unexpected visit. And, as the light drained away beyond the curtains, she had the familiar feeling that she had let everyone down.

MR MYKLEBUST AND THE TWO TROLLS

Magnus Myklebust hated the fjord. Every time he saw it he remembered that horrendous day when he had tripped over Henrik's skis, rolled down the mountain and ended up splashing into the cold water.

But the path that circled the fjord was the best place from which to spy on Henrik and Eda's house. After all, if he was spotted, he would probably just look like a night fisherman – though the only things he was fishing for were secrets.

'Oh, Henrik,' he whispered to himself as he stared through his binoculars. 'You may have fooled Tomas Thomassen, but Magnus Myklebust is not so stupid.'

A light went on upstairs. The light in Samuel and Martha's bedroom. He saw a shadow pass across the curtains. It didn't look like a human shadow. But there was no point taking a picture of a shadow – what proof was that?

Then he heard something.

Distant voices carried over from the forest. He looked through his binoculars, half expecting to see some monsters emerge from among the trees, but there was nothing.

'You big baby,' he told himself. 'Stop imagining things.'

Turning back to the house, he saw a light go on downstairs. This was much more promising, as the curtains weren't closed properly.

I bet that's the troll in there now, moving around.

He pulled out the camera that was lying beside the ten beef sandwiches in his picnic hamper.

Through the zoom lens he could definitely see someone moving about in the living room, but it wasn't clear if it was a troll or a human.

If he were to find the kind of evidence that would put Henrik in prison, he would need to get a closer look. So he left the hamper where it was and started walking towards the house.

So intent was his gaze on the window that he didn't notice the two silent figures who had just left the forest.

Even as they approached, Magnus remained perfectly unaware. He bent forward, or as forward as his vast stomach allowed, and kept as low as possible. When, finally, he reached the house, he waited to catch his breath with his back against the timber walls.

It was as he was putting a new film into the camera that he felt a hand grip his arm. He turned and saw them. The trolls. But these weren't child trolls. These were full-sized, scary-looking things that could have been capable of anything.

The one who held onto his arm was wearing a long coat, and had a smart, slicked-down hairstyle that did nothing to disguise the profound ugliness of his long face. The lumpy nose, the broad chin, the lipless mouth full of rotten teeth and the red warts on his forehead were all horrible enough, but it was the eyes that most frightened Mr Myklebust. They were eyes that, even in the gloom of night-time, shone terror like windows in a haunted house.

The creature next to him didn't have any eyes – simply a single empty eye-socket in his forehead that caused Magnus to gasp out loud – so it was hard to tell precisely how evil he was, but he looked just as hideous. In contrast to the smart hair and overcoat of the taller troll, this one had tattered clothes and a raggedy beard.

Magnus tried to stay calm. After all, the troll that was in the house seemed harmless. Maybe these trolls were harmless too.

This hope vanished when the taller one pulled a piece of thin wood out from inside his overcoat. Magnus had never seen a Bettering Branch before, but he knew it was something to fear.

'Please . . .' he said. 'Please . . . don't hurt me.'

Perhaps he should scream for help. After all, Henrik would hear him . . . No. Even if he could find the courage, it was too risky, and the Bettering Branch was too close to his neck – twitching like a curious snake – to take that risk.

The eyeless, bearded troll was the first to speak. 'We be not going to hur–'

'Ssssh,' said the other troll sharply.

'Who . . . who . . . are you?' Magnus asked, trembling.

'I'm the Betterer,' the taller one said, in a voice so cold and quiet it was as though it came from the chill night air.

'And I be Troll-Father,' said the one who clung to

the Betterer's arm. 'We be trolls, sir. Humble trolls, that's all we–'

'*Ssssh,*' said the Betterer, even more impatiently than before.

The Betterer's terrifying eyes glanced over Mr Myklebust, observing him the way a scientist observes a test tube. A rather *round* test tube.

'I never realized humans could be so feeble,' he said, noticing Mr Myklebust's shaking hands. 'Or so *fat.*'

'Please . . .' Mr Myklebust said. It was the only word he had to offer. 'Please . . . please . . . please . . .'

'Be you seeing my son, sir?' said Troll-Father.

'We're looking for a troll boy,' added the Betterer. 'A troll boy we believe has run out of the forest to stay with a human called . . . What was the name again?'

'Samuel Blink,' said Troll-Father.

The Betterer nodded, and stared down at the camera hanging around Mr Myklebust's neck. He'd never seen a camera before, and wondered if it was a kind of weapon. If it *was* a weapon, then Mr Myklebust seemed too scared to use it.

'Do you know this Samuel Blink?' the Betterer asked, his voice so sharp it seemed to carve the air. 'And you had *better.*'

Mr Myklebust nodded frantically. 'Yes, I know Samuel Blink. And I know the troll is with him.'

'You're lying.'

'No. No I'm not.'

Troll-Father's frowning face melted with relief. 'Be my son alive?'

Mr Myklebust kept nodding. 'Yes.'

'That be such good news.'

The Betterer clenched his eyes shut, as if Troll-Father's happy voice caused him pain. 'Just tell us where they are,' he said.

Mr Myklebust hesitated. 'They're . . . ver . . . I . . . they're . . .'

'*Tell* us.'

'They're here.'

'Here?'

'In this house.'

The Betterer touched one of the timber planks that clad the outside wall. '*This* house?'

'Yes.'

'Very good. Very good indeed.' He stroked the timber as if it were an animal he'd just bought.

'My boy,' added Troll-Father, with glorious relief. 'My boy be here.'

THE COMPANY OF TROLLS

Everything was ready. The sandwiches were made. The batteries were in the torch. The backpack was stuffed with blankets, sleeping bags, a tent, a portable gas fire, a Swiss Army knife and camping lanterns. Uncle Henrik had doubted whether they needed anything more than a torch – he was sure they would be home by dawn – but Aunt Eda wanted them packed just in case.

'Right, Troll-Son,' said Uncle Henrik. 'I'm afraid this is it. It is time to take you home. Samuel, are you ready? Will you be warm enough?'

Samuel yawned, wishing he'd managed to get some sleep. 'Yes, I'm ready. And I'll certainly be warm enough.' Instead of the thin jacket he'd brought with him to Norway, he was wearing the jumper Aunt Eda had given him. It was a thick jumper and very big, but perfect, Aunt Eda had said at the time, for a Norwegian winter. Samuel hated it, but agreed with his aunt when she'd told him to put it on tonight. After all, he knew how night-time could feel in Shadow Forest.

'Oh, how I wish you were taking the Hek bracelet,' said Aunt Eda.

'Why don't we go round to Cornelia's house and ask for it back?' Samuel knew his suggestion was ridiculous even as he made it. After all, someone as cunning as Cornelia would not only deny having the bracelet, but would also have made sure it was so well hidden it could never be found.

'I think we'll be all right,' Uncle Henrik said. 'Hek bracelet or not.'

Aunt Eda was moving quickly about the place like a bluebottle trapped in a jar, checking everything.

'Eda, don't worry,' said Uncle Henrik. 'Everything is fine. It's not like last time.'

And Aunt Eda nodded as she looked down at Troll-Son's miserable face. She knew Henrik was right. She knew the forest was safe for humans now. But still she had this *feeling* – this unsettled feeling that sat in her stomach like a kind of seasickness – as though she were on a boat in rough water heading towards a waterfall.

'Yes, well, I suppose we should fetch Martha down. Samuel, do you want to call your sister? I'm sure she would be ferry upset if you left without saying goodbye.'

Martha was upstairs, lying on her bed. Not singing, not humming or talking away the silence. She was miserable, you see, because she knew it was her fault the Hek bracelet had gone missing, just as it had been her fault Cornelia had come round in the first place.

'All right,' said Samuel. 'I'll get her.' And he went to the foot of the stairs and called his sister's name. 'Martha! Mar–'

Right then, much to everyone's surprise, there was a knock at the door. A rather feeble-sounding knock, but a knock all the same.

'Who on earth can that be at this time?' wondered Aunt Eda.

'I don't know,' said Uncle Henrik. 'Shall I get it?'

'No. You must hide. With Troll-Son. We don't want people asking any more questions. Go. Into the laundry room. Go on, quick. Me and Samuel will see to it.'

And so Uncle Henrik took Troll-Son by the hand

and led him quickly through the kitchen into the cool darkness of the laundry room. The knock came again, just as feeble as before.

'Don't answer it,' said Samuel.

Aunt Eda looked confused. 'What?'

'Don't answer it. Just don't. We don't have to.'

Aunt Eda paused. Considered. She looked around the living room, as if the rocking chair or the oil-painted mountains or the old bookcase were about to offer advice. 'They know we're in – the lights are on.'

'So? We don't have to answer it.'

The knock came a third time, and with more force. Aunt Eda shook her head. 'No. We haff to. It might be something important.'

'But–'

Aunt Eda left Samuel in the living room and went to open the door. 'I'm coming, I'm coming . . .'

And as she twisted the door knob, the feeling in her stomach intensified. It was as though the imaginary boat had reached the imaginary waterfall and was tipping her forward, fast, towards untold horror.

Samuel poked his head round into the hallway to see the identity of the mystery caller. It was with some degree of relief that he realized it was Mr Myklebust.

True, Mr Myklebust wasn't exactly Samuel's

favourite person, but in his tired and anxious state he had been imagining someone even worse.

'Magnus,' said Aunt Eda. 'What on earth are you doing here?'

She noticed, as Samuel did, that Mr Myklebust wasn't quite himself. He looked even worse than usual, which was quite some feat. Paler, sweatier, more out of breath. He had a camera around his neck too, which struck Eda as most suspicious.

'Magnus, have you been . . . *spying* on us?'

At first it seemed that Mr Myklebust wasn't going to say anything at all. He just stood there, his bald head shining with sweat despite the cold weather, his eyes bulging with a strange terror.

'Magnus? Magnus? What is it? What's the matter?'

'Is . . . is . . . is . . . is Samuel in?'

'Samuel? What do you want with Samuel? Is this still about that troll we're supposed to be hiding?'

She noticed Mr Myklebust's trembling hands.

'No,' he said, and looked to his left, like an actor waiting for a prompt. 'I just wondered if . . . Samuel . . .'

'Yes,' said Aunt Eda. 'Yes, but he's about to go to bed. Now, whatever it is you have to say to him you can say to me, I'm sure. Go on, tell–'

Samuel heard his aunt gasp, and then saw the reason why. Two strange figures emerged out of the dark, stepping behind Mr Myklebust. *Trolls.* One was as tall as the door, with a sinister face, and a smart long overcoat. He had the rough skin and broad nose of a troll, but his hair was slicked down into a neat parting. This troll had two eyes, in roughly the right places, unlike the other troll, who had only one eye-socket with no eyeball inside it.

This eyeless troll was a bit shorter, with a kinder face – one instantly familiar to Samuel. He had met him in the forest. He had sought shelter in his house after being chased by huldres. 'Troll-Father . . .' he whispered.

'Oh, hello,' said Aunt Eda, most confused as to why Mr Myklebust should be arriving on her doorstep in the company of two trolls. 'And who are you?'

'They need . . . need . . . to see . . . Samuel,' said Mr Myklebust.

'Samuel? Whateffer for?'

'We're looking for a troll boy,' said the tall troll in a deep and whispery voice.

Aunt Eda stared into Mr Myklebust's face, wondering whether to keep the lie alive. 'A troll boy? We haffen't seen a troll boy. No, I can assure you that if we'd seen a troll boy we'd know about it.'

It was at that point that the tall troll's eyes caught sight of Samuel. 'You,' he said. 'Are you Samuel Blink?'

Samuel came into the hall, but said nothing.

And then, during the silence, the Betterer produced the thin wooden branch, which twisted into the shape of a question mark and prodded into Mr Myklebust's flabby side. The Bettering Branch then began to grow and curl around his vast stomach, tightening and causing him to choke. Mr Myklebust was pushed forward into the house before Aunt Eda could shut the door. A moment later, both trolls, and their captive, were in the hall.

'Oh, good Heffens, who are you people?' asked Aunt Eda.

'I will ask you again, dear boy. Are you Mr Samuel Blink?'

Samuel swallowed, and saw how terrified his aunt looked. He had to do it again, he realized. He had to act like a hero, even though he didn't feel anything like one. But still he forced himself to say it.

'Yes,' he said. 'I'm Samuel Blink.'

THE BETTERER PRODS TROLL-FATHER INTO REMEMBERING SOMETHING HE HAD LONG FORGOTTEN

'Stop,' said the Betterer and his Bettering Branch duly uncoiled itself from around Mr Myklebust's body. Then he pointed the branch towards Samuel. 'Now, perhaps you can tell us where Troll-Son is?'

Samuel looked at Aunt Eda, whose eyebrows were insisting he tell the truth.

'I don't know what you're talking about,' he said.

'Oh, very good,' said the Betterer. And then he looked at Troll-Father, who was clearly confused about what was going on. 'Observe, Troll-Father. Observe very carefully. Oh – of course, you can't. Well, listen instead. For here we encounter the true sophistication of a human. Not a quiver in his voice. Not a doubt in his eyes. And yet we know he is lying.'

Troll-Father frowned. 'Samuel Blink be a good

boy, Mr Betterer, sir. We be not wanting any trouble.'

'Trouble, Troll-Father? Trouble? Am I a lowly thug? I am here to find your son, that is all. I am here to better him, so he will never do anything like this again.'

Troll-Father winced. 'Now, Mr Betterer, sir, I be thinking about that and I be thinking perhaps Troll-Son be not really needing to be betterered – not just yet–'

'Not *needing* to be bettered?' The Betterer was clearly appalled by the idea and, in his distraction, failed to notice Mr Myklebust shuffle backwards out of the front door and disappear from view.

The Betterer then pressed the tip of the Bettering Branch against Troll-Father's stomach and, with a flick of the wrist, brought it to life once more. Troll-Father's empty eye-socket was wide open in yawning horror as he felt the wood coil around him.

'What be happening?' he said. 'What be happening? What be happening?'

'Leave him alone,' said Samuel.

'Yes, leef him alone,' said Aunt Eda, whose face didn't quite know if it was cross or frightened.

It was at this point in the proceedings that Uncle Henrik emerged from the laundry room. He carefully closed the door behind him, making sure Troll-Son was still inside.

He grabbed a knife from the rack in the kitchen, but the Betterer already seen him from the hall.

'I suggest that if you want your wife and boy to remain alive, you will put that down,' he said, the branch still squeezing around Troll-Father.

Uncle Henrik put down the knife and came towards the hallway, his hands in the air. 'Please,' he said. 'We can talk about this. Why can't we act like gentlemen?'

The word 'gentlemen' seemed to have a strange effect on the Betterer: he looked as if he had suddenly swallowed too much mustard.

'You arrogant human,' he said. 'You see my trollish nose and skin and you assume I am not a gentleman. You think I do not understand what it means to have a refined mind?'

'No,' said Uncle Henrik, stepping closer. 'That is not what I meant.'

'Silence! Stop right there!'

Uncle Henrik felt strange, hearing this command, but knew he couldn't afford to have one of his funny turns. *I'm not a dog,* he told himself, and despite a fleeting desire to run on all fours and grab the branch, he stayed in control, and in the kitchen.

The Bettering Branch had also seemed to obey the

Betterer's command. But although it stopped moving, it stayed wrapped around Troll-Father's body. Samuel looked at Uncle Henrik to see if he had a plan, but found no sign of it on his face. A face which by now was a grim shade of pale.

So, there they all were. Aunt Eda and Samuel standing close together in the hall, Uncle Henrik forced to stay in the kitchen, and all three of them watching the Betterer and his eyeless, branch-coiled hostage.

'Oh, Troll-Son!' called the Betterer, in a voice loud enough to reach every corner of the house. 'Oh, Troll-Son! Come out, come out, wherever you are! It is time for your first lesson . . . Let's call it Family Loyalty. I have your father, Troll-Son. I have his life in my hands . . . I only have to give the command and the Bettering Branch will take him from you for ever. And if anyone else moves, including you, Troll-Father, it will be over anyway.'

'I be not understanding,' said Troll-Father, choking from the branch that was still coiled around his chest and stomach. 'I be not . . . understanding . . . Why be you doing this? You be wanting to help me, that is why you be here.'

The Betterer laughed so loud it made Samuel jump.

'Help *you*? That is funny, Troll-Father. For an

imbecile you really do have a remarkable sense of humour. Or perhaps you mean I should help you in the way you helped me, by teaching me the painful and cruel nature of this life.'

'I be not understanding . . . I be not teaching you. Never I be teaching–'

'Oh, can you not remember? That important lesson you taught me by the lake?'

Samuel looked at Aunt Eda, then at Uncle Henrik. It was clear none of them had the faintest clue what the Betterer was talking about. Neither, it seemed, did Troll-Father.

'By the lake? I be not–' he said, and choked again as he tried in vain to free himself from the branch.

'Yes, by the lake. A very valuable lesson it was too, given from one troll boy to another. "Look at your face," you told me. "You be not a human. You be a troll." Oh, what does it matter if a lesson causes untold pain. For what is pain but truth? And truth is always the key point of every lesson, is it not.'

Troll-Father's mouth widened with his eye-socket: he suddenly remembered that day in his childhood when he had met the peculiar troll boy who thought he was a human. 'It be . . . *you.*'

ANOTHER RUDE INTERRUPTION FROM THE AUTHOR

Yes, yes, I know. It's rude to interrupt. Especially when you're getting towards the end of a book. And feel free to skip this interruption and flick to the next chapter to find out what the Betterer does next. I promise I won't mind. And even if I did mind, what could I do? It's not like I could make the rest of the book disappear until I'd forced you to read this bit. And really, this bit isn't that important to the story. I mean, if you didn't read it you'd still know what was going on. Because all I want to do is tell you about what Troll-Father remembered, with the Bettering Branch coiled around him.

Oh well, just in case you are actually still reading, I might as well get on with telling you. Even if you're not still reading, it won't stop these words from actually being here. Or maybe it will. Maybe when you close the book the words all disappear, and only come back when you open it up again. But either way, they're here now, and are about to describe what Troll-Father remembered. Look:

Many, many years ago, when Troll-Father was a little boy and called – like most troll boys – Troll-Son, he used to go fishing at the magical saltwater lake in Shadow Forest. It was his favourite thing in the world. To sit on the edge of Still Lake and try and catch a trunklefish. Of course, he couldn't cook or eat these fish. They are so poisonous that one mouthful would have killed him before he had a chance to swallow. No, as soon as he had caught a trunklefish he always put it straight back in the water. And besides, he always managed to catch another one. The joy was in sitting there on his own, without his parents nagging him.

He rarely ever saw anyone. It was usually just him, the still water and the trunklefish. But one day he *did* see someone. Another troll, about his own age. Only this troll was walking not from Trollhelm, but from the opposite direction. Another thing that struck the young Troll-Father as rather odd about this troll boy was the way he was dressed. He had never in all his life seen a troll looking so smart.

The troll boy came over to talk. And for a short while they enjoyed a most agreeable conversation about trunklefish. Troll-Father (who was then called Troll-Son) told the boy that trunklefish move slowly in the water and act dopey because of the salt.

'It be making them sleepy,' he said.

'Sleepy? I should take a cup of water and let it evaporate, so all the salt will be left,' said the boy in smart clothes. 'Then I could fall asleep just by sniffing it.'

'Evaporate? I not be understanding that word.'

'That's because you're a troll.'

'So be you.'

'No,' laughed the smartly dressed boy. 'I am a human. I am called Martin. A troll! Honestly, that's so funny.'

Troll-Father-who-was-then-called-Troll-Son pointed to the water. 'You be not a human with a face like that. You be a troll. There be no humans in Shadow Forest. Be looking there in the water. You not be having one eye like me but you be having a lumpy face like mine. And be looking at your big nose. That be a troll's nose, that be.'

The smartly dressed boy was silent for what seemed like ages. Then he leaned over the water's edge and stared into the still surface at his reflection.

'Be you all right?' asked Troll-Father-who-was-then-called-Troll-Son.

Eventually the smartly dressed boy answered, in the quietest and saddest voice you can imagine: 'I . . . I . . . I . . . be . . . a . . . troll.' He looked at Troll-Father-who-was-then-called-Troll-Son. 'I hate you, I hate you, I hate you,' he told him. 'You disgusting troll!'

And Troll-Father remembered him running away, disappearing into the woodland on the north side of the lake. Never to be seen again – or so he had thought.

Right, OK, that's it. Did that add a certain depth to Troll-Father's tragic plight? Did it add a psychological insight to your understanding of the Betterer's sinister mind?

Oh, who cares? I'm off.

Bye.

A FISHING LESSON

The Betterer commanded the Bettering Branch to tighten its grip around Troll-Father's body, and called again, 'Troll-Son! So far you are failing the lesson . . . I think we need to apply a little pressure. A deadline, you could call it. I will count down from ten. When I reach zero, your father will be dead unless you come out from your hiding place. Ten . . . nine . . . eight . . .'

'Please,' said Troll-Father, turning a greyish colour. 'Be not doing this.'

'. . . seven . . . six . . . five . . .'

'We told you,' said Samuel. 'We don't know where he is. You really might as well go home.'

'Samuel,' hissed Aunt Eda, out of the side of her mouth. 'Sssh.'

'. . . four . . . three . . .'

'Can we just talk about this reasonably?' said Uncle Henrik. 'Man to . . . er . . . troll? Let's not do anything hasty.'

'. . . two. One . . . Very well, Troll-Son,' said the Betterer. 'Your father must–'

'No,' said Samuel. 'Wait!'

Just at that moment the laundry door creaked open and Troll-Son shuffled out.

The Betterer flicked his wrist, and the Bettering Branch stopped.

'Father,' said Troll-Son, blinking in bemusement at the scene.

'Troll-Son? Troll-Son?' Troll-Father's voice was weak, but still contained a thousand emotions as he blindly turned towards the kitchen and his son's soft approaching footsteps.

The Betterer stood back and let the reunion take place. He watched Troll-Father, with the branch wrapped around his middle, hugging his son tightly, breathing in his smell. 'I be sorry,' said Troll-Father, choking. 'I be sorry . . .'

Samuel wondered what was going to happen to Troll-Son now. What was the Betterer going to do with him? He couldn't imagine.

'Of course,' said the Betterer, 'as a former fisherman, Troll-Father knows what happens to the bait . . . It is pierced with a hook, used for its purpose, and then thrown away. *Coil, branch, coil . . .*'

The Betterer flicked the end of the branch he was holding one more time, and it tightened around Troll-Father. Within moments he was pure grey.

'No!' Troll-Son cried. 'No! Father!'

Troll-Father gasped and clutched the branch, then fell to the floor. Samuel ran towards the Betterer. 'Stop it! Let him go!'

'Samuel! No!' cried Aunt Eda and Uncle Henrik both at once.

But too late. It was now Samuel's turn to be held in a headlock.

This time, though, the Betterer reached into his pocket for something else. A bottle containing a dark greenish liquid.

He undid the bottle with his misshapen teeth and then flicked it forward to create a large green puddle separating the two trolls and Samuel from Aunt Eda and Uncle Henrik.

Meanwhile Troll-Son was crouched over the dying body of his father, watching in despair as the flesh became greyer and greyer, gradually turning to stone.

'I too be sorry,' said Troll-Son.

'Be taking care of your mother . . . She be meaning well . . . I be–' Troll-Father's words slowed as his face stiffened, becoming petrified.

'No!' screamed Samuel.

But Troll-Son spoke quietly. 'Yes, I be doing it,' he said to his dead father. A tear fell from his eye and ran down the bridge of his nose. 'I be taking care of her.'

The Betterer realized he could now uncoil his branch from Troll-Father's neck and put it back in his pocket; then he dragged Samuel over and pressed a handkerchief into Troll-Son's crying face. A handkerchief containing a hundred tiny sleeping salts. 'Looks like you'll be needing this.'

And Samuel watched as Troll-Son collapsed, fast asleep, then tried to resist as the same handkerchief came towards his face. 'No, get off! No, get–'

But then his mind slipped into darkness and he could no more fight it away than the day can fight off the night. His body fell back against the Betterer, who hoisted up both the sleeping bodies, one over each shoulder.

Uncle Henrik and Aunt Eda both ran forward to try and save Samuel, but the moment they stepped into the dark green puddle they couldn't take another step.

'Gripgrass Juice,' explained the Betterer usefully. 'My own special recipe. Don't worry – you'll only be standing there a day or so. It wears off after a while.'

Uncle Henrik strained to pull his socks out of the puddle, or his feet out of his socks, but it was no good. Neither he nor Aunt Eda could drag themselves free. So they had to watch as the Betterer carried Troll-Son and Samuel out of the house. They could do nothing as he headed out towards the forest, leaving the stone corpse of Troll-Father lying on the floor like a fallen statue.

MR MYKLEBUST'S RETURN

Martha had been on the landing, listening to everything. Realizing the Betterer had gone, she now went downstairs to witness the most incredible scene.

Not only were her aunt and uncle rooted to the floor in the middle of a green puddle; the stone body of a troll lay in front of them. The doormat and the row of shoes were all still in place, along with all the coats on their hangers. In the kitchen she could see the packed gjetost sandwiches Aunt Eda had prepared for Uncle Henrik and Samuel. And the backpack lying ready in the living room.

All these normal things only seemed to add to the horror of what had just happened, the way light helps cast a darker shadow.

'Martha, don't come any closer,' said Aunt Eda. 'If you step in the liquid you'll stick to the floor like us.'

'Where's Samuel?' asked Martha.

'I think the Betterer's taken him back to the forest. He used some kind of sleep potion and carried him away with Troll-Son,' said Uncle Henrik.

Martha felt weak at the news, and tightened her grip on the banister. She hadn't felt quite so scared – or quite so alone – since the day her parents died.

'Wait,' said Aunt Eda. 'Someone's coming.'

And she was right. They heard heavy footsteps outside, and even heavier breathing. For the second time that night Mr Myklebust appeared in their doorway, only this time he was alone.

'Magnus?' said Henrik. 'What happened to you? Where did you go?'

Mr Myklebust wiped his brow and loosened his collar as he stared at the stone formerly known as Troll-Father. 'I went back to my car and I rang the police and spoke to Tomas. I told him about the trolls, but of course he didn't believe me. I told him people were in danger, but he just got cross with me. He said I was wasting police time. Wasting police time! In Flåm! That's a joke. Ha!' Mr Myklebust realized no one was laughing, so he asked, 'Where is the boy? Samuel?'

'The Betterer – the troll who nearly killed you – has taken him,' said Uncle Henrik. 'With Troll-Son. The troll boy.' There was no point in lying. Not now Mr Myklebust had seen trolls with his own eyes.

Mr Myklebust nodded. He saw the sadness in Henrik's face and felt something he had never expected to feel towards the man who had turned him into a human snowball all those years ago. He felt *sorry* for him.

'I suppose you are happy,' said Aunt Eda, rather sharply, 'now that you know the truth.'

'No,' said Mr Myklebust, surprised by his own answer. 'No, it doesn't make me happy at all. And I'm sorry I left you – and that I tricked you when I knocked on the door.'

'It wasn't your fault,' said Uncle Henrik.

Martha was getting quite annoyed at all this talking. 'We've got to find Samuel,' she said. 'We've got to rescue him.'

Aunt Eda looked at Uncle Henrik. 'What shall we do?'

Uncle Henrik again tried to raise his foot out of the Gripgrass Juice, but he couldn't. 'It doesn't look as though *we* will be able to do anything.'

'Well,' said Martha, already making her way

carefully around the puddle. 'It looks like it is down to me and Mr Myklebust.'

'Me?' said Mr Myklebust. 'Oh . . . no . . . I . . . er . . . I've got a very important meeting–'

'At eleven o'clock at night?' said Martha, looking at her watch.

'Well . . . I'm . . . I'm sure I wouldn't be much help. Look at me. I'm a big fat . . . a big fat coward.'

'And I'm a ten-year-old girl. But what's that got to do with it?'

Aunt Eda was looking terribly worried. 'Martha, I'm afraid Mr Myklebust is right. There is really nothing he or you can do. Or any of us.'

There was a long and hopeless silence, punctuated only by the ticking of the longcase clock in the living room. During this silence Mr Myklebust stared down at the face of Troll-Father, immortalized in stone at the moment he said goodbye to his son. All his life he – Magnus Myklebust – had wanted to be a hero. But it was only then that he understood what precisely was required to fulfil that wish. It wasn't about winning medals, or being the fastest skier down a slope, or becoming the richest man in Flåm. No. Being a hero was about something rather different. It was about taking a risk for someone else. And so, for the very first time in his life, he decided to do something heroic.

'No, Eda,' he said. 'I was wrong. I was weak. I didn't even *try* to stop that evil troll from entering the house. And I might not be as fit as I used to be, but I am sure there is something I could do to bring Samuel back.'

'You're right,' said Martha, before Aunt Eda or Uncle Henrik had time to consider an answer. 'There *is* something you can do. You can take me to Cornelia.'

Mr Myklebust looked confused. The last thing he expected was for Martha to tell him to drive *away* from the forest. 'Cornelia?'

'Yes,' said Martha. 'She's got something we'll need.'

PERSUADING CORNELIA

Mr Myklebust lived in a very large and very beautiful house, reached by a long and winding driveway. But Martha hardly noticed the tennis courts, or the stables, or the vast entrance hall, or the gymnasium, or the numerous bathrooms she encountered on her way through.

Nor did she really pay any serious attention to the woman she assumed was Mrs Myklebust, lying on a very long pink couch (or was it purple?), drinking a large glass of white wine and watching a TV the size of a cinema.

'Magnus,' the woman said, not taking her eyes off the soap opera on the screen, 'I have been thinking . . . It would be nice to have a husband who took me out for a meal once in a while. To a nice restaurant. A man who wasn't just obsessed with work, work, work. Magnus? Magnus? Are you listening to me? And who is that plain-looking thing?'

'It's – *she's* Martha Blink. Cornelia's friend. Where is she? Cornelia, I mean.'

'Upstairs in her room. Magnus, come back! Did you hear a word I just—?'

Of course, Cornelia wasn't going to give the Hek bracelet up just like that. And Martha knew that at first she would pretend she knew nothing about it at all. Which is precisely what *did* happen.

Cornelia was sitting at her desk. She had found it impossible to sleep and so was busy doing the thing that relaxed her most – really difficult sums. The desk she was sitting at was, like everything else in the house, ginormous, and had ample room upon which to perch a very expensive computer, a globe, numerous pink fountain pens and a pile of encyclopaedias. Cornelia was in the middle of doing some very complicated trigonometric equations, and didn't welcome the interruption.

'You're the only one who could have taken it,' Martha said.

'Listen, Cornelia,' said Mr Myklebust. 'This is very

important. A boy's life is in serious danger. Martha's brother, Samuel.'

'So?' said Cornelia, wondering what precisely had got into her father. 'Why would you care?'

'I was there. A troll came and–'

'A troll?' Cornelia now found the conversation interesting enough to put down her fountain pen and turn round to look at Martha. 'So you believe me now? There really *was* a troll hiding in your house, wasn't there?'

'Yes,' said Martha. 'But it wasn't our fault. He ran away and sneaked into our house. And the reason he ran away was because he didn't want to go to the Betterer, who is a really evil troll.'

Mr Myklebust nodded. 'And he is *really* evil. I've met him.'

'He's a murderer, in fact,' said Martha.

Cornelia shrugged. 'So?' And then she turned back to calculate the next equation.

'So we need this bracelet Martha's told me about. This Hek bracelet,' said Mr Myklebust.

'If a is equal to b . . .' muttered Cornelia as she stared into her maths book.

Mr Myklebust looked at his daughter and wondered precisely what kind of creature he had managed to raise. He looked around the room. At the various rosettes and trophies she had won from show jumping and spelling contests. At the three wardrobes, at the vanity dresser, at the audience of dolls she had acquired over the years, at the clarinet, at the music stand, at the ten hairdryers, at the pottery wheel, at the exotic plants imported from Africa, at the microscope, at the telescope, at the bookcase filled with first editions, at the video camera, at the artefacts of the Sumi civilization, at the collection of silver hairbrushes – at the million and one things she had asked for and he had given. The presents which were designed to make her the cleverest or the prettiest, but which still left her far from the happiest. How on earth would they find the Hek bracelet among all these things?

'Listen,' said Martha. 'It's up to you. I am going into the forest to rescue my brother . . . And then I will be in the newspaper as the first girl ever to see trolls and all the magical things that live in the forest.'

Of course, Martha didn't really care about getting into the newspaper, but she knew Cornelia did. And indeed, the tactic was already working. Cornelia was still staring at the various equations and isosceles triangles, but Martha could see from her face that she was no longer concentrating on them.

'But obviously,' Martha went on, 'if you came too, with the Hek bracelet, they'd be far more interested in writing about *you*. After all, who would want to write about Martha Blink when they could write about Cornelia Myklebust?'

Cornelia didn't turn round, but took a deep breath as if the decision had a scent that needed to be inhaled before it could be taken.

'I will want *five* new ponies,' she said, in a voice as cold and precise as the equations on the page. '*Trakehner* ponies,' she specified, as they were her favourite breed. 'And I'll want new stables too.'

Mr Myklebust was on the verge of nodding his head when he changed his mind.

'No . . .' he said, and he felt strange saying it. 'I am starting to realize, Cornelia, that a father cannot buy his daughter's respect. I nearly died tonight – the Betterer nearly killed me. And do you know what I wished for?'

Cornelia shook her head. 'No,' she said.

'I wished for you to grow up to be a happy person. A truly happy person.'

'So why are you saying "No" to me?' said Cornelia, a confused frown creasing her forehead.

'Because happiness isn't always about how many

ponies you have. Sometimes it's about being pleased with who you *are*, not what you've *got*.'

Cornelia may have been a genius in other areas but this was an idea too complicated for her brain. All she knew was that if anyone was going to have their name in the paper, she wanted it to be her.

'Pleeease,' begged Martha.

'All right,' she said. 'I'm coming.'

'Good girl,' said Mr Myklebust. 'Now, you must get the Hek bracelet. There's not a moment to lose. We've got to save that boy's life.'

And as he said that last sentence, Mr Myklebust realized just how heroic he sounded. And it felt good to be a hero. *Yes*, he thought as imaginary trumpets sounded in his ears, *it feels very good indeed.*

THE HANDY HANDBOOK OF HUMAN HABITS

Samuel woke up from the longest and deepest sleep of his life to the sound of wailing.

His eyes opened, but at first everything was a blur.

He thought he was in bed, staring at the vertical rows of flowers on the wallpaper. But as his vision sharpened into focus, he realized he wasn't in bed at all. He was lying on rough, splintered wood, staring not at vertical rows of flowers but at bars to a cage.

He was exhausted, but as the miserable wailing continued, he remembered everything. He remembered the visit by the Betterer. He remembered what had happened to Troll-Father. He remembered the handkerchief that had been placed over his face, and that sudden very sleepy feeling.

Slowly, and with enormous effort, he lifted his head

off the floor. As he did so, he noticed it wobbled. The floor, that is. And then he realized why. The cage he was in wasn't on the ground – it was dangling in the air.

He looked around but saw nothing beyond the cage except grey walls and a tiny circular window. Through it he could make out the dark shape of forest trees against the night – pine trees, like those that surrounded Trollhelm – and strange sharp-beaked birds flying in the sky.

He wondered how much time had passed since the handkerchief had sent him to sleep. An hour? A night? Two nights? It was impossible to tell.

As the wailing continued, he felt as though his vision were going foggy again. Maybe he was falling back to sleep. But no, he was feeling more and more awake.

'Can I ask you a question, human?'

Samuel moved to the edge of the cage, looked down towards the voice and saw the Betterer sitting in his long overcoat right by the cage, next to a large lever.

'Let me out,' was the only answer Samuel offered.

The Betterer smiled at the request, as though it were a greeting. 'Tell me, Mr Samuel Blink, if you saw me walking down a human street in one of your human towns out there in the world of humans, what would you think? I mean, if you had never seen me before. Tell me, I'm curious – what would you think of me?'

His voice sounded more gentle than Samuel remembered.

'I don't know,' he said, as it seemed a bit better than saying, *I'd think 'Who's that evil-looking monster in the long overcoat?'*

'I mean, from the distance we are now. Look at me. Would you think I was human?'

Samuel stared down at the Betterer's misshapen face. At his rough skin and troll nose and big chin. 'I don't know. I don't care. Just let me out of this cage.'

The Betterer ignored this request. 'Out of ten, what would you give me? If ten was *Happily, happily human* and one was *Terribly, terribly troll*, what number would I get? A seven? An eight? Eight and a half? I mean, I'm well dressed. I've got two eyes. I'm not like that snivelly little freak up there, am I?'

Samuel looked over to where the Betterer was pointing and saw someone dripping wet with soapy water, pegged with iron pegs to a kind of washing line that ran the length of the room. At first Samuel didn't recognize this wailing, pink-faced, one-eyed creature.

But then he realized: it was Troll-Son, but Troll-Son *clean*.

'He's not a freak,' said Samuel. 'He's my . . . friend.'

The Betterer flinched at the word 'friend' as if it were a wasp flying too close to his face. When he spoke, his voice cooled once more. 'I will ask you again. Out of ten, how human do I look?'

Now, here is a piece of advice. If ever you should find yourself trapped high in a cage in a Bettering Tower with an evil-hearted troll asking how human he looks, tell him, *'Oh, yes, you look very human.'* Or *'Ten-out-of-ten human.'* Or, even better, slap your thigh and say, *'What, do you mean to tell me you're not really a human? You are joking! You are the most humany human in the whole of humankind. In fact, if you looked any more human, it might be a little bit too much and other humans would start to wonder if* they *were the ones who were trolls. No, seriously, trust me – human is a great look for you and you work it so well.'*

Yes, say any of those things. But whatever you do, don't do what Samuel did.

Don't say: 'You're missing the point. Troll-Son's more human than you'll ever be.'

Not unless you want the Betterer to give you a

look so threatening that your heart stops for five whole seconds.

'Oh, and why's that?'

Samuel gulped. He was frightened of the Betterer but he was also angry. There were millions of other twelve-year-old boys in the world who were, right at that moment, doing perfectly ordinary things. Their parents hadn't been crushed by a falling log. They hadn't had to move to Norway and live with their aunt on the edge of a forest full of trolls and tomtegubbs and other weird things. And they weren't now stuck in a cage having to answer a kidnapper's stupid questions.

Such anger gave Samuel the courage to look down at the Betterer and speak in an untrembling voice. 'Being human's not about what you look like. It's about how you treat other people.'

As Samuel said this, he thought of how he had treated Troll-Son. Yes, it hadn't been particularly *pleasant* sharing a toothbrush with someone with cabbage breath, but he should have made an effort to understand Troll-Son. After all, he'd only been trying to avoid being sent to the Bettering Tower.

The Betterer laughed and pulled a small booklet out of one of his inside pockets. He read out the title on the front for Samuel's benefit:

'*The Handy Handbook of Human Habits*.'

He then started flicking through the pages, which were arranged alphabetically, and stopped to read little bits from the middle.

'K is for Kidnapping . . . L is for Lying . . . M is for Murder . . . Apparently these were all invented by humans. Along with bullying, name-calling, poisoning, prejudice and warfare. Oh, and rice pudding. In fact, after reading this handbook I am rather sure my treatment of other people has been very human indeed. A textbook case.'

Samuel looked over at Troll-Son, who was blinking the itchy soap out of his eye while weeping for his father.

'No,' said Samuel. 'There are evil humans just like there are evil trolls, but most aren't like that. Most humans are kind. Most humans want to be good.' He was thinking of his own parents as he said this, but he was also thinking of Aunt Eda and Uncle Henrik. Both of them had tried to save his life before, and he knew they would have been trying to save his life now if they hadn't been stuck to the hall floor.

'Very good, human. You are lying to me, but that is all right. I want you to lie. I want you to teach me, as

I said. Perhaps, deep down, you are quite as evil as a human can be.'

'I'm not evil,' said Samuel, watching as the Betterer began to turn the giant lever. The lever was connected to a rope – a rope which in turn ran in a tight, straight angle to somewhere directly above the cage. As the Betterer worked the lever, the cage kept getting lower and lower.

'I must admit, it is quite an honour. I have never had a human reside with me. But don't worry, I don't intend to waste the opportunity. I assure you that you will get precisely the same treatment as any of the other useless cretins who stay here, starting with a little spell in the tub.'

'Hey, what are you doing?'

'What do you mean, "What are you doing?" You are a human. What kind of host would I be if I didn't offer you a bath? Of course, the soap might be a little *itchier* than what you are used to.'

The Betterer laughed, and turned the lever faster. And Samuel noticed it was getting steamier and steamier, and felt his skin start to itch.

'Hey! Let me out! Let me out!'

'Now let's see just how clean a human can get.'

Samuel felt the cage descend, very quickly now –

quicker than the roller-coaster he'd made his dad go on. Then there was a splash, and a flood of hot Itch Water washed into the cage.

'Argh!' Samuel said, finding the energy to hop to his feet.

The Itch Water was horrible even when it was lapping around his ankles, but it kept on getting higher and higher, itching like fleas.

'Argh! Stop! Argh!'

The cage sank so fast that it was under the water in seconds.

That must be the Betterer's plan. He's going to kill me, just like he killed Troll-Father, thought Samuel.

But no.

The Dunking Cage rose out of the water, swung round and came down in a puddle. Samuel coughed, and saw that his hands were speckled bright red.

When the Betterer opened the cage door and yanked him out, Samuel was too weak and too itchy, to put up a fight.

A soft 'No' was all he could manage as the Betterer lifted him onto his shoulder, carried him up a kind of rickety stepladder and clipped him by his sleeves to the washing line so that Samuel was hanging there, like a pair of Aunt Eda's long-johns. It was the worst feeling in the world, as he had so many itches that he couldn't scratch.

The Betterer clapped his hands once he was back down on the floor. Samuel could only see him by straining his eyes, because he couldn't move his head. But after the hand-clap he was sure the Betterer was smiling and stroking his chin, viewing Troll-Son and Samuel in rather the same way certain people look at old paintings in art galleries.

'Much better,' said the Betterer. 'Much, much better.'

SILENCING SWEETS

Samuel could remember a time when being hung from a troll's washing line would have seemed a most unlikely thing to happen. But as he watched the drips fall onto the wooden floor, he realized there was no point thinking of likely or unlikely things. There were just things, and they happened whether you wanted them to or not, and so although Samuel was not happy to be locked in the Bettering Tower, listening to the thoughts of this rather mad, smartly dressed troll, the fact that it was happening did not surprise him at all.

'I should have got rid of Troll-the-Wisest . . .' the Betterer was saying as he licked his Lertwick Root to keep himself awake. 'No. It's better that he's alive. He won't remember anything. And now he'll help me . . . Yes, Troll-the-Wisest is the most stupid troll of all. He'll believe every word I tell him. Yes . . . I'll say he fell asleep. He was tired and he wanted us to go on ahead. I'll say we got attacked by humans. Humans who blamed us for stealing their goats. And they attacked Troll-Father with a pitchfork – which he obviously didn't see coming – and despite my best, most valiant efforts to defend him, he was killed and I ran back to the forest, which the humans were too scared to enter.'

Troll-Son was thinking of his father, lying dead outside the forest, and anger overcame every urge to itch. 'You be not getting away with this! Mother be finding me.'

The Betterer laughed. 'My poor, stupid troll! It was your mother who sent you here in the first place.'

He looked up to Troll-Son, whose wails had faded to medium-volume sniffles. 'Oh yes, but it will be so hard for your mother when I tell her that not only was her husband murdered but I was unable to find her son.'

'But . . . but I be here,' said Troll-Son, in a sad voice.

'Yes, you are. And you always will be, along with the human. You see, I know you have potential, Troll-Son.'

'No,' said Troll-Son, who didn't know what potential was but was pretty sure he didn't want it. 'I not be having potential.'

The Betterer shook his head. 'You ran away to be with this boy. You wanted to be like him in every way. You wanted to escape your troll parents and live with the humans. You are clearly not happy with who you are, and nor should you be. Now you will have Samuel Blink all to yourself. With my guidance you will be able to observe him and become more like him. I will show the forest precisely how much better a troll child can be!'

Troll-Son felt a double sadness. There was truth in what the Betterer was saying. He *had* wanted to escape his parents, and he *did* want to be like Samuel Blink. But he remembered the taste of orange juice and toothpaste, and the uncomfortable hell of carpets and attics, and began to think he had made a mistake. Perhaps trolls were trolls and humans were humans *for a reason.*

'You will never get away with this,' said Samuel, struggling in vain to release one of the pegs that was attached to his sleeves – a peg that the Betterer had specifically designed to be impossible to open from below.

The Betterer smiled. 'Witness, Troll-Son, the correct use of the future tense. *You* will *never* . . .' He then held out his hand underneath Samuel and Troll-Son as if checking for rain. 'Still dripping,' he said. 'Looks like you'll be hanging there all night. But don't worry – as soon as you are dry we'll see how differently trolls and humans cope with the lessons. The first one is the Strong-Stomachs-Are-Never-Sick Spinning-Wheel Challenge, which is always rather fun. But it won't be too long before someone comes knocking, and I will have to explain the tragic situation. So . . . time for your Silencing Sweets.'

He positioned the rickety stepladder under where Troll-Son was hanging and climbed up to press a Silencing Sweet into his mouth.

'No,' said Troll-Son. 'No sweet, no sweet, no–'

The Betterer pushed the sweet onto Troll-Son's tongue, and it dissolved instantly. Samuel could see Troll-Son trying to shout, but it was like watching someone from behind soundproof glass. There was no noise at all.

Samuel knew this was his last chance to be heard beyond the Bettering Tower, and so he screamed at the top of his lungs, 'Help! Help us! We're kidnapped! Help! The Betterer's got us! Help!'

But the Betterer had already positioned the ladder and was now climbing up towards him. The Betterer squeezed Samuel's nostrils to make him gasp for air and then pressed the sweet onto his tongue.

'There,' said the Betterer. 'That should keep you quiet for a while.'

Samuel felt his tongue go heavy inside his mouth, like a dead fish. He tried to lift it and speak, but he couldn't.

But then something rather brilliant happened. The doorbell rang. The Betterer winced at the sound and looked out of the tiny circular window, up towards the purple sky, where birds that had once pecked skulls now sang songs of love as they flew. Samuel looked at that sky too, and wished he could fly out and join those former skullpeckers under the vast freedom of the clouds. Maybe whoever was ringing the doorbell had come to save them.

'Who is that?' the Betterer wondered aloud. 'Oh well, let the performance begin.'

THE STICKY GREEN PUDDLE

At this time Aunt Eda and Uncle Henrik were still very much stuck to their hall floor. Their legs ached, their stomachs grumbled with hunger, and they both were exceptionally tired from so much standing. Oh, and they rather needed the toilet.

'I feel so useless, just standing here,' said Aunt Eda, looking out of the window towards the dark outline of the trees, blacker than the night. 'The forest is so close but so far away at the same time.'

'I know how you feel, Eda. But until this sticky stuff evaporates some more, there is nothing we can do.'

'But they need us, Henrik!' said Aunt Eda, getting into a bit of a flap. 'When they were in Shadow Forest last time, they had us to help them. If I hadn't gone and got them, they would never have lived to tell the tale. Oh, they are helpless! Helpless!'

Uncle Henrik stared at Troll-Father's stone body lying in front of them. It would have been very easy for him to be as bleak as Aunt Eda about the situation, but somehow he wasn't.

'Helpless is not the word I would use, Eda,' he said.

Aunt Eda looked at him a little crossly. 'No? Well, tell me, Henrik Krohg – which word would *you* prefer? Two young people in our care are in that forest. One of them is kidnapped by an evil and murdering troll, and the other one popped in to tell us she is on her way to visit the same evil and murdering troll, all while our feet are stuck in the middle of the stickiest green puddle in the history of sticky green puddles. Tell me what isn't "helpless" about that?'

Uncle Henrik left the question unanswered for a while, giving time for Aunt Eda to calm down. Then, finally, he said what he felt needed to be said.

'It is indeed a very terrible situation, Eda. But I do not agree that those children are helpless. I believe quite the opposite in fact. They might be children but they are also two of the most extraordinary people I have ever met. When I was still an elkhound, I accompanied Samuel through the forest. I saw how brave he was. I know he can get himself out of the most desperate situations. Consider everything that those children have been through this summer. As I said, when it comes to Samuel and Martha we are dealing with something quite extraordinary. We owe it to them to believe that they can do this, and to believe everything will be all right. Come on, Eda – you can do this. You can believe in them.'

As Aunt Eda struggled to pull her feet out of the Gripgrass Juice, she looked away from the forest to see the half-eaten jar of pickles in the kitchen. She was still very worried, but she knew Uncle Henrik was right. Samuel and Martha were not helpless. They had both proved that.

She also thought of the time, long ago, when Uncle Henrik had disappeared into Shadow Forest. Everyone had told her there was no way she would ever see him again, but she'd kept on believing. And maybe it was that belief itself that had got her through, and brought him back to her.

Yes, to make it through a horrible time you need someone to believe in you, just as an onion needs pickle to preserve it, and so she knew she had to believe in Samuel and Martha.

She took a deep breath and, for a moment, stopped trying to free her feet. 'Yes, Henrik,' she said. 'You are right. I believe in them. The truth is, I believe in them as much as I believe in anything. If anyone can escape that evil troll, then I know they can.'

She turned again to the window, towards the dark, dark trees. And as she looked, she tried to send her belief out into the forest, as a wish or a prayer might be sent, to give Samuel and Martha extra hope.

THE BETTERER'S PET

As soon as the Betterer had left the Bettering Chamber and locked the door behind him, Samuel began to try and wriggle out of his jumper. All of a sudden he was rather pleased that Aunt Eda had bought him one that was too big – even though it had shrunk a little in the water, it might be possible to free himself from the washing line.

As he wriggled away, he could hear the distant sound of Troll-Mother on the ground floor.

'Oh no,' she was saying. 'Oh no, not dead! He not be dead! Not Troll-Father!' She began to wail. 'And where be my son, Mr Betterer? Where he be?'

'I couldn't find him. I had to come back to the forest. It was too dangerous. I am afraid there are a lot of very dangerous humans out there,

Troll-Mother. They are murderous creatures, in the main–'

'Samuel Blink be not like that,' she said, confused as well as sad.

'Well, I never got to meet Samuel Blink,' said the Betterer. 'But I assure you, all the other humans I met were the most vicious and violent creatures you could imagine.'

'Liar!' Samuel would have screamed if only he could have moved his tongue. He was nearly there now. He almost had an elbow out of the sleeve.

'So where he be?' said Troll-Mother. 'Where be Troll-Son? Be you thinking he be alive?'

There was a pause, and then the Betterer gave some kind of answer which Samuel couldn't hear. But it was clear what that answer must have been, because a moment later, Troll-Mother began to cry out in despair.

'No! Oh no! Oh no! My poor boy! Killed by them savages! Tell me it be not true, Mr Betterer, sir! I never even be having the hopperunity to tell him I be sorry for all my crossnesses. I be being such a bad mother! A most bad mother I be! Oh! Oh!' Her voice became louder still as she raised it towards heaven – which happened to be in the same direction as the top floor of the Bettering Tower. 'Oh, Troll-Son, if you be up there in troll heaven, I hope you be listening! I hope you be hearing how sorry I am! I be so sorry of all my hipperty tempers I be getting in! If only I be having another chance to be making mends, I'd be not sending you for bettering. I be 'cepting you for who you be and be not seeking no changes, I be! I . . . I . . . I be saying then what I be saying now – that I be loving you, Troll-Son. I be loving you and loving Troll-Father too, even if I not be showing it before. I be not knowing how to go on without you. Oh! You be mine! You be my own! Oh! I be lost! I be lost! I be so much sorry . . .'

Troll-Son, of course, wasn't in troll heaven but he could still hear every word his mother was saying.

'Mother, I be up here,' were the words he was trying to shout at the top of his voice. But ever since the Silencing Sweet had dissolved on his tongue he couldn't even reach the *bottom* of his voice, let alone the top of it.

'Well, Troll-Mother,' said the Betterer. 'I am truly sorry for your loss. To lose a husband and a son at the hands of those vicious humans is a tragedy beyond all imagining. But I'm sure you'll eventually have fewer sleepless days – you'll get over it.'

'If only I could be touching their stony bodies!' Troll-Mother wailed.

'Yes, yes . . .' said the Betterer. 'I know, I know. Those evil humans. It's unthinkable, what they did.'

Samuel was now out of his jumper, but holding onto it, dangling high above the ground. Troll-Son strained his eye as far to the left as he could to see what Samuel was up to. But even Samuel himself didn't quite know. After all, it would be quite a drop down to the floor.

But that was the point, wasn't it?

After all, the louder the landing, the more likely it was that Troll-Mother would get suspicious.

So he let go.

Aargh, he screamed silently.

Thud.

He might have hurt himself, but he was still so itchy he hardly noticed. He stood up and stamped his feet as hard as he could.

'You'd better be going, Troll-Mother,' he heard the Betterer say urgently, between stamps.

'What be that sound?' asked Troll-Mother.

'There's no sound.'

'Yes. There be a sound. A banging sound.'

Samuel kept jumping up and down on the wooden floorboards, and Troll-Son offered the faintest glimmer of a smile. A painful, scared kind of smile, but a smile all the same.

Thump. Thump. Thump.

'Oh, *that*,' said the Betterer. 'That's my pet.'

'Pet?' said Troll-Mother.

'Yes, I've got a pet. A caloosh. You know, one of those large three-headed flightless birds. It's a lively thing. I'm thinking of letting it back into the forest, actually. But it's nothing for you to worry about. You go home and . . . mourn.'

'But it be sounding like–'

'Well, I told you what it is. And now I must leave you. Good night, Troll-Mother.'

'But–'

'Good *night*.'

And Samuel heard the front door of the Bettering Tower close again, and the Betterer start to lock the thirteen locks.

Samuel stopped stamping and moved the stepladder over towards Troll-Son. There wasn't much time. The plan hadn't worked. Troll-Mother had gone without realizing they were trapped up there. And now he had to get Troll-Son down off the washing line before the Betterer came back to the Bettering Chamber.

He climbed to the top of the rickety stepladder, and had to stand on tiptoe to reach him.

'Be still,' Samuel wanted to say, because Troll-Son

was wriggling. And it was a particularly hard job to unclip the heavy iron pegs.

The Betterer had locked the last lock and was running as fast as he could up the spiral staircase.

Then, just as Samuel was unpegging the last peg, the key turned and the Betterer was there, standing in the doorway, with a face that could have frightened sharks out of the ocean.

Well, maybe not. But it was certainly enough to frighten Troll-Son off the top of the stepladder. He lost his balance, and came crashing down onto his bright red face. In the process, he knocked over the rickety ladder, and Samuel flew backwards into the air.

'You will pay for this, human,' said the Betterer.

Samuel tried to push himself up off the floor, but the Betterer grabbed his wrist with one hand and felt inside his overcoat with the other. He pulled out a brown leather pouch. 'In this pouch, curled very, very tight, is the Bettering Branch. Would you like it to teach you a lesson?'

Samuel didn't answer, but he noticed Troll-Son crawling on all fours behind the Betterer.

Just as he was about to pull the branch from the pouch, the Betterer felt a sharp pain in his left heel. He turned round to see Troll-Son biting into him with the teeth that had ruined Samuel's toothbrush.

It *nearly* worked: Samuel was *nearly* able to snatch the pouch out of the Betterer's hand and Troll-Son *nearly* managed to avoid getting the Betterer's large foot in his belly.

'It's the ingratitude that upsets me,' the Betterer said, picking Samuel up by the scruff of his neck, while Troll-Son struggled with the Betterer's foot. 'All I wanted was to better the badness out of you, Troll-Son. Smooth the rough edges. The ill manners and disobedience. I thought the human would want to help, but he's no use. It's too risky. I'm very much afraid you're going to have to die. And without any pupils, what good is a human to observe? No, I will have to kill both of you. Starting with you, Mr Samuel Blink.'

Then, with no warning, a faint voice made it through the window. A sound more wonderful to Samuel's ears than even the most beautiful huldre hymn.

'Mr Betterer, be you there?'

It was Troll-the-Wisest. He must have woken up and walked back to Trollhelm. And as he was leader of the Troll Council, he was going to be the Betterer's chief ally in explaining everything to the villagers. So it was important for the Betterer to tell Troll-the-Wisest his made-up version of events as soon as possible.

'Mr Betterer, be anyone at home?'

'Right, you two little cretins, come with me.' The Betterer put away his Bettering Branch and dragged Troll-Son and Samuel over to the door at the far side of the chamber – the one painted black – pushed them into the room, then locked them in.

'Welcome to the Room of the Unbettered,' he said, before locking the door to the Bettering Chamber and going downstairs.

Samuel looked around the room, but saw nothing as it had no windows. It was silent too. The quiet made it seem like it was a hundred miles away from the rest of the Bettering Tower, and Samuel became worried. How could they escape?

Filled with the sudden energy only fear can bring, he tried banging on the door, and Troll-Son joined in, but they both knew it was no good. They'd seen how thick it was. There was no way anyone downstairs would hear them.

But still they kept banging, with their hands and their feet, because if life had offered Samuel a positive lesson alongside its multitude of miseries and torments, it was that you must never give up.

Never.

For hope is always there, shining smaller than the thinnest slither of light through a door-crack. And sometimes – just sometimes – hope decides to listen, and give its believers one last chance.

A SURPRISE VISIT

The Betterer unlocked thc thirteen locks and turned the door handle.

'All right, Troll-the-Wisest, I'm com–'

He opened the door to see Troll-the-Wisest standing there, with his long grey beard and nervous eyes. But it wasn't this that gave the Betterer such a shock. No. It was the three humans standing behind him. The fat bald man he had seen before, and two girls. One of whom – the one with dark hair and a frowning forehead – was the first to break the silence.

'Where's Samuel?' she said in her crossest voice. 'My brother. What have you done with him?'

The Betterer shut the door and leaned against it, wondering what to do as the doorbell kept ringing.

'It would be most wise to be letting us in,' said

Troll-the-Wisest. 'It be market night in Trollhelm and in some time soonish, three hours before sunrise, the whole village be being out and about, wondering at the commotion on your doorstep. Look over yonder, they be setting up some stalls this minute.'

The Betterer saw Hurgle-Troll in the distance, setting up his hurgleberry wine stall, and sighed. It was the wisest thing he'd ever heard Troll-the-Wisest say. He couldn't have anyone else know about what had happened in the Outer World. His only option was to let them in. Yes. He would let them in, and he would never let them out again.

He opened the door a second time.

'We're not after any more trouble,' said Mr Myklebust, trying his very hardest to keep a nervous quiver from taking over his voice.

'We just want my brother back,' said Martha.

'And Troll-Son,' said Troll-the-Wisest.

'Ugh,' said Cornelia, staring at the Betterer's face as though it were a disgusting meal placed before her. 'You're *ugly*.'

Martha elbowed her in the ribs. 'Sssh! You'll make him angry.'

The Betterer looked at the human faces in front of him, and felt such envy for their smooth skin that it hurt. 'All right,' he said. 'If Troll-the-Wisest can assure me that this whole business will remain a secret, then I'll show you where they are. To be honest, it would be doing me a favour. Troll-Son is the most troublesome pupil I've ever had. Beyond all bettering. And even the human is a major disappointment. So, if Troll-the-Wisest offers me an official pardon, I will promise to hand them over and retire from my profession.'

'You be having my word,' said Troll-the-Wisest. 'I be promising the most officialest pardon there be.'

'Very well, follow me,' said the Betterer, and led them all up the spiral staircase. Then, when he was at the top, he told them to wait. 'I won't be a moment,' he said, before disappearing inside.

Some clanking and creaking noises followed.

'What's he doing?' asked Mr Myklebust.

'He's getting Samuel and that troll boy,' said Cornelia, as if her father had just asked the most stupid question in the world.

'Yes,' said Troll-the-Wisest. 'He must be.'

Only Martha begged to differ. 'No,' she said. 'I don't think so. He wouldn't give them up *that* easily.'

But what could she do? She needed to find her brother. And so when she heard the Betterer call them inside, she followed Troll-the-Wisest and the rest of them into the trap.

They opened the door and walked straight into the Dunking Cage that the Betterer had moved right up to the door.

'Quick,' Martha shouted. 'Back out!'

The cage door fell shut before they could escape, and they were hoisted up into the air, just as Samuel and Troll-Son had been. This time, though, there was a difference. The Betterer's plan wasn't just to dunk the cage in the giant wooden tub full of Itch Water. No, he was going to leave it there, and never raise it again.

MARTHA BLINK IS DANGEROUS (THE FIZZUPY FRIZZUP CHAPTER)

Cornelia whimpered in panic. 'I thought you said this Hek bracelet would keep us safe,' she whispered crossly.

'I thought it would,' said Martha as the cage filled with steam. 'I'm sorry.'

'It be not meant to be ending like this,' said Troll-the-Wisest, clutching his beard for comfort. And then he shouted down from the cage: 'You be making me ashamed to be a troll!'

The Betterer laughed. '*I* make *you* ashamed? That's a good one! Well done, Troll-the-Wisest – after all these years of boring me with your council meetings you've finally developed a sense of humour.'

As the cage was lowered, Martha heard something. A very soft and distant knocking. She looked over towards the black door on the other side of the room and made the connection.

'Samuel!' she called. 'Samuel!'

But if he could hear her, he wasn't answering back.

It was Cornelia, though, who was most afraid. 'Oh no,' she said. 'Why isn't it working? I should never have believed you, Martha Blink.'

'I'm sorry,' said Martha.

'Sorry? How's "sorry" going to help?' snapped Cornelia. 'I knew it couldn't be true. I knew I shouldn't have believed in magic.'

And she began to cry, and her head leaned against the softest and most comfortable thing to lean against, which was her father's stomach.

'It's all right,' said Mr Myklebust – quite ridiculously, given the circumstance. 'It's going to be all right.'

'Oh, how touching,' laughed the Betterer as he stopped working the lever and let go, deciding to end this the quicker way.

'Aaaaaaargh,' screamed Martha, Cornelia, Mr Myklebust and Troll-the-Wisest all at once as the cage fell through the steam.

But then something rather odd happened. A short distance above the water, the cage, with only the slightest of shudders, stopped in mid air.

'It worked,' said Cornelia, stroking the bracelet on her wrist. 'It actually worked.'

'Yes,' said Martha, equally relieved. 'It really did.'

The Betterer couldn't understand it. He went up to the giant wooden tub and reached into the air between the water and the cage, as if testing a magic trick.

'It's impossible,' he hissed.

And then he dragged the stepladder into place, and climbed up into the cage.

Martha turned to face him. 'Let us go,' she said. 'Please, just let us go.'

'You,' said the Betterer, pointing at her. 'It's you, isn't it? You're doing this . . . to the cage. With your magic human powers.'

'No,' said Martha, her voice trembling as he got closer, the Bettering Branch now in his hand, uncoiling towards her. She made wild eyes as she stared at the Hek bracelet around Cornelia's wrist. Cornelia got the hint, and pressed the bracelet into Martha's left hand, out of sight of the Betterer. Martha squeezed the bracelet tight and closed her eyes. Nothing happened. Then, when she reopened them, she saw the Betterer desperately trying to force the half-uncoiled branch towards her neck.

'Urghhhhh! What . . . is . . . wrong . . . with . . . this . . . stupid . . . thing?' He couldn't do it – the branch wouldn't go near Martha.

She looked around at all the other faces, and saw how worried they were that the Betterer might try and squeeze them to death instead of her.

'Yes,' she said, realizing she had to do something. 'I *do* have magic powers.' She remembered the witch who had once owned the bracelet – the kind Snow Witch she had met the last time she had gone into the forest. 'I can make it snow. And . . . um . . . you'd better let us leave or I'll freeze you to death.'

'It's true,' added Cornelia, relishing the lie. 'She's killed before and she could kill again. Martha Blink is dangerous. Say her name and you can strike fear into the heart of every human being.'

Martha knew the Betterer needed more convincing, so she started to chant words in a kind of tomtegubb rhythm: '*Fizzupy frizzup fizzupy froo, watch what my ice-cold heart can do . . .*'

She found it quite easy making up the words – it wasn't too different to making up song lyrics (something she had always done in the back of her parents' car). She knew it was a skill that would come in useful one day.

The Betterer began to panic. 'What's she doing?'

'You'll see,' said Mr Myklebust.

The Betterer looked deep into Martha's eyes but couldn't decide if she were telling the truth. There was a chance that she *might* have special powers – and again *The Handy Handbook of Human Habits* hadn't been clear on the subject of magic, so he decided not to take the risk. After all, he was a bully and, deep down, bullies are generally the most scared creatures there are.

He lowered the Bettering Branch.

'It be the right decision you be making,' said Troll-the-Wisest, who was the first to leave the cage. Cornelia was next, followed by her father, who checked to see that Martha was all right before stepping onto, and nearly breaking, the stepladder. Then Martha inched past the Betterer, keeping her eyes firmly locked on his and trying her hardest to look scary.

Of course, the moment she stepped out of the cage, it stopped floating in the air and dropped, with the Betterer inside, down into the Itch Water.

THE HUMAN SNOWBALL STRIKES BACK

'Aaaaaaaaaaaargh!' screamed the Betterer as he plunged into the water.

'We should try and lock the cage door so he can't get out,' said Mr Myklebust.

Cornelia shook her head. 'Daddy, don't be so stupid. He's got the keys. He'd be able to escape anyway. According to my calculations our best option is to run.'

'She's right,' said Martha. 'You go. Quick. Before he gets out of the tub.'

'But what about you?' said Mr Myklebust.

Martha looked over to the far side of the room. Samuel had risked his life to find her when she had got lost in the forest, and now it was her turn to repay the favour. 'I'm going to get my brother.

And Troll-Son. They're over there. Behind that black door. I'll be all right – don't worry. I'll meet you back in the forest – where we found Troll-the-Wisest. Here, take the bracelet. I'll be fine.'

Mr Myklebust stared down at the bracelet. 'No,' he said, his face pale but determined. 'We stay together. We came here to get Samuel and that's what we'll do.'

'Daddy, are you mad?' asked Cornelia.

'We stay together. *All* of us.'

Mr Myklebust turned round and realized Troll-the-Wisest had already fled. 'Well . . . the *rest* of us.'

Cornelia didn't want to risk running away alone so she followed Martha to the black door. She and Martha ran. Mr Myklebust puffed along at half the speed, cursing his weight.

The two girls tried to push the door open, but it wouldn't move.

'Samuel. We're here! But the door's locked!'

'It's no use,' said Cornelia. 'We haven't got the key.'

Mr Myklebust panted to a stop. 'Stand back,' he said in a booming voice. 'If you can hear me inside there, stand back!'

Cornelia looked confused. 'Daddy, what on earth are you doing?'

Martha tugged her aside as Mr Myklebust used every last bit of energy he had to charge forward into the door. He closed his eyes and imagined himself once again as that giant unstoppable snowball rolling heavily down Mount Myrdal. It worked. He hit the hard wood with his right side, and the lock broke immediately. The lock, after all, had been designed to withstand troll children and thieving pixies, not a Mr Myklebust.

'Samuel!' said Martha, seeing her brother – wet, itchy and missing his jumper. 'Are you all right?'

Samuel tried to move his tongue, and discovered the effects of the Silencing Sweet were beginning to fade. 'Yes,' he said slowly. 'We're OK.'

'I thought he'd killed you,' Martha said as a feeling of relief sang through her body. 'I thought–'

'Quick,' interrupted Cornelia. 'You can do all that "I'm so glad you're alive" rubbish later. The Betterer could be out of the tub by now. We must get out of this place quick.'

'OK,' said Samuel. 'Come on, Troll-Son – we're going.'

'I be understanding, Samuel Blink,' said Troll-Son, who was still trembling in the corner.

'Come on then!' said Samuel. 'Let's go!'

They rushed towards the outer door, Cornelia urging her father on.

'It should be all right,' Martha told Samuel. 'The Betterer thinks I've got magic powers that could kill him. He doesn't realize it's just the bracelet on my wri–'

'Martha! Quiet, you imbecile!' said Cornelia from behind her. 'Look!'

She pointed towards the steaming wooden tub – and more specifically to the dripping figure of the Betterer, who had just climbed out of it. His skin was now bright red from having been so long in the steaming Itch Water.

'Quick!' said Samuel.

But the Betterer had heard every word, and now knew Martha had been lying. All he had to do was grab the bracelet off the girl's wrist and use the Bettering Branch on all of them. He strode towards them, his overcoat leaving a wet trail on the floorboards.

Samuel reached the door first, then Martha. Troll-Son was next.

'Daddy, quick!' shouted Cornelia, seeing the Bettering Branch hook her father around the ankle.

'Got you!' shouted the Betterer.

The others ran back, Samuel taking Mr Myklebust's

right hand, Martha helping Cornelia pull on his left. With their help he managed to pull his foot free before the branch tightened further, even though he lost a shoe in the process.

'Let's go,' said Samuel, getting behind Mr Myklebust and pushing him for extra speed.

They all sped down the spiral staircase.

'Where are we going?' said Martha.

'Troll-Son home,' said Troll-Son.

'Good idea,' said Samuel.

'We'd better be quick,' said Cornelia sharply. 'He's on the stairs already.'

It was true. Before they'd even reached the front door, the Betterer was speeding down the spiral staircase two steps at a time. Fortunately, though, the thirteen locks were all unlocked, as Troll-the-Wisest had already escaped.

They ran out onto the grass, hardly noticing the fresh night air that greeted them. And in the dark they failed to see the two figures hiding by the doorway. Indeed, they didn't notice them until they heard an almighty clang.

Samuel was the first to stop and turn. 'Look,' he said. 'She got him.'

The 'she' in question was Troll-Mother who, having

been told by Troll-the-Wisest what had happened, had dragged him along with her back to the Bettering Tower. She had left Troll-Daughter playing at home, and had brought her rabbit pan – the only weapon she had to hand. Having heard the footsteps running down the stairs, she and Troll-the-Wisest had waited by the doorway, ready to attack.

Well, Troll-Mother had been ready to attack. Troll-the-Wisest had wanted to cover his face with his beard. But he didn't. He had been the eyes of the operation and had whispered the order – 'Now!' – just at the right time.

'That be for Troll-Father,' said Troll-Mother, after swinging her rabbit pan and whacking the back of the Betterer's head.

As it turned out, that was all she needed to do. You see, the Betterer had been running with the Bettering Branch out in front of him, so as he fell forward with the force of the blow, it coiled around his neck.

'Aaargh!' he howled as it squeezed tighter. He stayed still for a moment, before slowly lifting his head to look around. 'Sto–' He couldn't finish the command – the branch was clamping his throat shut.

Everyone watched as purple blood leaked from his mouth.

The Betterer gasped one final time, and struggled to utter his last words:

'*That's . . . better.*'

Meanwhile Troll-Son ran over to his mother, and she dropped the rabbit pan to reach out for him.

'Where you be?' she said. 'Where you be, my boy?'

'I be here,' he said, throwing his arms around her.

'Oh, my boy, I be so sorry,' she said.

'I too be sorry,' he said, and he pulled his eyeball out of its socket and gave it to her, so she could cry the tears she had stored away.

Cornelia saw this and decided to hold her father's hand. 'I was thinking,' she said. 'Surely I deserve some more ponies *now*.'

'Really?' said Mr Myklebust.

'Yes. But I was a bit greedy asking for five. I think I'll go for four instead,' she said, and he laughed.

It was only Samuel and Martha who stayed silent, staring at the Betterer's hateful face as it slowly turned to stone.

TEARS AND CHEERS AND TROLL-MOTHER'S WISDOM

It was a busy market night in Trollhelm, and somewhere deep in the crowds Troll-the-Left and Troll-the-Right were arguing by a stall selling hurgleberry wine.

'No, we be not buying any,' said Troll-the-Right. 'It be upsetting my stomach.'

'It be my stomach too,' said Troll-the-Left. 'And I be saying it be all right. We be having three bottles, please, Hurgle-Troll.'

'Look,' said Troll-the-Right. 'Over there.'

And so Troll-the-Left turned to see the sight that by now most of the village were seeing. The runaway had returned, and he was walking through the market with his mother, followed by Troll-the-Wisest and four humans.

As the crowds gathered round, Troll-the-Wisest decided to do some explaining. He told the full story of what had happened, and the village gasped when they heard the Betterer was dead, and many cried when they found out about Troll-Father.

'Such a horrible thing!'

'He be such a kind man!'

'Never a bad word about nobody!'

'Poor Troll-Mother!'

And someone started singing a song with a very sad tune, and soon all the trolls were singing it. The song was called: 'For him who be loved be living for ever in our hearts, he be', and when it was over, Troll-Mother spoke to the whole village.

'I be knowing you all be thinking I be a good wife and mother, but to be honest I be a bit cross and clouty too often because I be never knowing really just how much I be having, and now I not be able to make it better with Troll-Father. But our son still be here, and now I be apprecipitating him for what he be and I be not bathing him or wanting him no more better nor worse than what he be. He be an unbettered troll, and I be proud of him because there be goodness in his heart. And in all them troll hearts that be accepting who they be. I must also be thanking Troll-the-Wisest for telling me the truth.'

Someone shouted: 'Three cheers for Troll-the-Wisest!'

And Troll-the-Wisest was about to stand back and smile and lap up the cheering crowds when he decided he probably shouldn't.

'No, no,' he said. 'It not be me you must be cheering. It be Troll-Mother, and these brave humans.'

'What be they called?' shouted another troll mother, who had brought her troll twins out to watch the commotion. And then everyone was suddenly asking to hear the names of the humans, as they had heard that humans had proper names.

Cornelia was the first to step forward. 'I'm Cornelia. Cornelia Myklebust,' she said, smiling and offering a slight curtsy.

'Three cheers for Cornelia Cornelia Myklebust!'

'No, there's just one Cornelia, you dimwits,' she said crossly, but was drowned out by the crowds.

'And I'm Magnus Myklebust,' said Mr Myklebust, stepping forward and raising his arms like an Olympic champion.

The crowds cheered again, and Magnus knew in that moment that he would never want to move these creatures out of their homes. Just as he would never want to get Uncle Henrik into trouble. No amount of money could beat this strange feeling of *being good.*

Troll-the-Wisest raised his hand towards Samuel and Martha, indicating it was their turn.

'I'm Martha,' said Martha shyly. 'But I didn't do anything really . . .'

The crowd cheered even louder than before, especially Troll-the-Left and Troll-the-Right, who remembered Martha from their days in prison. 'Good to be seeing you, human girl,' shouted Troll-the-Left.

And then the crowd fell silent, waiting for Samuel to give his name. He wanted to say something about Troll-Father, but he didn't know the right words.

'He be Samuel Blink,' said Troll-Son eventually. 'He be the best human of all!' And he meant these words very sincerely, but was still relieved that he no longer had to live like his human friend. A world of orange juice and daily baths and toothpaste was one he was more than happy to leave behind.

Following that last and most resounding cheer, Samuel went over to talk to Troll-Mother.

'I'm sorry,' he said. 'About what happened to Troll-Father. He was a great troll . . . He saved my life when I was fleeing those huldres in the forest. You both did.'

'Don't you be sorry, Samuel Blink,' she said, with a smile. 'It be no one's fault but that evil Betterer. And yes, Troll-Father be a very great troll, he be, though I be not always showing him the softness and niceness he be deserving. If we could be living our lives from the end to the beginning, then I be thinking that we be all making less mistakes. But that not be life, be it? Life be from the beginning to the end and it be learned as it be lived. But all I be knowing is that the dead never be dying proper when the living be there to remember them. And so we must not be dying with them and drowning in our old wrongnesses. We must be going on like they be wanting us to and be showing more nicenesses to them who be there by our sides.'

And she squeezed Troll-Son close to her, and added something else: 'He be looking up to you, Troll-Son be,' she said. 'He be not wanting to live with humans now but I be still thinking you be his hero.'

Samuel remembered how he had shouted at Troll-Son for using his toothbrush. 'I'm not as great as he thinks,' he said.

Troll-Mother shrugged, and gave him a doubtful look. 'Well,' she said, 'he be seeing the goodness in you, even if you be not seeing it yourself. Just as Troll-Father be seeing the goodness in me, when he be having no reason. When you be having only one eyeball to share all around, you be knowing that sometimes we be needing others to see the truth of how things be, and of who we be. And from what he be telling me, you be good, Samuel Blink – there be no doubting that.'

Samuel smiled as Martha came over.

'It's time to go back,' she said softly. 'To Aunt Eda and Uncle Henrik.'

'Yes,' he said. 'I suppose it is.'

And as they said their goodbyes and went to join the other humans, he wondered if it was slightly silly to have his younger sister as his hero.

He thought it probably was, so he kept that information to himself.

THE END

by MATT HAIG

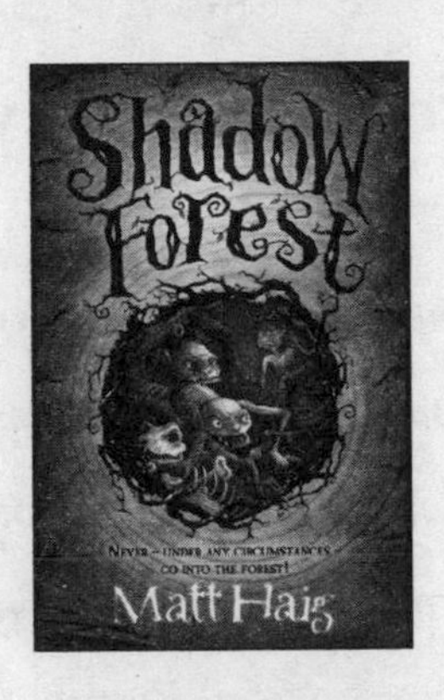

Samuel Blink is the hero of this story, but he doesn't know it yet.
Right now, he and his sister Martha are in the back of his parents' car.
He has no idea a giant log is about to fall from the sky and change
his life for ever. He doesn't know that he and Martha will be forced
to move to Norway and eat their Aunt Eda's smelly brown cheese.
He hasn't the slightest clue Martha will disappear into Shadow Forest.
A forest full of one-eyed trolls, the sinister huldre-folk, deadly truth
pixies and a witch who steals shadows. A forest ruled by the evil
Changemaker. A forest so dangerous that people who enter never return.

No. Samuel Blink doesn't know any of this.
So don't tell him. It might ruin the book . . .

'Weaves horror and humour into a terrific tale'
THE TIMES

978 0 552 55563 0

by

Joseph Delaney

'The Spook's trained many, but precious few completed their time,' Mam said, 'and those that did aren't a patch on him. They're flawed or weak or cowardly. They walk a twisted path taking money for accomplishing little. So there's only you left now, son. You're the last chance. The last hope. Someone has to do it. Someone has to stand against the dark. And you're the only one who can.'

Thomas Ward is the seventh son of a seventh son and has been apprenticed to the local Spook. The job is hard, the Spook is distant and many apprentices have failed before him. Somehow Thomas must learn how to exorcize ghosts, contain witches and bind boggarts. But when he is tricked into freeing Mother Malkin, the most evil witch in the County, the horror begins . . .

978 1 862 30853 4

Into the Woods

by

LYN GARDNER

Aurora Eden's List of VERY Important

Things to do Today

1. Tell Storm off for making fireworks – AGAIN!

2. Bake chocolate-coated madeleines.

3. Dust behind the kitchen cabinets – IMPORTANT!

4. Ask Storm if she knows anything about that funny-looking musical pipe I found behind the pickle jars.

5. See if Desdemona has laid any eggs.

6. Set Storm ESPECIALLY hard maths test as punishment for crying WOLF.

7. Make sure no one finds out we are living without a Grown-up.

8. Convince Storm that Witches Aren't Real.

9. Rearrange linen cupboard.

10. DON'T GO INTO THE WOODS!

978 0 552 55459 6

The NEW POLICEMAN
by
KATE THOMPSON

There is never enough time in Kinvara. When Helen Liddy is asked what she wants for her birthday, she says, 'Time. That's what I want. Time.'

Fifteen year-old JJ is continuing the Liddy family tradition with his fiddle-playing. But one day he discovers that music might not be the only thing that runs in his veins. Can it be true that his great-grandfather was a murderer?

When JJ sets out to buy his mother some time he discovers the answer, as well as some truly remarkable things about music, myth and magic.

Who knows where the time goes?

JJ does.

Winner of both the Whitbread Children's Book Award and the 2005 Guardian Children's Fiction Prize

978 0 099 45627 8

The Toymaker

by

Jeremy de Quidt

What good is a toy that will wind down?
What if you could put a heart in one?
A real heart. One that beats and beats
and doesn't stop.
What couldn't you do if you could
make a toy like that?

From the moment that the circus boy, Mathias, takes a small roll of paper from the dying conjuror, his fate is sealed. For on it is the key to a terrifying secret, and there are those who would kill him rather than have it told.

Pursued by the sinister Dr Leiter with his exquisite doll and malevolent dwarf, preyed on by the circus master and his vicious, painted wife, Mathias is drawn into a elentless nightmare. A nightmare that will lead him to the Toymaker, and to a knife as cruel as frost.

978 1 849 92004 9